MW01611273

FRESH DOUBT

AN INGRID SKYBERG THRILLER

EVA HUDSON

VENATRIX

First published 2014.
This version published by Venatrix 2020.

978-1-9160195-7-7

Copyright © 2020 Eva Hudson

Eva Hudson has asserted her right under the Copyright, Designs and Patents Act 1988 to be identified as the author of this work.

This book is a work of fiction and, except in the case of historical fact, any resemblance to actual persons, living or dead, is purely coincidental.

All rights reserved. No part of this publication may be reproduced, stored in a retrieval system, or transmitted in any form or by any means, electronic, mechanical, recording, or otherwise, without prior permission of the copyright owner.

For Mum - Thanks for believing in me

FRESH DOUBT

PROLOGUE

Dear Lauren,

They make you write letters here. One to your parents. One to mine. One to my future self, that sort of thing. Apparently, the fact you're dead is supposed to free me to write the truth about my feelings. The doctor running the rehabilitation programme has fewer psychology qualifications than me—fewer than you, in fact—so it's fun to play with his head. And let's face it, he's the only one who's going to read this, isn't he?

So how do I feel, Lauren? I believe they want me to say I'm sorry, or remorseful, or sad. But the truth is I'm angry. Angry with you for putting me here. If I'd never met you, I honestly think I could have been happy. But you had to come along and ruin everything.

At the beginning it was fun, I'll admit. It was just the two of us against the world, remember? We had this crazy, intense connection but when the spell was broken you couldn't keep your mouth shut, could you? I warned you to keep it to yourself, to hold your tongue, but you didn't, did you? So what happened was... inevitable.

There's something that really bothers me. Can you guess what it is? It was that look you gave me when you were lying on the floor. You were still alive then—I checked your pulse—and there was this moment when you seemed to see me and recognize what was happening. I want to know if that look—that narrowing of your pupils, that tightening of your features—was that you hating me, or thanking me?

I picture that scene often. Your head at an odd angle, the gash in your skull starting to glisten. God, the sound you made when you fell. It was almost metallic, like the crunching of a car when it goes into the back of another. Although that wasn't the last sound you made, was it? There was that wheezing rasp as the air left your lungs.

I don't know if you care, but I thought you should know I didn't hate you when I killed you. Like I said at the time, I only wanted to shut you up, to put an end to things. But by God I hate you now. You've caused me so much trouble.

This is such a ridiculous exercise. It's not like you're going to write back is it? And how am I supposed to sign off a letter like this? Best wishes? That's all for now? Rest in peace? Ah. I know…

See you soon,

Prisoner A2441AC

1

"Somebody stop him!" the woman shouted. "Please, someone!"

Special Agent Ingrid Skyberg saw it all happen in slow motion as she ran past on her early morning run along the Thames river path. A moment to shove the woman sideways, another to drag the straps of the bag from her shoulder, then a second to snatch and scoop the bag into his arms. The young Caucasian male sped away, barging into a crowd of commuters near the London Eye. The woman fell hard onto the concrete path, her mouth forming a wide silent O as she hit the ground.

Ingrid had just been getting into her stride, feeling her muscles warm, absorbing the faint heat of the early morning April sun on her face. She pulled up fast—the man was escaping behind her—turned on a dime and ran back under Jubilee Bridge toward the Royal Festival Hall. She accelerated through the crowd.

"Stop!" she shouted, pumping her arms faster. "FBI!" Then she remembered herself, threw a glance over her shoulder and yelled at the mugging victim to call 9-1-1. The woman looked at Ingrid blankly. "I mean nine nine nine, call nine nine nine!"

Ingrid turned face front again and scanned a sea of disgruntled faces to find the thief.

"Get out of my way!" she yelled, but most had headphones in and didn't hear. She scrutinized the edge of the crowd and

3

spotted him again, his shaven head appearing bright white above the throng of commuters. She memorized his description for later. White, male, five eleven, one-seventy pounds, bald head, no more than twenty years of age. And fast. Really fast. Her cell phone vibrated, tingling against her bicep. Whoever it was would have to wait.

The crowd cleaved in front of her, opening a central channel. Ingrid pumped her arms harder and dragged air down into her burning lungs. Thirty yards ahead, the perp darted quickly right, pushing a tourist out of his way before roaring up a concrete staircase to the terrace above.

Ingrid dug deep, gaining on him with every stride.

"Stop! Police!" she yelled.

She took the first four steps in a single leap, drove the balls of her feet hard into the concrete and propelled herself upward. A bottle of water hurtled down toward her. She ducked left, and the half liter of Evian bounced harmlessly off her shoulder.

"Son of a…"

Ingrid reached the top of the steps and located her quarry as he crossed an expanse of concrete paving. This part of the South-bank was home to an arts complex built in brutal, bare concrete, with walkways and staircases connecting concert halls, galleries and theaters on several stories. Ingrid knew the center well: she met other parkour athletes here once a week for training sessions, jumping from level to level to find new and inventive ways to get from A to B. She smiled: she hadn't been this exhilarated since her last Bureau fitness assessment. She'd been training for some-thing like this for years. She was going to enjoy herself.

He ran toward a narrow passage leading between two build-ings, discarding items from the woman's bag as he went, briefly disappearing from sight. Ingrid ran after him, spotting him as he headed for another concrete spiral of steps down to street level. She lengthened her stride, reached for the waist-height wall and vaulted over it, twisting and holding onto the other side before dropping down to the flight below. He appeared at the bottom of the staircase and showed no sign of flagging. Ingrid jumped over the wall and dropped down, landing a few feet behind him.

"Fuck off, bitch."

Ingrid rolled to disperse the impact and sprang up to give chase. He reached into the handbag, fetching a pink leather wallet then discarding the bag as he ran. It caught under Ingrid's foot. Her ankle twisted, and she stumbled, but she kept on running. Her phone buzzed again. She was five yards back now. He ran into a graffiti-covered undercroft where skateboarders practiced their jumps. They zigzagged around each other, not paying any attention to her or the thief. The noise of the wheels on the hard standing echoed off the walls.

He darted between the boarders. Ingrid was within lunging distance now. She ran up one of the ramps and launched herself up into the air, cycling her legs before bringing her right foot down on the back of his calf, sending his face crashing into the hard concrete below and forcing the pink wallet out of his grasp.

She rolled him over; a huge graze covered his face from chin to ear. The skateboarders gathered round. One picked up the wallet.

"Who the fuck are you?" the thief managed.

"Ingrid Skyberg," she said, breathing heavily. "Special Agent Ingrid Skyberg to you, Federal Bureau of Investigation."

"FBI? Is this a joke?"

A uniformed police officer riding a bicycle came to a stop at the edge of the skate park, ditched the bike and scrambled over to them. He spoke urgently into his radio. "Suspect apprehended." He turned to Ingrid. "Where'd you learn to do that?" Behind him another cop ran over, and behind her was the woman whose bag had been snatched. The cops bent down and yanked the youth up to a seated position.

Ingrid's phone was still buzzing. She lifted it out of her armband and answered. "Agent Skyberg."

"You sound terrible." It was her boss.

"What's up, Sol?" She breathed heavily, her chest heaving with exertion.

Sol Franklin cleared his throat, then coughed. He really needed to stop smoking.

"Sol?"

She heard a deep inhale. "Got a case for you. An American citizen has been murdered. I'll text you the details, but you need to get there super quick."

"I'm on it."

The male police officer, with help from one of the skaters, had the thief in restraints. Ingrid approached his colleague. "I'm real sorry," she said, still out of breath, "but I don't have time to give you a statement right now." She pulled out a business card. "Call me this afternoon if you need one."

The officer looked at the card. "For real?"

"Phone the US Embassy after lunch. They'll patch you through to me."

The cop looked up and down the river path, searching for something. "FBI? Where are the cameras?"

"What?"

"You're filming something, right?" The cop nudged her colleague, whose mouth dropped open. "Is this another parkour video for YouTube?"

One of the skaters turned to her. "No. You're that... erm... that actress... the one who—"

"No." Ingrid tucked her short blond hair back under her baseball cap. "I'm not." She forced a smile.

The mugging victim stared at her intensely. "I can see it myself. You do look a bit like her. Except for the short hair, of course. What's her name? Charlize... thingummy..."

The skaters already had their phones out and were filming her. She really didn't need to end up on a viral video on Facebook. "Call me," she shouted, and accelerated back along the river path to continue her run. If it wasn't for the huge smile on her face, it was almost as if nothing had happened.

Her phone buzzed as she was slipping it back into the armband, and she glanced at Sol's message. Her smile quickly disappeared: the murder victim was only twenty-two. She didn't have time to waste: she took the steps up to Westminster Bridge three at a time and flagged down a black taxi.

2

Ingrid reached her hotel in Marylebone in fifteen minutes. After a quick shower, she chose a somber dark gray pantsuit from her small collection of work clothes. Yet again, she made a mental note to visit Banana Republic to purchase one or two alternative suits. She had only intended to stay in London for five days, and living out of a suitcase was getting tiresome. Her posting to the FBI's overseas Legal Attaché Program was supposed to be temporary, but it had stretched out to four months, and she was bored of wearing the same clothes. She was also over the glamor of hotel living. Ingrid dabbed a smudge of mascara under her left eye and promised herself she'd do something about her wardrobe and her living arrangements soon.

Ingrid picked up her helmet and belted leather jacket and took the stairs down into the hotel's underground parking lot. Her Triumph Tiger 800 didn't compare to her beloved Harley back home, but it was perfectly suited to weaving in and out of rush-hour traffic in central London.

The GPS led Ingrid to New Cross, a suburb she hadn't been to before, south of the Thames. She parked the bike at one end of a wide side street lined with cherry trees in full blossom. Fifty yards from where she stood, blue and white police tape fluttered in the stiff breeze outside a large, detached, five-story Victorian villa.

Her cell phone buzzed in her bag, vibrating noisily against her metal water flask. She swiped it and checked who was calling. Marshall, her fiancé. Not for the first time in the past few weeks, Ingrid didn't feel like talking to him and let it go to voicemail.

She locked her helmet into the top box and smoothed down the pants of her suit. A few feet from the police tape was a frizz-haired, middle-aged woman in a dark raincoat and patent leather boots arguing with a weary constable. The woman wagged a finger in his face, and Ingrid heard her shout something about press freedom. Ingrid recognized her from her very first assignment at the embassy: Angela Tate, an investigative journalist for the main London newspaper, the *Evening News*. Tate, Ingrid had learned, had a knack for finding out about stories before any of her colleagues. Press freedom? Tate seemed to have plenty.

Ingrid approached the police cordon and flashed her ID. None of the officers were armed. Strict UK laws meant only specialist firearms officers carried weapons, a rule that also applied to Ingrid and her Bureau colleagues.

"Don't I know you?" Tate said.

Ingrid pushed through, keen for the hack not to remember who she was.

"I never forget a face," Tate shouted after her.

In the entrance of the house, standing at the top of wide stone steps, was a familiar face Ingrid was much happier to see. Detective Inspector Natasha McKittrick was the closest Ingrid had to a friend in London. They had met at a training session Ingrid had delivered to the Metropolitan Police on child protection, the area of law enforcement she had specialized in before her deployment in London. The two women had discovered a similar sense of humor and taste for tequila and had enjoyed several 'putting the world to rights' sessions. She beamed at the detective.

"You got here fast," McKittrick said.

"I've been trying to tell you to get your motorcycle license."

"And I've tried to tell you how much I like my limbs in their current unbroken state."

Any anxiety Ingrid had about working with her friend

instantly evaporated. "So what have we got?" Ingrid asked. "Murder one?"

"Pathologist says it's too close to call. Could just be an accident. We'll have to wait for the preliminary autopsy report."

Ingrid peered beyond McKittrick into the main hallway of the house. There were two doors on the left, another on the right, with a flight of stairs in the center leading up to the next story. The walls were scuffed, and a bicycle leaned against the banister.

"Cause of death was most likely severe loss of blood," McKittrick said as they turned to go inside. "Victim has a huge gash in her head. Seems a hard, sharp object went into her temple with a lot of force."

"You found the murder weapon?"

"If you can call a glass and steel coffee table a weapon, sure."

"She fell and hit her head on a table?"

"You sound disappointed."

Ingrid checked herself. She was a little.

"The next question I'm sure you're itching to ask me is 'was she pushed, or did she fall?'" McKittrick said.

"And?"

"That's what we're here to find out." McKittrick stopped on the stairs. "It's not that I'm not pleased to see you, but why exactly are you here?"

There wasn't a quick answer.

"Please don't say 'protocol.'"

"Well, when an American citizen dies in mysterious circumstances, it's diplomacy," Ingrid said, deliberately avoiding the word *protocol*, "for us to assist local law enforcement in any way we can."

"So you're not here to spy on me?"

She kind of was. "Of course not. I'm here to look out for the interests of American citizens, and that means ensuring the crime, if one has been committed, is thoroughly investigated."

They reached the top of the stairs. "So you are here to spy on me!"

Ingrid cleared her throat. "The US Embassy has total confidence in the investigatory competence of the Metropolitan Police."

"You rehearsed that." McKittrick gestured toward a pile of overshoe bootees and all-in-one Tyvek suits. "We'd better get togged up."

Togged up? Ingrid imagined she could live in England for the rest of her life and still not understand everything that came out of Brits' mouths. Once they were in the protective clothing, McKittrick filled her in on what they knew about the victim.

"Her name is Lauren Shelbourne. Twenty-two. Postgrad psychology student at Loriners College, which is part of the University of London." McKittrick led Ingrid up to the third-floor landing, then through a narrow door into a single-room apartment. Bright lights bathed the studio room in a magnesium glare, making every surface and object look strangely artificial, as if on the set of a horror movie. The CSI team fussed round the crumpled body lying next to the low coffee table, taking photos and collecting samples.

Ingrid was engulfed by sadness when she caught sight of Lauren Shelbourne's body. She was fully clothed, her arms flung out in front of her, her legs folded awkwardly beneath. A dark red pool of congealed blood had spread across the floor. A piece of her forehead was missing. Ingrid pulled herself together. "Estimated time of death?"

"Some time between midnight and four a.m."

"You've spoken to the other residents?"

"Working through them, one by one. They're not all home."

"Inspector!"

Angela Tate was hovering by the door.

"Care to make a comment, detective?" Tate said. "Or perhaps the US Embassy would like to make a statement?" She smiled insincerely at Ingrid.

"How the bloody hell did you get past the cordon?"

The reporter took a step inside the room.

"Stay exactly where you are!" McKittrick rushed toward her. "You're contaminating the crime scene."

"So you are treating this as murder?" Angela Tate held her ground.

McKittrick grabbed the reporter's arm. "Mills!" she hollered.

A flush-cheeked face appeared in the doorway, an embarrassed, almost pleading look in his wide brown eyes. "Sorry, boss. I thought the uniforms had everything under control."

Tate snatched her arm away from McKittrick and pointed at the tall man. "You lay a hand on me, Ralph Mills, and I swear my paper will sue the arse off you."

The apologetic detective held his hands up high, palms facing toward Tate.

"Are you linking this death to the suicide at Loriners last week?" the journalist shouted before Mills herded her toward the stairs.

"Get her out of my sight, Mills," McKittrick said.

"I'll just be outside, Agent Skyberg," Tate said. "You can speak to me later."

Ingrid admired the reporter's determination, but she had absolutely no intention of telling her anything.

After talking to the crime scene investigators, Ingrid followed McKittrick downstairs and back out into the front yard. "Who called the police?" Ingrid asked her. "Who actually discovered the body?"

McKittrick nodded toward a shell-shocked, ghostly-white young woman sitting half-in, half-out of a police car. She was shivering despite the foil blanket wrapped around her shoulders.

"Have you questioned her yet?"

"Not beyond the preliminaries. We'll interview her formally down at the station."

"She lives here in the house?"

"No. A few streets away, apparently."

Ingrid watched as the young woman rose unsteadily to her feet. She seemed completely disoriented. She was wearing a blue Tyvek suit like Ingrid's.

"She's not a suspect?"

"Not at this stage, but her clothes are covered in blood. She found her, so I'm not ruling anything out. We'll find out more when we question her." McKittrick turned to Ingrid. "I suppose you'll want to sit in when we do."

Ingrid frowned, not taking her eyes from the staggering figure wrapped in the silvery blanket. The young woman got out of the car and wandered toward the house. She stared directly at Ingrid and McKittrick. A uniformed female officer attempted to guide the girl back to the police car.

"Madison Faber—also studying psychology at Loriners," McKittrick explained. "Also an American citizen."

"Really?"

That meant Ingrid had to offer her consular assistance. "Are you planning to arrest her?"

"I expect her to come to the station voluntarily."

"Does she understand that? Maybe I should speak to her." The young woman in the blanket wriggled her arms free from the cop. "Looks as if she isn't about to volunteer to go anywhere."

Madison Faber dragged the foil blanket from her shoulders and threw it at the feet of the female constable, who glanced toward McKittrick for help before Faber shoved the uniformed cop, who staggered backward.

"What the hell does she think she's doing?" McKittrick ran out onto the street.

Two more officers tried restraining the ashen-faced student, who batted their hands away and drove her fist into the face of the nearest officer. "Don't touch me!" she screamed.

Ingrid ran toward her as Angela Tate fired questions from the cordon. Faber looked up at Tate, the confusion on her face obvious. "Who are you?" Faber yelled.

A male officer stepped forward and grabbed both Faber's arms. The bewildered student kicked out at him, her right foot hitting hard against his shin.

"Let me go! I have to get out of here!" She struggled, kicking him again to slip from his grasp. She ran down the street.

"How was she when you first spoke to her?"

Ingrid and McKittrick hurried into the road.

"Shocked. Quiet. Traumatized."

"Let me speak to her."

McKittrick held firmly onto Ingrid's arm. "It's OK. We have this under control."

Her friend's expression told her she was in danger of taking over. Ingrid nodded.

Two more officers ran toward the distraught young woman, arms held out wide, as if capturing a wild animal. One grabbed her shoulders, another held onto her arms, and a third attempted to attach wrist restraints. Faber screamed at them to let her go.

McKittrick looked at Ingrid. "Contrary to my earlier statement, it seems we are indeed arresting her. You might want to sort out legal representation for her."

3

The interview suite in Lewisham police station smelled of freshly laid carpet. Ingrid sat next to a blank-eyed Madison Faber now wearing a gray sweatshirt and pants the police had given her. She hadn't spoken since Ingrid had introduced herself over an hour ago. They were waiting for the embassy-appointed attorney to show up, even though Ingrid had put the request in while she was still outside Lauren Shelbourne's apartment.

Faber had sat perfectly still for over twenty minutes, staring straight ahead at a bulletin board crammed with local notices. She was prim looking, with a neat mousy bobbed hairstyle and single pearl earrings. Her large blue eyes gave the impression of seeing everything while revealing nothing. There was something owl-like about her.

"Can I get you anything?" Ingrid asked her. "A glass of water?"

Faber turned and stared at her as if seeing her for the first time. She tried to speak, but only managed a low croak. "I've got to get out of here."

"You will, don't worry. Just as soon as—"

"No! I mean now." She stood up.

Ingrid pulled her back down. "Everything's OK. A lawyer will be here real soon, and I'm here for you in the meantime."

"How can you say that? Everything's not OK!" She struggled against Ingrid's grasp.

"You don't have to answer any of their questions if you don't want to." Ingrid was deliberately trying to sound calm. The girl had just been through one of the most traumatic experiences of her life, and she implicitly understood why Faber had lashed out when the cops restrained her. "You have the right to remain silent, just like back home. Is that clear?"

Faber's face was expressionless.

"It's important you understand me. Are you clear about the questioning?"

Faber nodded slowly.

"Good." She patted Faber's arm. "I'm on your side. Everything is going to be OK." She regretted the platitude the moment it left her lips.

"Everything is *not* going to be OK! My friend is dead." Faber pulled away from her and got to her feet. "I have to get out of here. I need to call Lauren's parents. They should hear the news from a friend, not some English cop." She could not keep the sneer from her voice when she said 'English cop.'

Ingrid stood up. "The embassy has that under control. Lauren's parents have already been informed." She kept her voice low, gentle, reassuring. "Right now, my job is to worry about you."

"Me?" Faber's eyes widened. "I'm fine."

She was anything but. "You don't seem it, Madison. You've seen something awful this morning; it's bound to have an impact."

The girl peered into Ingrid's face, scrutinizing her. Ingrid found her impossible to read.

"I'm scared." Faber dropped her voice to a whisper.

"That's understandable. You want me to call someone for you? Your parents?"

Faber clenched her jaw. "No."

"I can stay with you just as long as you need."

Faber slumped back onto the couch.

"The lawyer should be here any minute," Ingrid said. "He'll

explain your rights, but like I said, you can remain silent if you choose to."

"Why would I want to do that?" Faber's eyebrows knitted together. "My friend is dead. I want to help the police all I can."

"They've arrested you, Madison. Yes, you want to help them with their enquiries into Lauren's death, but you hit a police officer."

The girl sniffed and stuck out her bottom lip.

"Though I'd say it's likely they'll drop the charges, given your evident distress."

Ingrid stared into Faber's face, and an unbidden image filled her mind. She screwed up her eyes in an attempt to banish it. In an instant she was back in Minnesota, fourteen again and feeling more helpless than Faber did now. *Not this, not here.*

"Are you OK?" Faber asked her. "What just happened?"

Ingrid forced a smile. "I'm fine."

"You don't look fine."

"It doesn't matter."

"Obviously it does. You said I could trust you, but now you're scaring me."

Ingrid placed her hand on Faber's knee. "I'm sorry. Old memories."

Faber looked puzzled. "Oh my God, this happened to you, didn't it?"

Those eyes didn't miss much.

"Not quite," Ingrid said. "But I did lose a friend."

"I'm sorry."

"It was years ago."

"But you're not over it."

"Creeps up on me sometimes."

"Was your friend murdered?"

Ingrid had said too much. "This isn't about me. Let's focus on what you need."

"But I thought—" The door to the interview room opened, and McKittrick entered with Ralph Mills, the tall detective who had escorted Angela Tate from the house in New Cross.

"Feeling calmer?" McKittrick asked Faber. There was no trace of sympathy in her voice. Ingrid had never worked with McKittrick before, so had no idea how her friend operated professionally. "We won't talk about the assault charge without your solicitor here—"

"Go ahead. Agent Skyberg is looking after me." Faber grabbed Ingrid's hand.

"—but I would like to get a statement from you about what happened this morning. Are you up to that, Madison? I can call you Madison, can't I?"

"Sure." The girl shrugged.

"Thank you." McKittrick sat down and opened a fresh notebook. DC Mills did the same. "Can you tell us the exact time you discovered Miss Shelbourne?"

Faber nodded almost imperceptibly. "I went to her apartment early. We'd arranged to meet before class. So I guess it must have been eight. Certainly no later than eight thirty."

"This morning?"

Faber glanced at Ingrid, her confusion evident. "Of course this morning."

"How did you gain access to the property?"

"I have a key. We used to be roommates. Lauren has—had keys to my apartment too."

"So you were close?"

"We looked out for one another, you know? Us 'Yanks' gotta stick together." She made air quotes with fingers raw from the forensics swabbing process.

"So Lauren was expecting you this morning?" McKittrick asked.

"She wanted to discuss her thesis with me. She was getting a little anxious about it, and I said I'd help."

"And the apartment door was locked when you arrived?"

Faber nodded. "I went straight up to the third floor. Banged on the door, waited. When there was no response, I used the key. The door was stiff, sticky. I had to force it open."

"Then what did you do?"

"I called her name from the hallway outside the apartment."

"And she didn't answer?"

Faber wrinkled her nose. "Of course she didn't."

"I'm sorry if my questions seem obvious, but we do have to be very precise."

Faber took a shaky breath and swallowed. "I stepped into the apartment and called her name again, louder this time." She blinked. "That's when I saw her. Just lying there." She snatched a Kleenex from the box on the table. "Who would do something like that to her?" She stared at McKittrick, her eyes wide, as if she were actually waiting for an answer.

Faber's hands dropped into her lap, and she picked at the Kleenex. She hadn't dabbed her eyes or blown her nose.

McKittrick pressed ahead. "Do you know if Lauren had fallen out with anyone recently?"

"What?"

"Did Lauren have any enemies?"

Faber snorted. "No way. Not Lauren. She never fought with anyone."

"How about boyfriends?" McKittrick asked. "Was Lauren in a relationship?"

Faber wriggled in her seat and pulled a face.

"What is it?"

"I don't know if she was seeing anyone. Whenever I asked, she got evasive. She'd change the subject. But she had that look sometimes, like she was keeping a secret. And sometimes she had that other look." She turned to stare at Mills. "Like she was getting laid."

The detective's face blushed, and Mills looked down at his notepad. How could a thirtysomething homicide detective be so easily embarrassed?

"Can you hazard a guess?" McKittrick asked. "Someone she studied with, perhaps?"

"Why do you want to know? Do you think he could have killed her?"

McKittrick took a deep breath. "In a case like this, we're particularly interested in her close relationships. Can you think of any reason she wouldn't want to tell you who she was dating?"

Faber shrugged. "Maybe she just wanted to keep it a secret. Maybe she was embarrassed."

"About what?"

"Whoever was screwing her."

Ingrid flinched. She had been expecting Faber to say 'sleeping with.'

"What about other friends? Would they know who she was seeing?"

Faber shook her head. "If she was going to tell anyone, it would've been me."

Ingrid was taken aback by her certainty.

"Can you give us a list of her friends' names at college? We will need to speak to all of them." McKittrick scribbled something in her notebook.

"You can find them on her cell phone," Faber said. Her tone was now infused with a teenager's snark, a brooding petulance.

McKittrick's nostrils flared ever so slightly. "A list from you would be very much appreciated."

"Sure, it won't take long."

"Are you saying Lauren didn't have many friends?"

Faber pinged the elastic cuff of the Tyvek coverall. "She didn't really click with many people. She could be a little... What's the word you Brits use?" She played with the stitching while she tried to remember. "Brittle. That's it."

"Brittle? Lauren had mental health issues?"

"Not exactly. At least... none I know of. She could just be a little... off beam now and then."

McKittrick scribbled more notes. "Thank you, Madison, we really appreciate your cooperation. Now, when was the last time you saw Lauren?"

Faber's mouth dropped open. "You know when."

McKittrick drew a breath. "I'm sorry, I meant *before* this morning."

"You mean when was the last time I saw her alive?" Faber shuddered.

Ingrid had heard enough. "I think we need to take a break."

McKittrick gave Ingrid a stern stare and raised an eyebrow. Where was her compassion?

"I'm fine to carry on," Faber said in such a way that it sounded like a rebuke to Ingrid's concern. "We had lunch together on campus yesterday." The girl wasn't helping herself: she was coming across as cold and uncaring. Ingrid remembered her own odd behavior when she lost her best friend. She understood that shock can make a person appear unhinged.

"How did Lauren seem to you?" Mills asked.

Faber pursed her lips as she considered her answer. "Fine. No, more than fine, actually. Happy even. Maybe the happiest I've seen her."

McKittrick made more notes, then flipped back through the notebook. After a few moments of concentrated reading, she looked up and stared at Faber. "When did you and Lauren stop being roommates?"

McKittrick's sudden change of direction took Faber by surprise. She turned to Ingrid for guidance, and Ingrid nodded encouragingly.

"In January. I went away for a long weekend. When I came back, she'd moved out."

"Why?"

Faber shrugged. "She said something about wanting to be more independent."

"What did she mean?" McKittrick asked. She was questioning Faber like a murder suspect, and Ingrid's concern was mounting.

"She didn't really explain. But I guess, if I think about it, I had assumed the big sister role. I took on most of the responsibilities. You know, making sure the rent got paid on time, settling the bills, cooking. I guess she wanted to prove she could survive on her own."

"And how did that make you feel?" McKittrick's questions were taking advantage of the late arrival of Faber's lawyer.

"Feel? It didn't make me feel anything. I was a little surprised she hadn't discussed it with me in advance."

"You weren't at all upset by her departure?"

Ingrid didn't want to tread on her friend's professional toes, but she would be handling this interview completely differently. After four years working in the Violent Crimes Against Children Unit, Ingrid knew how to handle adolescents. Faber might legally be an adult, but she was nevertheless vulnerable.

"It's almost as if she was snubbing you," McKittrick continued, "throwing everything you'd done for her back in your face?"

"No, I was happy for her." Faber bristled: McKittrick was getting to her.

After a pause, Mills picked up the questioning. "Did you ever fight with Lauren?"

"Why are you asking me that?"

"Please answer the question, Madison." His tone was gentle but urgent.

"What are you trying to say?" Faber jumped up. "We never fought!"

Ingrid and Mills also got to their feet.

"We are taking a break now," Ingrid said. She turned to McKittrick. "Madison is a young woman experiencing one of the worst days of her life. I must insist you wait for her lawyer to arrive."

McKittrick, still seated, looked up at Faber. "Just one last question."

"She was like a sister to me. I can't believe you're suggesting—"

Faber's flow was interrupted by the door bursting open. A steel-haired woman in a power suit and dangerously high heels marched into the room, a bewildered uniformed cop trailing in her wake. She pushed past Ingrid and Mills and stopped next to Faber. She slipped an arm around the student's shoulders. "That's quite enough, detective. This interview is now terminated."

4

"Mr Brewster?"

Ingrid flashed her ID toward the narrow gap. The door closed and opened again. Ingrid slipped in from the hall to see a shoeless fat man padding down the plushly carpeted interior hallway of his luxury hotel suite.

"Well, come on!" Brewster yelled over his shoulder. "I don't have all goddamn day."

On the phone Sol had told her to 'play nice': he was aware of Brewster's reputation and wanted to make sure Ingrid didn't rise to the businessman's bait. From what she'd seen of Brewster already, it was going to be a struggle. She wasn't happy being taken away from chaperoning Faber, but Sol said it was important Brewster knew the embassy was taking his case seriously.

She entered the bedroom and found the red-faced businessman tying a dressing gown over his fleshy belly, the fat undulating like Jell-O. Diabetes and heart failure were just waiting to happen. The lack of wrinkles on his doughy face made it hard to determine his age. He could be anywhere between thirty-five and fifty.

"How long is this going to take?" Brewster barked. "I have better things to do with my time."

You and me both. "I'm sure you want this dealt with thoroughly, sir."

"I don't want it 'dealt with' at all." He tapped his watch, the leather strap secured on the very last hole.

"You called us, sir."

"Not through any choice of my own. I have an obligation to inform the authorities when something like this gets stolen. Let's get on with it, shall we?" He gestured toward an empty space on a narrow desk opposite the bed. A power cord snaked into thin air.

"Your laptop has been stolen?" Ingrid had meant it to sound more like a statement than a question.

"You don't know?"

"Just confirming the facts, Mr Brewster." She was pushing a boulder up a steep incline.

"Laptop, credit cards, cash."

"And you won't report this to the police, is that correct?"

"It's a diplomatic incident, not a criminal one." His sneer was threatening to turn into a snarl.

"I see." She didn't. She was grasping in the dark. "I'm going to need a bit of background, Mr Brewster. What line of business are you in?"

"What level of security clearance do you have at the embassy?" Brewster looked her up and down.

"That's not something I can discuss."

He shook his head. "Well, that tells me plenty."

"Sir?"

"Unless you have level five clearance, I cannot tell you what I do, or what was on the laptop, but there are documents on there of a sensitive nature."

"National security?"

"It would be more accurate to say commercially sensitive with security repercussions." He looked out the gothic arched window of his hotel down onto the busy four-lane highway of Euston Road. "The content is encrypted. I'm confident the information is completely secure, but there are people in government who need to know about the potential for a breach."

"Sir, I work for the FBI. I understand embassy officials are informing relevant parties via the regular channels. I am a criminal investigator, and as it is my understanding there was information on your laptop that belongs to the United States government, it is my job to retrieve it."

He huffed.

"Do you have the make and model? The serial number?"

"I can get my secretary to email you that sort of thing."

"That would be helpful. Now, do you know an approximate time your possessions were taken? I'll need to interview the staff on shift."

"No, you don't."

Her cell phone buzzed in her bag, vibrating noisily against her metal water flask. No doubt it would be her fiancé again. They hadn't spoken for days, possibly weeks. She ignored it.

"The robbery had nothing to do with the hotel staff."

"How can you be so—?"

"I had a… guest last night." He leaned his plump forearms on the window ledge. "It's an agency I've used every other time I've visited. I've never had any trouble before." He held up a hand, his wedding ring digging into the flesh of his finger. "Before you ask, I've already been in touch with the agency. All the contact information they have is fake."

"An escort agency?" His dressing gown made him look like a sleazeball.

"I'm a businessman on a long trip from home." He turned to face her. "It's not exactly unusual."

Ingrid took a notebook out of her bag. "Can you give me a description of your visitor? I should be able to track her down."

Brewster's shoulders tensed.

"A description?"

"What did she look like?" She joined him at the window and caught sight of a skyline of modern glass spikes and ancient religious spires. His eyes were screwed tight shut.

"I can assure you I will be discreet." *You cheating bastard.*

Brewster let out a long sigh. "Dark short hair, mid to late twenties. Six feet two, one-eighty pounds, muscular." He opened his eyes and studied her face, daring a response.

Ingrid fought hard not to appear surprised. "Ethnicity?"

"White."

"Nationality?"

"How the hell would I know? I wasn't paying to make chitchat with him."

"Did you notice an accent?"

"He sounded British; that's the best I can do."

"I'll need the name of the escort agency and a complete list of what was taken."

He glanced at a large flight case shoved beneath the narrow desk.

"What's in the case?" she asked.

"Nothing was taken from it." He stepped between her and the case. He was hiding something.

"How long are you in London?" she asked him.

"Another forty-eight hours. And then I will be back again in a week."

"And you're sure no one else had access to your room? Only the escort?"

"Correct." He was getting agitated.

"I have to ask you, sir. Is there anything personally compromising on the laptop?"

His eyes narrowed. "It is my *work* laptop."

"I'm trying to ascertain a motive for the theft, Mr. Brewster. If, as you suspect, the thief wants to access whatever sensitive information is on the device—and if that's the case, I imagine he'll be easier to find—but if his intention is merely to blackmail you"— she looked deliberately at his wedding ring—"he might be harder to track down."

Brewster said nothing.

"I need to ask: were you conscious the entire time the escort was in your room?"

She could tell he wished he hadn't called the theft in. "I may have nodded off."

"Might you have been drugged?"

He looked puzzled.

"Rohypnol," she explained. "The 'date rape' drug. There may

be other crimes he could be charged with if we can't prove the theft."

Brewster had had enough. He looked at his wrist. "Dear God, is that the time?" His flesh bulged around his watch strap. "I really do think you should be going, Miss Skyberg."

The man was objectionable.

"It's *Agent* Skyberg." She dropped her notebook into her bag and turned for the door. "I'll show myself out."

When she reached the door, she glanced back and saw Greg Brewster crouching down for the aluminum flight case. She paused, suddenly needing to straighten her collar in the mirror.

He looked up at her. "You can go now."

She let herself out. Ingrid had no desire to help him out, but every single piece of her wanted to know what he was hiding.

5

Ingrid arrived at the embassy building in Grosvenor Square shortly before lunch. She fired up her computer, determined to do a bit of background research on Greg Brewster. While she went through the long-winded log-in procedure, her mind drifted back to the scene in Lauren Shelbourne's apartment. She saw again the lifeless body and was overwhelmed with sadness. She wondered which of the embassy staff had told the girl's parents.

Ingrid closed her eyes, and inevitably an image of her lost school friend appeared, the way she'd looked the last time Ingrid had seen her. The last time anybody had seen her. Ingrid took a moment to offer up a silent wish. *One day I'll find you.* Then she puffed out a breath, snapped her eyes open, and focused on her computer monitor. She tapped Brewster's name into the database search field and tried hard to concentrate on something other than dead girls. There was no record of him. She tried another database, and this time an alert flashed up: 'access denied.'

On her way through the bullpen to Sol's office, Ingrid passed a couple of other agents. One acknowledged her politely with a nod; the other totally blanked her. She knew her role in the criminal division was seen as lowlier than the counterterrorism work her colleagues were involved in, but sometimes the way she was treated felt like more than rudeness.

She reached the end of a wood-paneled, airless corridor and rapped on the frame of Sol's half-open door. The office was empty. She checked the hallway both ways. No sign of Sol. Or anyone else. After one last glance up and down the empty hallway, she slipped inside the office and behind Sol's desk. She looked for a scrap of paper and a pen. Sol's computer woke from sleep mode. Ingrid stared at the cursor flashing enticingly at her from the search field in the center of the screen. Maybe Sol had a higher clearance level—he was bound to, wasn't he—and she wouldn't get the access denied message if she searched for Brewster on his computer? Her fingers hovered over the keyboard.

"Can I help you with something?"

"Sol, hi." She swallowed hard. "I, um, thought you always ate a sandwich at your desk."

"I'm not sure that's the correct way to address a superior officer." He folded his arms and glared at her. A moment later his face broke into a wide grin, but as he walked toward her, Ingrid got the feeling he was scrutinizing the merest flicker of movement in her expression. He slipped behind his desk and checked his monitor. He glanced up at Ingrid and narrowed his eyes.

"What was it you needed, agent?" He reeked of cigarettes. He always did.

"I don't think I have sufficient security clearance for this Brewster assignment. I can't find out who he is, or what he does."

Sol raised an eyebrow. "You don't actually need to know, Ingrid. All you have to do is find his laptop."

"Which would be much easier if I knew what someone's motivation for stealing it was."

He scratched his salt-and-pepper beard. "I appreciate that, but it's national security. Need-to-know. Just put a trace on the serial number and do your best."

Ingrid felt her fury rising. "Is there something I've done, Sol? Some reason I don't have clearance?"

He pulled off his wire-frame glasses and cleaned them with a cloth. "What makes you say that?"

"Am I still on probation?"

He leaned back in his chair. "You shouldn't be. We've made your appointment permanent, haven't we?"

"Not as far as I know."

He replaced his spectacles. "Are you happy here? At the embassy? In London?"

Where the hell had that come from? She thought about the dark looks she got from her colleagues. "Mostly."

"Good. We should probably do something about finding you an apartment."

It would be nice to leave the hotel. "I'd rather you did something about my clearance level."

Sol laid his hands flat against the desk and stared at them for a moment. "I'll see what I can do. But in the meantime, find the laptop. Impress the people who need to be impressed."

He might as well have said 'run along, little girl.' Ingrid had warmed to Sol. He was usually an avuncular, easygoing presence who was slow to anger and didn't rush to judgment. But if he didn't have her back, if she wasn't sure he was on her side, then she should think about moving home to DC. Ingrid wandered slowly in the direction of the criminal division office. Jennifer, her assistant, had returned from lunch.

"Hey," she said brightly. "Did David Eustace turn up at the interview this morning?"

Ingrid, still rattled from Sol's stonewalling, sat down heavily. "Who's Eustace?"

"He's, like, the embassy criminal lawyer." Jen was a total Valley Girl, down to her sunny Californian personality and the inclusion of the word *like* in every sentence.

Ingrid pictured the smartly dressed woman who had terminated the Met's questioning of Madison Faber. She definitely didn't look like a David. "No," she said. "A woman turned up."

"Strange. He's normally very reliable."

"Can you give me his number?" Ingrid said. "I'd like to give him a call."

"Sure thing." Jen swiveled breezily in her chair and flipped through an old-fashioned Rolodex. It matched the rest of the office, which could easily be described as 'vintage.' It could also be called 'dated.' It looked like the set of an '80s cop show.

Ingrid nudged her mouse, and her computer flicked into life. The 'access denied' alert was still in the middle of her screen. It was clear Sol wasn't going to give her any more information, but there had to be another way to discover what Brewster's business trip was really about.

All she had to do was figure out how.

6

The arrival of Faber's high-powered lawyer, paid for by the girl's family, had resulted in Madison being released without charge. Now that Faber no longer needed embassy assistance, Ingrid's job was to ensure Lauren Shelbourne's death was investigated properly.

Ingrid made an early start, arriving a little after nine at Loriners, the college where Lauren Shelbourne had been studying. The young woman's grieving parents wanted her body repatriated, and for that to happen, all the paperwork—including Ingrid's report—had to be completed.

Loriners was a mix of impressive twentieth-century brick buildings and ultramodern concrete, glass and steel structures, haphazardly stacked cubes, their doors and windows painted in bright primary colors. A network of walkways at various levels connected the muddle of architectural styles together. It was a glorious spring day, and the students were in short-sleeve tees, with a handful braving shorts and cutoffs. The weather was in contrast to the mood on campus: everyone seemed quiet and subdued, speaking in hushed tones and moving slowly.

Ingrid claimed her visitor's badge from the administration block and memorized the map of the campus. She surveyed the piazza in front of her and spotted the building she was interested in. Just to the left of it was Detective Constable Ralph Mills chatting to a uniformed colleague. She ducked behind a tree: she was there to report on the thoroughness of the Met's investigation, and she'd rather they weren't aware she was on site.

There was a quality about Mills Ingrid had warmed to. He was tall, slim, with collar-length hair and substantial sideburns. He looked like he could have been the bass player in one of the Britpop bands that had dominated the charts in the 1990s. Maybe that was who he reminded her of—there was definitely something unnervingly familiar about him. Unlike most homicide cops she'd known, Ralph Mills gave the impression he was caring and compassionate. She imagined he was very good at dealing with bereaved families. His height gave him presence, but his slight stature and easygoing nature meant he wasn't intimidating. He would probably be a good person to ask for the preliminary autopsy report.

When Ingrid had called Natasha McKittrick the previous evening to request it, the person who'd answered the call transferred her not to the detective inspector, but to a press officer, who told her precisely nothing and treated her like a journalist rather than a fellow law enforcement officer. When she'd complained, she was told to go through 'proper channels.' Which was what she'd thought she'd done calling McKittrick in the first place. She could understand why McKittrick was keeping her at arm's length—no one likes another investigator scrutinizing how you run a case—but it was as if their friendship counted for nothing.

With Mills safely occupied on another part of campus, Ingrid made her way to the large cafeteria housed in one of the traditional Edwardian redbrick buildings. Inside, it was furnished with long wooden refectory tables and benches, coats of arms decorating the walls below the high ceiling. Despite the dark wood and stone floors, the cafeteria was actually quite a welcoming space. The students were more relaxed than they had been outside, most of them chattering noisily to one another, raising their voices to be heard above the general din. She grabbed a plastic tray and joined the line waiting for a cooked breakfast, hoping to tune in to any conversations where Lauren

Shelbourne's name was mentioned. She didn't have to wait long. Two excited teenagers lined up behind her. They were already in full flow, speculating about the death.

"Martina said they found her naked. Raped, Martina said. The police think it might be a serial killer."

"Who else has he killed?"

"Well, no one yet—no one we've heard about. But all serial killers have to start somewhere, don't they?" She shuddered.

"Makes me glad I'm still living at home. I bitch about the commute, but being two bus rides away actually makes me feel safer."

"I wonder who's going to be next." There was a mawkish thrill in her tone.

Ingrid took a good look at them. They were ordinary students, even a little bookish. One sported Harry Potter–style spectacles, the other had a wild head of red hair stuck up in a ragged bun held together by an HB pencil. Nice girls. Why were they talking about the suspicious death of a fellow student as if it were an episode of their favorite soap opera?

Ingrid reached the bakery display and helped herself to a rubbery-looking raisin pastry. It didn't really matter if it tasted as bad as it looked, she had no intention of eating it. She paid and found a place at the center of one of the long wooden tables, where she could listen to as many conversations as possible while she played with her food.

As soon as she sat down, the surrounding chairs were vacated. Just as she was wondering whether she'd forgotten to apply deodorant after her run that morning, a gawky, geeky teen shoved his food tray onto the table and sat heavily on the hard wooden bench directly opposite her. His plate was stacked high with fries, eggs, and a pie buried beneath a landslide of baked beans. He definitely wouldn't be starting class on an empty stomach. She watched as he smothered the whole lot in tomato ketchup and dove and attacked the fries as if they were an enemy army. She looked away as soon as he shoved the first forkful into his baby-bird gaping mouth, and considered switching tables. She picked a flake off her pastry and popped it into her mouth. She chewed slowly and glanced up at her uninvited companion.

"What's in the pie?" she asked.

When he'd recovered from the shock of her dialog opener, he answered with a full mouth, "Steak." He swallowed. "And mushrooms. Thankfully though, not many. Mushrooms make me gag."

"Then why did you choose the pie?"

"Halal, innit? Only meaty thing on the menu that is."

"But it's OK?"

He shrugged back at her. "S'all right."

She smiled at him, taking a proper look at his face. His greasy complexion mirrored the fatty mess on his plate.

"Is the campus usually this... subdued?" she asked.

"Is it? Hadn't noticed." He carried on shoveling his food, barely chewing it before each noisy gulp. "Might be something to do with that girl who died."

Ingrid sat up straight. "You knew her?"

"Do you?"

"Me? How would I know her?"

"You're American, aren't you? She was American."

"Hey, it's a big place." She smiled again. "I've just heard a few people talking about her this morning."

"You're new here. I would definitely have noticed you before otherwise. Are you a lecturer?"

She shook her head.

"Admin staff?"

"I'm just checking the place out. Prospective PhD student."

"Mo," he said and nodded at her. "Short for Mohammed."

"I figured it wasn't short for Maureen."

"Nice—an American with a sense of humor." He narrowed his eyes. "What's your name?"

Ingrid paused a beat before answering. "Sarah." She glanced down at her visitor's badge and quickly shoved it inside her jacket.

"OK, Sarah... so what can I say to persuade you to come here?"

"I'm not sure you can say anything. I've heard people talking about a serial killer on the loose."

"You shouldn't listen to rumors. Most of the students here are complete morons."

"That's not exactly a glowing recommendation."

"Not all of us!" He put down his knife and fork. "The post-grad stuff is all right. But I wouldn't be here if I'd got the grades for Imperial."

Ingrid tore off a corner of pastry and rolled it between her fingers like a ball of modeling clay. "So far you're not convincing me."

He shrugged and grabbed his cutlery from the table. "Shame. You'd improve the scenery round here a bit." He stared unashamedly into her face.

Ingrid eyeballed him until he dropped his gaze to his plate. "Just saying," he mumbled.

"I'll take it as a compliment."

"How many other colleges are you visiting?"

Ingrid paused before answering, she hadn't gotten that far working out her cover story. How many would sound right? "Oh, um, a few."

"Which ones have you rejected?"

"None so far."

"I suppose… if you're gonna make an… informed decision…" He stared at his plate. "I should tell you about the girl who died last week."

"Another girl?" Ingrid remembered the question Angela Tate had fired at McKittrick when the reporter had barged into Lauren Shelbourne's apartment. "So there *is* a serial killer?"

"Nah, nothing like that." He shoveled another quivering pile of meat, gravy and pastry into his mouth. "It was suicide. I saw it happen. She jumped from the top of the admin block."

"You saw her jump?"

"I saw her fly. Until she stopped. Splat! Guts and brains all over the shop. They still haven't managed to clean it all up." He shook more ketchup onto the remains of his pie.

"Must have shaken you up."

"Not really. I don't mind the sight of blood. I'd be a useless doctor if I did, wouldn't I?"

"You're studying medicine?"

"I like cutting stuff up."

Ingrid glanced at the knife he was wielding over his plate.

"Did you know her? The girl who jumped?"

"No."

"But as far as you're aware, her death isn't connected to the one that happened yesterday?"

"There isn't a serial killer—you don't need to worry."

"I don't suppose you knew... what was her name... Lauren?"

"Depends on your definition of 'knew.' I'd seen her face around. The psychology grads like to put themselves about a bit. But they're a stuck-up bunch. Especially the Americans. No offense."

"None taken."

"They're all too important to speak to lowly undergrads. Until they need another recruit for one of their Mickey Mouse experiments. Always looking for volunteers for them. Then it's all 'Hi, Mohammed, how are you? Come and have your testicles wired up to an electrical current and we'll measure how loud you scream.'"

"Wait a minute—you're not telling me they're *torturing* students?" Ingrid leaned forward.

"No, I was exaggerating." He chewed another mouthful of fries. "But not by much."

"What kind of experiments, then?"

The young medic inched toward her, clearly excited to have anyone listen to what he had to say. "I know for a fact that they —" He pulled away suddenly, distracted by something or someone across the room.

"What is it?" Ingrid turned to follow his gaze and saw two male students deep in conversation. They were wearing matching green and purple polo shirts.

Mohammed slumped in his seat, making himself smaller. "Nothing."

"You were telling me about the experiments."

He pulled a face. "I don't really know anything about them. Don't listen to me. Loriners is a good college. You should definitely do your PhD here." He shoveled the last of his fries in his mouth and stood up. "Are you planning on finishing that?" He nodded at the pastry.

"Be my guest."

He produced a used square of aluminum foil from his bag, smoothed out the wrinkles on the table and carefully transferred her uneaten breakfast onto it. He wrapped it up in a neat cylinder and slipped it into his backpack. "I'm not a big fan of the sugary stuff, but there's no point in wasting it."

"Those two guys..." Ingrid gestured to where the students wearing the purple and green shirts had been standing. "What are they, in a sports team or something?"

"Don't know what you're talking about. I didn't see anyone." He nodded a goodbye, weaved quickly around the table and disappeared through the main door.

Ingrid shoved her dirty tray onto a nearby stack and followed him out. But by the time she'd reached the exit, Mohammed had melted into the crowd. There was no sign of the purple and green shirts either. Ingrid wondered what they might have done to have gotten Mohammed so spooked.

She crossed the piazza in search of the psychology department where Lauren Shelbourne had studied. Her attention was snagged by a man in overalls up a ladder, scrubbing at a scrawl of graffiti on one of the gray concrete walls. As she approached, she saw the first two words painted in bright yellow paint, previously obscured by the workman's ladder.

She froze.

lauren shelbourne = whore

7

Ingrid asked the janitor to stop: he was destroying evidence in a potential murder. He refused, and without UK powers of arrest, she had settled for him wiping some of the paint onto a tissue so she could get it forensically analyzed. She carefully folded the tissue, stored it inside a candy wrapper and went in search of the office of Lauren Shelbourne's psychology professor. She knocked on the door and opened it quickly without waiting for a reply.

"Can I help you?" A forty-something white man, with close-cut silver hair over his head and most of his face, stared up at her from his perch on the edge of a desk. He was lean, long-limbed and held himself with an athlete's poise and the confidence of a man used to students hanging on his every word. His eyes were red, as if he'd been up all night.

"I'm so sorry to interrupt." Ingrid nodded to the four young students, three men and a woman, sitting in a tight semicircle of chairs. One chair was vacant. "Professor Younger?"

"That much you must have gleaned from the brass plate on my door." He sounded irritated.

Ingrid flashed her ID at him. "Special Agent Skyberg. From the US Embassy."

Professor Younger tensed at the mention of her title, then again at the word *embassy*. She sensed a general stiffening in the students' postures.

"We were just finishing up, anyway." He glared at the students, who scraped back their chairs and got to their feet.

"Actually, if it's not too inconvenient, I'd like to speak to all of you." Ingrid smiled at the four suspicious faces, all of them scrutinizing her just as closely as she was studying them. The woman folded her arms across her chest and looked at the floor in embarrassment. Two of the young men wore Chinese-style collarless gray shirts and plain black corduroy pants, almost like a uniform. The third was more interesting to Ingrid. He was the only student to return her gaze, making eye contact for much longer than was polite. He was also wearing a purple and green polo shirt. She smiled and stared back at him, determined he should look away first. When he did, she said, "I want to talk to you about Lauren Shelbourne."

All four students mumbled at once, making vague noises that at no point threatened to coalesce into actual words.

"I'm sorry, what was that?" Ingrid stared directly at the female student.

"I didn't really know her," she said.

Ingrid pointed at the extra chair. "The registrar's office told me this was Lauren's study group. I'm supposing the empty chair is hers?"

The girl looked imploringly at Professor Younger.

"The whole group is very shaken by what has happened," he explained. "I'm not sure firing questions at them is entirely appropriate. They're clearly still in shock. Can't it wait?"

"So you did know Lauren?"

The students nodded and mumbled again.

"It's terrible, what's happened," the student in the polo shirt said. "Do you know if the police are treating it as murder?"

Professor Younger threw the young man a warning look.

"I'm sorry, I can't discuss that with you."

Younger levered himself off his desk and opened his arms wide. He moved forward slowly, shepherding his flock toward the door. "They should really be getting back to their studies."

Ingrid stood to one side and watched the students shuffle out of the room. The man in the polo shirt was the last to leave. "Which sport do you play?" Ingrid pointed at his shirt.

For a moment he was confused.

Younger came to his rescue, butting in before he could answer for himself. "Hockey. Thomas represents the college in the university league."

"Isn't this the off-season?" Ingrid had no clue which season the Brits played hockey. She just didn't want to let him off the hook that easily.

"We play all year round," the bemused student finally managed before leaving the room.

"Good luck!" Ingrid called after him.

He turned back. "I'm sorry?"

"In your next match."

"Right, yeah. Thanks."

Ingrid closed the door. "I'm hoping you have a few moments for me, Professor?"

"Please." He gestured toward a leather chair close to the desk. "Call me Stuart."

Ingrid remained on her feet. "I'm trying to get some background information. Perhaps you could paint me a picture of Lauren's life here at Loriners?"

Younger let out a long, quiet sigh.

"I guess it's hit you hardest of all," Ingrid said.

He blinked at her. "Why do you say that?"

"Lauren was effectively in your care during her time here."

"It's not as if I could have done anything to prevent what happened." He lifted a trembling hand and ran it over his short hair.

"Even so."

He nodded, bit his lip then made deliberate eye contact. "Why is the American embassy involved? Surely the police are investigating the circumstances of her death?" He scratched the side of his face, the pale skin beneath his beard reddening in long streaks.

"It's a matter of routine."

He frowned at her. "I've already spoken to the police, a chap named… Mills, I think. I answered all his questions. Can't you liaise with him rather than asking me the same things all over again?"

"My role is to make sure the police investigate thoroughly, that if a crime has been committed, they deliver justice for American citizens."

"I see. I didn't know you did that sort of thing." He blinked nervously.

"Tell me about Lauren."

"I'm confused. Are you saying Lauren was murdered? The police didn't give that impression."

"I really can't comment." Ingrid moved toward him. "What kind of student was Lauren?"

He blinked again. "Lauren was, um, an exceptional student. Quiet. Reserved. Always impeccably polite. Her parents brought her up that way." His eyes focused on an invisible distant object. "She'll be missed."

Ingrid smiled at him. "As far as you're aware, Lauren hadn't made any enemies here at college?"

"Enemies?" His eyes bulged. "What makes you say that?"

"You must have seen the graffiti?"

"Graffiti? I don't understand."

"On one side of the science block. It was—"

At that moment the door burst open so hard and fast Ingrid had to jump to avoid getting hit.

"Why are you ignoring my calls?"

Madison Faber stomped into the room, and Younger held up his hands defensively. Following his gaze, Faber spun round.

"Oh," she said.

"Hello, Madison," Ingrid said. "How are you doing?"

Faber cleared her throat. "Why are you here?"

"Actually, I'd like to talk to you. We didn't really get the chance yesterday. After the lawyer arrived." She smiled warmly at the student. "I'm glad to see you're well enough to come into college."

It took a few seconds for the scowl on Faber's face to soften. She turned back to the professor. "We have to talk," she told him. "I'll find you later."

8

Ingrid thanked Younger for his time and raced to catch up with Faber as she crossed the piazza. The girl was very pale, her large eyes bloodshot through lack of sleep. Ahead, the janitor had water-blasted all but the final *r* and *e* of the word *whore* from the concrete facade.

"That must have really upset Lauren. Did she speak to you about it?"

Faber raised an eyebrow. "It was new this morning."

"It was?" Ingrid hoped Mills and his colleague had spotted it before the cleaning operation started.

Faber studied the janitor as he water-blasted the *r* of yellow paint. "It's the first time I've seen it."

"Any idea who would have written it?"

She shrugged in response. "How would I know?"

Ingrid shook her head. "Who would want to say something like that about Lauren, in these circumstances?"

Faber stared at the wall. "People never fail to appall me. The more I study, the more convinced I am in the limitless human capacity for cruelty. Some people are just plain evil. Surely I don't need to tell you that, with your job?"

Ingrid turned to her. "You still believe Lauren had no enemies?"

"Everything I've learned tells me that says more about the

person who wrote it than Lauren." Faber inhaled sharply, her nostrils narrowing. "They heard her name on the news and decided to make a little news themselves. Make a mark. Shock the college authorities."

"You're the psychology student," Ingrid said. "You'll no doubt have some insights."

"Are you making fun of me, Agent Skyberg?"

"Absolutely not. No."

The girl looked offended.

"No, I meant it. I wasn't being glib." Ingrid needed to change the subject. "I'm glad I ran into you today. I wanted to make sure you felt you were treated properly by the Metropolitan Police yesterday."

Faber's pace slowed. "I guess they were only doing their job."

"Was it tough?"

"Finding Lauren was horrific enough." Ingrid's thoughts seized on the image of Lauren's crumpled body, emptied of blood, and the gaping wound in her forehead where she had smashed into the coffee table. "Reliving it for the cops was almost as bad."

Ingrid pushed her hands into her pants pockets. "I hope they were gentle with you."

Faber bristled. "Like I say, it's their job."

"That's a good attitude to have. It'll help with future interviews."

Faber pulled up. "How many more are there likely to be?"

"Um, well, I'm not entirely familiar with procedures here in the UK, but given you were the one who found Lauren, they will want to rule you out as a suspect. That's standard in every case."

"But Miriam said there was no need for me to worry."

"Your attorney? I'm sure she's right. But nine times out of ten, the perpetrator is either the boyfriend or the witness who reports the crime. Don't take it personally if they want to speak to you again. And the autopsy may well say it was an accident, anyway." Ingrid rested a hand on Faber's shoulder. "Between the embassy and your attorney, we have everything covered. You don't need to be overly concerned." She tugged gently on Faber's arm.

Faber wouldn't be budged. She was staring into space, chewing her lip. "You don't think I had anything to do with Lauren's death, do you?"

"Of course not."

Faber put her hand on top of Ingrid's. "It helps to know you're in my corner."

"You have no need to doubt that. Come on, let me buy you a coffee."

"I guess... after losing your friend... you understand what I'm going through."

Ingrid said nothing. She didn't like that Faber knew, and she certainly didn't like that the girl had brought it up, but Ingrid wasn't about to give her a hard time. Faber was alone in a strange country, thousands of miles from home: at least when she had lost Megan, Ingrid's mom and grandma had been around to look out for her. "I'm here for you." She pulled out a card from her jacket pocket. "However I can help."

"Thank you." Faber tucked Ingrid's contact details into her bag, and they walked to the cafeteria. "Can I tell you something?"

"Sure."

"I've been thinking things over since yesterday," Faber said, withdrawing her hand from Ingrid's arm. "There is something I forgot to mention to the police."

"Whatever it is, you should definitely tell them about it. The smallest of details can help."

"I'm not sure what made me think of it, but it just didn't make any sense."

"Go on."

"The desk in Lauren's apartment was empty. Where was her laptop? Or her iPad? We were supposed to discuss her thesis. She would have been using her computer, surely?"

"Maybe she left her stuff somewhere else?"

"Or maybe they were taken. What if it was a robbery gone wrong?"

"I can mention it to the police if you like?"

Faber, lost in thought, didn't answer. "Poor, poor Lauren. Her parents must be devastated. It puts my pain into perspective."

"Don't underestimate the impact losing Lauren, and finding her, will have on you. Has the college talked to you about counseling?"

Faber nodded vigorously. "That's what I went to see Younger about."

"Oh." Ingrid wasn't sure she believed her. "I'm glad. He seemed pretty upset too. Was Professor Younger close to Lauren?"

Faber shrugged. "I guess tutors and students form a special bond."

"And is he, I'm not sure how they phrase things in the UK, like your personal supervisor? Is that why you were talking to him about counseling?"

They neared the refectory block.

"The exact opposite, in fact."

Ingrid looked blank.

"I don't agree with his research methods. I have my own way of approaching the work. I don't want him getting involved in my personal affairs."

Ingrid hadn't warmed to the professor either. He exuded arrogance. The exterior wall of the cafeteria had a large patch of cleaned concrete. Ingrid pointed at it. "Do you remember what was written there before it was cleaned off?"

Faber shrugged. "No idea. You see a lot of graffiti in this neighborhood."

They entered the large refectory, and Ingrid ordered them both large black Americanos.

"For here or takeaway?" the barista asked.

"To go," Faber said firmly before Ingrid could answer. Ingrid looked over at the table where she'd spoken to Mohammed. "You're not the first person to comment about Younger's methods. What is it he does that you don't agree with?"

"You should ask Professor Younger himself. My work is paper based: I research other people's research. A lot of people think it's dull, but I happen to consider it groundbreaking." She was displaying more than a little arrogance herself. Ingrid marveled at the girl's confidence. If only she'd been so self-assured in her early twenties.

"I've heard he uses other students in his experiments."

The barista placed two paper cups on the counter. Behind him, a colleague scrawled the word *tonight* across a poster for a music gig.

"Students are cheap and eager. They'll do pretty much anything for a pizza and a few beers."

"What kind of experiments are we talking about?"

"As I said—you'll have to ask Professor Younger. I'm really not that interested in what my peers are doing. I need to be focused on my own studies." Faber locked eyes with Ingrid, her large blue irises catching the light. "Talking of which, I should get to work."

"Already? I'm sure the staff here would make allowances if you took some time off."

Faber took a sip of very hot coffee. "I'd rather keep busy."

"It's as good a strategy as any," Ingrid said. "You've got my card. Call me if there's anything I can do to help."

"Thank you. And thanks for the coffee."

Ingrid watched Faber walk away. The girl's gait was heavy, determined, and she didn't look back or wave. It was as if she'd switched from friendly chat mode to serious academic mode in a heartbeat. There was a Jekyll and Hyde split in Faber's personality, and Ingrid imagined that prickliness made friend-ships difficult: Lauren's absence would leave a huge hole in her life.

Before Faber reached the door, a tall, familiar figure stepped into the cafeteria. Faber pretended not to have seen DC Mills, but he reached out one of his long arms and placed a palm on her shoulder. Ingrid was too far away to hear what he said to her, but her response was to slap him out of the way and push past him out the door. He ran after her. Ingrid ditched her coffee and did the same.

In the piazza, Faber had been apprehended by Mills and his

uniformed colleague. "What's going on?" Ingrid asked. "Has there been a development?"

"I've been leaving messages for Miss Faber all morning," Mills said.

The girl shrugged. "My cell phone must be out of juice."

"I was beginning to fear you'd left the country." He smiled at each woman in turn. "Which wouldn't be a good idea: you need to come with us to the station. Right now."

9

Detective Inspector Natasha McKittrick wheeled round, arms raised ready for a fight, when Ingrid tapped her on the shoulder. She was waiting in line in a sandwich shop five minutes from Lewisham police station.

"Easy!" Ingrid held up her hands, surprised at McKittrick's extreme reaction.

"Christ almighty. What are you doing creeping up on me?"

"Just saying hello." Ingrid smiled at her. "But I can go again. If you'd like."

What was up with McKittrick? Ingrid had got to know her as an easygoing, sharp-witted woman who wasn't scared of an opinion or an extra drink. But for the past two days she had been weirdly uptight.

"How did you know I was here?"

"The desk sergeant told me you were between shifts." Ingrid peered at the chalkboard above the counter. She'd forgotten to eat lunch again. "Your boy Mills just picked up Madison Faber. Thought I'd sit with her till her lawyer came, but one of your team said she didn't want me hanging around."

"You've pissed her off too?"

Ingrid was taken aback. "I take it that means I've pissed you off?"

McKittrick curled a lip. "I know you're just doing your job."

"Sorry. No one likes anyone second-guessing the way they run a case." She thought about the paint-soaked tissue in her bag and decided to hold back from handing it over.

McKittrick studied the menu, giving Ingrid a chance to notice how run-down her friend was looking. Whenever they met for an after-work drink, McKittrick turned up in a tailored power suit, kitten heels and a designer handbag. She wouldn't be described as glamorous in any APB profile, but her hair was always fixed and her lipstick was always freshly applied. Right now, however, McKittrick looked considerably older than her thirty-five years and a bit scruffy. She reached the front of the line and ordered tuna salad on whole wheat. "Do you want anything?"

Ingrid nodded a hello at the weary woman behind the counter. "Make that two." She turned her attention back to McKittrick. "If it makes you feel better, you've not been singled out for special treatment. We do it for every American citizen who dies in unexplained circumstances."

McKittrick said nothing.

"It's just a box-ticking exercise," Ingrid explained. "I'm not keeping tabs on you."

McKittrick's shoulders finally dropped. "You're probably the only one who isn't, then."

Ingrid's eyebrows narrowed. "What's going on?"

McKittrick grimaced. "It's nothing I can talk about."

"No? My lips will be forever sealed."

"I'm sorry, but I've got to get back." McKittrick paid for both sandwiches, shoved one at Ingrid and pushed her way between the tightly packed tables to the door. Ingrid joined her on the sidewalk.

"Another time, then," Ingrid said. "Before I let you go, anything I should know about why you questioned Faber again? Has something been flagged on the autopsy?"

"We call it a postmortem. And no, we're just eliminating her from our inquiries," McKittrick said. "We've spoken to a couple of neighbors and just need to make sure she gives us the same information. If she does, she can sign a statement and we'll let her go."

"Has someone corroborated her time of arrival at Shelbourne's apartment?"

McKittrick sank her teeth into one half of her sandwich, took a messy bite and chewed vigorously for a few moments before answering. "A downstairs neighbor said she arrived at eight twenty. She had trouble opening the main door to the house. The key wasn't working properly. She buzzed all the other apartments until someone answered."

Ingrid handed her a paper napkin. "You have a little..." She pointed to her own chin. McKittrick quickly wiped the spot of mayo away. "So Faber shouldn't expect a four a.m. call from the boys in blue?"

"Not unless we discover something specific to link her to the death."

"And when will you be getting the *postmortem*?" Ingrid pulled a shred of lettuce from between the slices of bread and popped it in her mouth.

"This afternoon. I'll ask one of the lads to get it to you by close of play."

"You must have had a preliminary report by now?"

McKittrick swallowed another rushed mouthful and nodded. "No surprises. Apart from the massive trauma to the head, there were only insignificant injuries. It's looking like an accident to me."

"But that was one hell of a head wound."

"I know, so we're keeping an open mind."

"You have a time of death?"

McKittrick finished her sandwich and tossed the messy bag into a trash can at the curb. "Pathologist puts it between midnight and two a.m."

"Toxicology? Had she been drinking? Or taking drugs?"

"We'll get the bloods back later too." McKittrick's shoulders crept up toward her ears.

"Sorry, I'm adding to your stress. Wasn't my intention. Had thought maybe we could have a nice catch-up."

McKittrick sighed. "I think what we have here is a case of this being a higher priority for you than it is for me. You know how many cases I'm overseeing?"

Ingrid didn't.

"Five murders, and one of them is really, horrifically complex. For as long as it looks likely the girl tripped on her landlord's Axminster shag pile and collided with his chrome and smoked-glass coffee table, I've got other things that need my attention."

"Understood." Inside though, Ingrid was furious. The first twenty-four hours are crucial in every investigation. If the pathologist suspects foul play, the Met will have squandered a precious opportunity to gather evidence.

Ingrid looked down at her sandwich bag; the greasy mayo had started to leech through the paper. Suddenly her appetite vanished. McKittrick was already walking away, heading back to the station. Ingrid raced to catch up with her. "Lauren's parents are flying in tomorrow. I'm meeting them at Heathrow in the afternoon. They'll want to know if their daughter was murdered, the local police are doing everything possible to find her killer."

"I'll do my best to see you've got the latest developments by the time they land." McKittrick had picked up her pace.

Ingrid remembered the tissue. "Natasha, slow down."

She didn't. "And there's also something you can do for me."

"Name it."

"Stop teasing my constable."

"Your constable?"

"Mills. He's been asking about you. Wondered if it'd be OK to give you a call."

"Really, I've not spoken more than two words to him."

"Well, your movie-star good looks have done the trick, then." McKittrick smiled mischievously. At last, a little of the Natasha Ingrid was used to had made an appearance.

"You did tell him I was engaged?"

"No. Not really. Must have slipped my mind." Another smile. "Besides, the way you talk about Marshall, I don't really see you as the marrying kind."

McKittrick's throwaway comment almost winded Ingrid.

"Really?" She was rooted to the spot while McKittrick marched on. She caught up with her on the police station's front steps. Ingrid grabbed her friend's arm. "There's something Faber mentioned earlier."

McKittrick turned. "Oh yeah?"

"Lauren's laptop. Did you find it? Faber said it wasn't on the desk where she usually kept it."

"No, there was no laptop. Or tablet. We haven't even located a mobile phone. In the apartment or at the college. Perhaps you could ask her parents if they have receipts for her devices. The serial numbers would be extremely helpful."

"But you've put traces on her number, her email?"

"I'm sure my team are doing all of that. The moment anyone switches Shelbourne's phone on, we'll know about it." McKittrick turned to go. "So"—she looked over her shoulder—"what should I tell lovestruck Mills?"

Ingrid smiled. "Tell him I've got an appointment at an escort agency."

10

Ingrid's trip to Escort Angels, the agency who supplied Greg Brewster's nighttime companion, wasn't exactly fruitful. The address they had for Barry Cline was fake. The number they had for him rang and rang without diverting to an answering service. And the woman running the agency couldn't be entirely sure the photo they had on file for him was a good likeness. When Ingrid got back to the embassy, she unsurprisingly discovered 'Barry Cline' wasn't in any database because it was almost certainly a fake name. Ingrid arranged for the phone number to be monitored, and checked to see if the laptop had been handed into the police, or London Transport lost property, or a branch of Cash Converters. She had very low expectations of finding it. She still wanted to know, however, what the hell was on it that required it to be reported to the embassy. More than that, she really wanted to get to the bottom of why she didn't have sufficient security clearance to access Brewster's files in the archives.

Unable to face another night in her hotel room and a long conversation with Marshall or her mom, Ingrid got on the bike and returned to Loriners. She was meeting Lauren Shelbourne's parents in the morning and wanted to be able to tell them as much as possible about the circumstances around her daughter's death. She kept seeing the gash on Lauren's forehead and couldn't believe such a wound could be inflicted by simply falling over. Ingrid fully expected the autopsy report to indicate she had been murdered. The suicide of the girl the week before and the whore graffiti meant Ingrid wanted to do a little digging. She remembered the poster for a music concert on campus and thought it was a better use of her time than another self-flagellation session in the hotel gym.

After the gig—a poorly attended cacophony of discordant experimentation—Ingrid found herself on an almost deserted campus and decided to take a look around. Apart from the odd camera, there was no obvious sign of a security presence save for occasional signs warning of dogs and specially trained staff.

Ten minutes after the musicians left the stage, she seemed to be all alone on the campus. The main piazza was deathly silent. When she reached the science block, she stopped: even in the dim light cast by the distant streetlamps, she could see fresh paint dripping down the facade. She checked left and right, but the campus appeared to be deserted. The vandals had dispensed with words and chosen to spray three identical symbols on the newly scrubbed concrete:

$$\setminus / \setminus / \setminus \quad \setminus / \setminus / \setminus \quad \setminus / \setminus / \setminus$$

She'd never seen anything like it before. Was it a symbol from some ancient language studied in the linguistics department? She got her phone out to take a photo, when the silence was broken by a clang of metal hitting metal, the sound echoing around the piazza. She turned toward the noise and saw a spray can bouncing off walls and steel handrails as it fell earthwards. A level up from the ground, two dark-clad figures leaned over the walkway wall.

"Hey! What are you doing?" Ingrid ran toward them. They just stood there watching her, making no attempt to escape, no doubt confident that the only way up onto their level was via a long ramp at the far end of the piazza. They laughed as she approached. Determined to wipe the smiles from their faces, Ingrid accelerated and launched herself at the lower wall, landing cleanly on top and using her momentum to leap upward, high enough to grab the metal rail on the next level up. She swung her right leg out and up, the rubber toe of her sneaker catching the edge of the walkway wall. Though she couldn't see them, she heard the unmistakable shuffle of feet sliding over cement. They weren't laughing anymore. Using both arms and her right leg for leverage, she pulled her body over the rail and rolled onto the walkway. In the gloom she could just make out the two graffiti artists at the end of the walkway.

One turned left, the other right.

She got to her feet and ran. She went after the heavier of the two, thinking a slower man would be easier to catch. Ingrid leaped onto the wall running alongside the walkway, intending to jump on him from above, but in the dark she hadn't seen the wall was way too narrow to run at full speed. The vandal started to pull away. She stopped and was about to drop back onto the walkway when something slammed into her calves, pushing her forward into thin air. She struggled to stay upright. A second later she hit the ground feet first and rolled quickly, spreading the impact of the landing. The second vandal peered down at her from the walkway above, a short length of wood in his hands.

She scrambled to her feet. Her left ankle rolled sideways as she put her weight on it, forcing her back onto the ground, searing pain shooting from her foot up her leg toward the knee. She grabbed her ankle and watched helplessly as the black-clad figure escaped, disappearing into the gloom.

A sudden bright flash lit up the walkway. Ingrid turned. Another flash blinded her momentarily. It was quickly followed by another and another. Ingrid held a hand up to her eyes and tried to blink away the purple stain on her retinas. With each blink a shadowy figure that had materialized in front of her became more solid. She recognized the boots first: shiny black knee-lengths. Then the raincoat came into focus. Angela Tate. The journalist.

Goddammit.

After another bright flash, Ingrid realized Tate was taking pictures of her with her cell phone.

"What do you think you're doing? Stop that." She grabbed at the phone, but Tate pulled away swiftly and slipped it safely into her coat pocket.

"That was quite a display," Tate said. "Isn't that what the kids do? Parkour, isn't it?"

"Did you get a photo of them?"

"It was too dark. Besides, their faces were covered." The journalist held out a hand to Ingrid, which she batted away.

Ingrid slowly stood up and tested her left ankle, gradually easing her weight onto it. It was sore but still functioning. "What are you doing here?"

Angela Tate looked Ingrid up and down. "I could ask you the same thing."

A set of lights came on over the main concourse below them. Tate peered over the walkway wall. "It appears the security firm, dogs included, have chosen to make an appearance."

Ingrid grabbed the journalist and dragged her further into the shadows. She dropped her voice to a whisper. "What are you doing here?"

"Research. I'm working on a story about Loriners. You know about the suicide last week?"

"Why don't you tell me about it?" Ingrid folded her arms and nodded encouragingly.

"Not here. I was rather hoping you'd give me a ride home. I doubt I'll pick up a cab at this hour. Presumably your car's parked nearby?"

"Motorcycle."

A dog barked in the distance.

"I think it's time we made a swift exit. A motorcycle, eh? Sounds like fun. Haven't been on a bike for years."

"Sorry. I only have one helmet."

"Even better. I like to feel the wind in my hair."

"No way."

"Do you want me to tell you what I know about the suicide or not?"

Without another word, Ingrid led Tate through campus, managing to avoid security guards and their dogs, to where she'd parked the Triumph Tiger. Ingrid unlocked the top box and handed the helmet to the journalist. "You wear it. Just in case we have an accident."

"Let's just make sure we don't, shall we?"

11

After an uncomfortable ten minutes of the journalist squeezing her hands so tight around Ingrid's waist she thought her dinner might find its way back up her digestive tract, they finally arrived at Tate's home in Kennington, just a few miles from Loriners in south London. Tate led Ingrid down a flight of stone steps to the basement apartment of a tall, narrow house in the middle of a row of identical properties.

Ingrid hesitated on the threshold. "Should I take off my sneakers?"

"God, no. We don't stand on ceremony here."

"We?"

"Figure of speech. We're quite alone."

She joined Tate in a narrow kitchen at the far end of the hallway. The woman dropped her coat and gloves onto a chair and lined up bottles of liquor on the kitchen bench. "What are you in the mood for? A drop of brandy to keep out the cold? Or a shot of tequila to get the gray cells firing?"

"A glass of water is just fine."

"Don't be a party pooper. What about a wee dribble of whiskey in that water?"

"You were going to tell me about the suicide last week." She watched as Tate poured herself a triple brandy then downed the lot in one.

"My God, that's better. Are you sure I can't tempt you?"

Ingrid shook her head.

"Please yourself." Tate pushed past her, bottle in hand, and disappeared into another room off the hallway. She hollered, "Well, come on, then."

Ingrid hurried into the room, scanning it quickly, taking in the artful decor and antique pieces of furniture. Angela Tate might be an alcoholic old hack, she thought, but the woman certainly had taste. The journalist was standing over an old oak table in the corner of the room, busily rearranging photographs and sheets of paper that covered most of its surface.

"Tuesday last week. It happened in the afternoon. I think that's what shocked people the most—the extravagant and very public nature of it. You expect people to have suicidal thoughts in the early hours, don't you? Not on a bright spring day. Sun shining, birds singing."

"What do you know about her?"

"Young. Canadian. Studying fine art. Loriners has something of a reputation for the arts. Places are highly sought after. She was only twenty years old. Quite a talent by all accounts."

"How did she die?" Ingrid would have to ask McKittrick for the official report; the graphic version Mohammed had given her wasn't exactly illuminating.

"Top floor of the admin block. It was a miracle she didn't hit anyone on the way down."

"Did she have mental health problems? Was there a note?"

"No and no. According to her friends at college and the ones back home in Montreal, she could sometimes display an 'artistic temperament,' but any depressive episode lasted no longer than a day."

"Maybe she was going through one when she jumped."

Tate refilled her glass and took an unhealthy slug. "It's possible, but there's something not quite right about the whole thing. People at the scene said they thought she was drunk. Properly off her face drunk. Yet no one I've spoken to since can even remember seeing her so much as take a sip of the hard stuff."

Ingrid wasn't sure the Canadian student's death was relevant to Lauren Shelbourne's death unless it demonstrated criminal neglect of students' welfare by the university hierarchy. If it did, then it was something Lauren's parents might want to take action over. "Is there anything else you can tell me? Anything unusual you've discovered about Loriners?"

"I've been working bloody hard on this story for weeks; I'm not just going to hand it to you on a plate."

"Oh, come on. You might be working on a story, but I'm investigating the violent death of a young woman."

"Interesting way of putting it." Tate drained her glass and shoved it on a nearby bookshelf.

"I don't follow," Ingrid said.

"You would have said 'murder' if that's what the evidence has shown. What's the pathologist saying?"

"I honestly don't know. I haven't received the report yet."

Tate folded her arms. "Why are you investigating Lauren Shelbourne's death, violent or otherwise? Is that something the FBI would normally get involved in?"

"If a US citizen dies in a foreign country of something other than natural causes? Sure, we investigate."

"Can't trust the local plod, is that it?"

Plod? She meant the police. "I have full confidence in the Met."

"You must be the only person in London who does. Should we have called nine nine nine about the graffiti?"

Ingrid remembered the paint-covered tissue: she forgot to give it to McKittrick. "I'll mention it to the investigation team in the morning."

Tate returned her attention to the documents on her desk. "What did you make of their artwork?"

"The symbols?"

"Ever seen anything like it before?"

"Have you?"

"I asked first."

Ingrid's cell buzzed in her pocket. Relieved to escape the back-and-forth with an increasingly brandy-fueled Tate, she made her excuses and took the call.

"What is it? Has something happened?"

"I need to speak to you. Urgently." Madison Faber sounded scared.

"I'm listening."

"Not over the phone. Face-to-face. It's a matter of life and death."

12

Despite her initial demand that Ingrid meet her right away, Madison Faber had reluctantly agreed to a rendezvous in Hyde Park early the next morning. She had been quite insistent that they not meet on campus. Ingrid had told Faber her run route, and they had decided to meet at the Serpentine Café.

"I don't feel safe there," she'd whispered into the phone, her voice catching partway through.

Ingrid slowed as she approached the café on the shore of a long lake in the middle of the park, and checked her time and distance stats on her watch. The pain in her ankle had slowed her down considerably, but it seemed to be holding up. Faber was already waiting at the entrance, puffing impatiently on a slim cigarillo.

"I didn't know you smoked," Ingrid said.

"I didn't. Seems to help." Faber clocked Ingrid's look of disapproval. "For now."

There was a coffee cart outside the café, which didn't open until ten a.m.

"Can I get you anything?" Ingrid asked.

"An Americano?"

Five minutes later, coffees in hand, Ingrid found Faber pacing up and down the wooden decking beside the lake, obsessively checking her phone every few seconds. "Sorry about the wait.

You take it black, right?" She handed Faber the cardboard cup. "Shall we find somewhere to sit? It's such a lovely—"

"I want to keep moving." Faber set off toward a path running east-west through the park. "What's happening with the case?"

"I won't know any more until I get into the office. How did it go yesterday, with the police?"

The girl was walking briskly, her gait deliberate as if the placement of each foot required concentration. Madison Faber was a serious young woman. "The police told me not to leave the country. Can you believe that? They let me go, but then lay that on me."

Ingrid wanted to reassure her. "It's nothing personal. They need you as a witness at the coroner's hearing. Now, you said you were scared. Has something happened?"

Faber ignored the question. "When are Lauren's parents arriving?"

Two lines of kindergarten children walking in pairs appeared around a kink in the path, all dressed in gray and yellow uniforms. Ingrid ducked out of the way, but Faber didn't seem to notice them and stood in the center of the path, forcing the pairs to walk around her or unlink hands. She was buffeted and banged on both sides by the tide of tiny bodies. When the final pair had negotiated the unwelcome obstacle, Faber squeezed her eyes shut. Ingrid put a hand on the student's shoulder.

"I think you need to sit down." She guided her to a nearby bench bathed in dappled sunshine.

Faber allowed herself to be led and set her coffee on the wide wooden slat beside her. "You haven't answered my question. When do they get here? I'd like to speak to them."

"They're due in this afternoon. They might not feel up to visitors. And there's a lot of ugly official business they have to deal with."

"It wouldn't be a social call. I need to talk to them about Lauren."

"I'll have a word with them—pass on your condolences."

"No!" Faber's eyes widened, and Ingrid was caught off guard by the power of her gaze. "I mean really talk to them, not spew out platitudes. I'm sure they've had enough of those already." Faber checked her phone again, reached for her coffee, brought the cup to her lips and returned it to the bench without taking a sip. The girl was on edge. Faber seemed more distressed than after discovering Lauren Shelbourne's body.

"You haven't told me why you wanted to see me." Ingrid kept her voice low and gentle, trying to sound as soothing as possible. "What's happened?"

"You'll only think I'm crazy."

"Try me?"

Faber stared at two women, nannies judging by their age and ethnicity, pushing bulky three-wheel baby strollers along the path. The women chatted happily to one another in Russian. Ingrid tried to stop her ears tuning in to their chat, something she always did when she heard people speaking in her mother's native tongue. One woman shrieked a high-pitched laugh that made Faber jump. Ingrid placed a hand on Faber's knee. "What's going on, Madison?"

The girl nodded vigorously. "There's something at college. Something bad." She lifted a hand to push a stray lock of hair from her forehead. It was trembling. "The atmosphere in the psychology department is really jumpy. Especially Professor Younger's group."

"Really?"

"I said you'd think I was crazy."

"Jumpy in what way?"

"Really tense, like they're waiting for something bad to happen." She stood up abruptly. "I've got to keep moving." She checked her phone.

"Are you expecting a call?"

"No, just checking the time." She walked in the direction they'd just come. "Do you think whoever wrote that graffiti has something to do with Lauren's death?"

"What makes you mention that?" Ingrid asked. "You weren't taking it very seriously yesterday."

"I've had more time to think about it since then." She quickened her pace, glancing at her phone again.

What had gotten into the girl to make her this nervous? "Is there something you're not telling me?"

"I just... I'm scared."

"There's no need to be. The police have eliminated you from their inquiries."

"I'm not scared of the police."

"Then what is it?"

"I'm scared for my life."

"Has someone said something?"

"I think I'm next." Faber broke into a jog. Ingrid ran after her, grabbed her arm and pulled her to a stop.

"Next? What are you saying?"

"First that Canadian girl died last week, now Lauren..." Her eyes widened and she stared blankly at the ground.

"The student last week committed suicide. And Lauren... well, the police aren't connecting last week's suicide and Lauren's death."

"Well, they should. They're linked. I know they are."

"Even if they are, why would you be next?"

"I found Lauren, didn't I? Maybe whoever did that to her is worried I saw something, and they can't risk me telling the police."

Ingrid wondered if she could persuade Faber to see the embassy doctor. "You're in shock. What you're feeling right now is completely natural."

"You're patronizing me." Faber pulled away and hurried back toward the café.

"Please, Madison. I'm not. I'm really not," Ingrid called out. She jogged to catch up with her.

"You said you were here for me. I thought you meant it." Faber was speaking in an urgent whisper.

"I am here. I've got your back."

"Your friend—the one you lost..."

Not this. Not again.

"How did she die?"

"It's really not relevant."

"Why won't you tell me?"

72

Because it's none of your goddamn business!

Ingrid took a steadying breath. She needed the girl to trust her. "She was abducted. And never found."

"So she could still be alive somewhere?"

"It was eighteen years ago."

"But she could be? And what if the police looking for her hadn't turned over every stone? Wouldn't you want to know they did everything to find the truth?"

Ingrid stared into Faber's pleading eyes.

"You have to find out what's happening at college." Faber took hold of Ingrid's arms and squeezed tight. "You have to take me seriously."

"And you have to tell me what's happened to you since the last time I saw you."

Faber let go of Ingrid and visibly sagged, all the pent-up energy leaving her in one simple gesture. "If I tell you, you have to swear not to tell anyone else."

"That depends on what it is."

"Promise me!" Passersby stared, making them both realize Faber had been shouting.

"OK, I promise."

Faber dropped her gaze to the ground. "It happened last night. I was at college, in the psychology lab. I left my workstation for a few minutes, and when I returned from the restroom, there it was, just lying there, its guts spilling out onto the desk."

"What are you talking about?"

"A white laboratory mouse. Partially dissected." Her owlish eyes widened. "There was no one around. I'd assumed I was alone in the whole building. But someone must have been there, just waiting for me to leave my desk for a moment."

"What did you do?"

"I panicked. I ran. That's when I called you."

"Did you call the police?"

"I was too scared."

"So the mouse could still be there?"

"I doubt it. Whoever put it there got the result they were after. It terrified me." Faber chewed the inside of her cheek.

"Is it possible it was just a prank? A practical joke?"

"At close to midnight? With no one else around?" She blinked deliberately then looked into Ingrid's face. "It was a warning. I know it was."

"What kind of warning?"

"It's obvious, isn't it? They're making it clear that what happened to Lauren will happen to me. If I don't keep quiet."

"I don't think it's clear at all."

"The mouse on my desk... they hadn't just disemboweled it." She pulled a pained face. "They'd stitched its mouth shut."

13

The embassy car was stuck in traffic on the freeway. Ingrid's frustration was rising. If she'd taken the bike, she'd be waiting in Terminal 5 by now, in plenty of time for the Shelbournes' flight from JFK.

"There must be a faster route," she said from the back seat. It was all she could do not to grab the steering wheel.

"This is the only way to get to Heathrow. I have been there before."

The driver had already explained, repeatedly and at great length, he used to drive a black taxi, which he called a 'cab,' and that Ingrid gathered was some kind of badge of honor. She squeezed her fists into tight balls and took a few deep breaths as the line of traffic ahead ground to a halt yet again.

Madison Faber's revelation was preying on her mind. Ingrid hadn't been able to persuade the girl to go to the police about the incident in the psychology lab. Faber was convinced the police secretly thought she was involved in Lauren's death, but without having the mouse as evidence, Faber was worried they would take it as a sign of her mental instability. On reflection, Ingrid agreed: Faber's behavior and demeanor had been understandably erratic since she'd discovered Lauren's body, and without the mouse, even she wasn't entirely sure she believed the student.

Ingrid's priority for the next few hours was chaperoning the Shelbournes and bringing them, tactfully, up to date with the investigation into their daughter's death. When the driver finally dropped her off, she ran all the way to the arrivals lounge, aware of the soreness in her left ankle. She pulled down the bottom of her jacket and combed her fingers through her hair to tidy it as the first few passengers from flight 489 trickled through. She held up a printed card with the Shelbournes' names and directed it toward any couple who were vaguely the right age. Her research had revealed Anthony and Lisa Shelbourne lived in Greenwich, Connecticut. He owned an ad agency in New York City, and she collected art and good causes.

Ingrid hadn't needed the card.

Lauren's parents were easily identifiable by their strained expressions and gray complexions. Though they had dressed for first class, their clothes were crumpled and disheveled. Mrs. Shelbourne had done her best to refresh her makeup, but her eyes were puffed and lined. No amount of cosmetics could hide her distraught features.

Ingrid set her face somewhere between a concerned frown and a sympathetic smile, not at all sure she was pulling it off, and approached the couple with an outstretched hand. "Ingrid Skyberg, from the embassy," she said and steeled herself for her first platitude. "I'm so sorry for your loss."

Anthony Shelbourne squeezed her hand in his and nodded. His wife held onto him as if she might slide right onto the floor if she let go.

"We have a car waiting," Ingrid told them. "If you'd like to follow me?" She gestured toward the exit.

"We have to wait for my daughter," Mrs. Shelbourne said. "She's bringing the bags."

"Your daughter?" Ingrid hoped she'd managed to suppress her surprise, struggling to keep her expression and tone neutral.

"We left her at the baggage reclaim," Mr. Shelbourne explained. "Alex volunteered to wait for the suitcases."

A full ten minutes of awkward silences and painful small talk later, Alex Shelbourne emerged from the customs channel, pushing a baggage cart stacked high with suitcases and carry-ons. The girl had to be no more than sixteen or seventeen, a little over five feet five and less than a hundred pounds. She was struggling with the weight of the cart. Ingrid hurried to help her.

"It's OK—I can manage," the girl told her firmly.

She wore thick eyeliner, dark purple lipstick and had lilac streaks in otherwise jet-black spiky hair. Alex Shelbourne had cast herself as the rebel of the family.

Ingrid planted a restraining hand on the uppermost bag and guided the Shelbournes through the busy arrivals hall, navigating a channel through the crush of bodies. The embassy limousine was waiting at the curb.

"We can go straight to your hotel or deal with the formalities at the embassy first, if you'd rather," Ingrid told them as the driver loaded the bags into the trunk.

"Take me to the morgue. I want to see my baby." Lisa Shelbourne's voice was surprisingly clear and strong.

"I'll, um, I'll need to make a few calls to arrange that for you. At this time of day it may be difficult."

"Make as many calls as you like. We're going to see my daughter."

Ingrid sat next to the driver, who buzzed up the glass partition between the front and back seats. Each time she turned to check on them, the Shelbournes were gazing out their respective windows, never once looking at one another or exchanging a word.

Once they were making good progress on the freeway, Ingrid called Sol and told him about the unexpected arrival of the Shelbournes' youngest.

"I get the impression she's the type of teenager who can't be left at home alone," Ingrid told him.

"It's going to be tough on the kid."

She caught sight of Alex Shelbourne in the wing mirror. She was staring at her smartphone, earphones snaking from the device and disappearing into her ears. So far she seemed to be coping with the situation remarkably well.

"I need you to make some calls for me," Ingrid said.

"Can't Jennifer do it?"

"I need your help. Mrs Shelbourne is insisting we visit the mortuary first. I figure they might listen to you. I really need the body in a viewing room in ninety minutes."

Sol was good to his word. When they arrived, an orderly was waiting for them at the entrance of the hospital mortuary. Anthony and Lisa Shelbourne followed the earnest man in scrubs into the single-story building while Alex hung back.

"Is it OK if I don't come in?" the teenager asked her mother. "I feel like I need some fresh air."

Lisa gently rested a hand on Alex's arm. "You're sure you don't want to see her?"

"Not here. Not like this."

"OK. Don't go wandering off."

"I'll stay with her," Ingrid said. "You'll need some privacy."

"Thank you."

Ingrid watched the ashen-faced couple disappear through the sliding doors.

"I don't need a babysitter," Alex Shelbourne said.

"Good, because that's not my job." Ingrid gave her a smile.

"I'm just fine by myself."

"I know that."

The teenager, instead of taking herself for a walk, pulled the earbuds from her ears. "Was she murdered?"

The bluntness of the question caught Ingrid by surprise.

"Well? Was she?"

"The police are still investigating." Ingrid still hadn't had the final autopsy from McKittrick.

"You must have an opinion." Alex Shelbourne fished a pack of cigarettes from one of the many pockets of her black combat pants. She offered the pack to Ingrid, who declined.

"Do your parents know you smoke?"

"Give me a break." She lit a cigarette and inhaled deeply.

"It must be very difficult for you, coming here like this."

"I wanted to come."

"Were you close to your sister?"

"You're trying to change the subject. Do *you* think someone murdered Lauren?"

An ambulance parked nearby. Two EMTs opened up the back and pulled out a gurney. A black body bag was strapped to the guardrails. The EMTs wheeled the gurney toward them, so Ingrid grabbed the teenager's arm and walked her away from the entrance.

"It's OK—you don't have to shield me from it. I do know what happens in a morgue."

Ingrid wondered how long it would be before the hard exterior the girl was doing her best to project started to crack.

The teenager took a deep drag on her Marlboro. "You still haven't answered my question."

"You're asking the wrong person. Only the Metropolitan Police can tell you."

Alex Shelbourne shrugged her dissatisfaction at Ingrid's answer. "So what happens now?"

"That depends on what the police find."

She ground her half-smoked cigarette under her sneaker. "Do you trust the local cops? To do a thorough job?"

Where did her cynicism come from? "I have every confidence in the ability of—"

"Don't give me the official crap."

Ingrid made deliberate eye contact. "I do. I trust them."

"You don't sound too sure."

"They're doing a good job. Believe me." This time, Ingrid heard the doubt in her own voice.

Alex Shelbourne put the earphones back in her ears. "They'd better be. Otherwise my dad's gonna hire a private investigator to do the job for them."

14

"Look, can this wait? We're up to our eyeballs." DI McKittrick shoved Ingrid out of the way and hurried from her office in Lewisham police station, her arms full of case papers and card files.

"I've just come from the morgue. They need answers." Ingrid followed her down a long corridor and into the elevator.

"Number six."

Ingrid punched the button with a knuckle. "Where are you taking all this stuff, anyway?"

"The main incident room is being remodeled. All the case files have to be transferred."

"Don't you have people to do that for you?"

"Supposedly." The elevator arrived at the sixth floor and the doors slid open. McKittrick hurried through. "Only it's much faster if I do it myself."

Ingrid felt much the same way about delegation. By the time you'd prepared for it, explained the situation, then dealt with whatever was thrown back at the end of the process, it was just simpler and more effective to do everything yourself. She tried to get a glimpse of the file on the top of the pile.

"Do you have the final autopsy report?"

McKittrick inhaled slowly. "I do."

"Great—"

"But I can't let you see it until my boss has approved it for release."

"And how long will that take?"

"You can see how busy we are."

Ingrid tried to see what case files McKittrick was carrying. "Is that the Shelbourne case?"

"I'm sorry to say this, but in the scheme of things, Lauren Shelbourne's death barely registers as an event. It's certainly not worthy of a dedicated incident room."

"You make it sound like you've closed the investigation."

"We're not far off." McKittrick, more harassed than ever, marched down another long corridor lined with closed doors glazed with opaque glass on either side.

Ingrid matched McKittrick's pace stride for stride.

"Lauren's parents have arrived."

"I know. Who do you think organized the viewing at the mortuary?" McKittrick stopped abruptly and kicked open a door. It swung wide to reveal Detective Constable Mills standing at the far end of the large, brightly lit office. He was rubbing marker pen off a wide whiteboard with a paper towel. He turned as they approached.

"I'll take those, boss."

McKittrick dumped the files into his arms, and Mills let out a grunt, his forehead puckering as he concentrated hard on not letting any of the loose paperwork slide to the floor. In that instant, Ingrid realized who the detective reminded her of and blushed.

Clark Swanson.

Her first crush in junior high. The boy who broke her heart without knowing it. He hadn't even known she existed. The extra forty pounds she was carrying at the time effectively made her invisible to all but the geeks and weirdos. Geeks and weirdos like her. She found herself involuntarily smiling at the memory. Mills made eye contact and quickly looked away. Was he blushing? She definitely was and she didn't like how it felt.

Ingrid turned back to ask McKittrick a question and discovered the overworked inspector disappearing into the corridor.

She ran after her, her left ankle still complaining. "I spoke to that journalist yesterday," Ingrid told her as she caught up with her again. "Angela Tate."

"Not someone I'd recommend having cozy chats with. What did she want?"

"I just happened to run into her."

"Knowing Tate, I expect she planned it that way. I suppose she wanted the details on the Shelbourne investigation?"

"She's writing about the suicide on campus. Thought you'd want to know."

McKittrick wiggled her nose.

"She thinks the girl didn't kill herself."

"Well, there'd be no angle for Tate if she had."

"Did you hear anything about it?"

"Didn't get as far as my team. The detectives on duty called it in as a suicide. No one else involved. Cut and dried. No need for HSCC to wade in with our size nines."

"There'll be an inquest though?"

"That's a formality."

"Tate told me she was drunk."

"Hardly surprising, she's a gin-soaked old hack."

"She meant the student, as you well know."

"So?"

"So the girl never drank."

"And your only source of information is Tate?"

The elevator doors opened and three uniformed officers stepped out with a nod of acknowledgment for McKittrick. Ingrid and her friend stepped back inside. Ingrid reached into her bag and pulled out a candy wrapper.

"What's this?"

Ingrid opened it to reveal the paint-soaked tissue. "It's a sample of the paint used in the graffiti on campus. The one that said Lauren Shelbourne is a whore?"

McKittrick peered at the tissue. "You're serious. You're handing me an old tissue?"

"I meant to give it to you yesterday. The janitor cleaned it off before your team would have had a chance to take a sample."

"You know I can't take that, Ingrid." She glowered at her. "A Twix wrapper is hardly an evidence bag. It would be inadmissible."

Ingrid scrutinized her friend. "But you're tempted though, aren't you? You suspect there's something odd going on at Loriners too, don't you?"

The elevator reached McKittrick's floor and the detective shot through the half-open doors as if a starter pistol had just gone off.

"The only thing worth looking at was the fact security around the admin block—the building the Canadian girl jumped from—was found wanting. It's the highest point on campus."

"Found wanting?"

"A maintenance crew inadvertently left a door unlocked. The incident was fully investigated. Why are you so determined to link the suicide to the Shelbourne case?" she asked Ingrid. "Please don't tell me it's a hunch."

Ingrid was still holding the tissue. "I'm just following the evidence."

McKittrick rolled her eyes. "I can't spare anyone to investigate a teenage prank."

"Lauren's parents want to repatriate her body as soon as possible. I want to be sure we know what happened to her before we lose a vital forensic asset." She hated referring to Lauren that way. "You might not have the manpower, but I do. And if I don't look into it, Lauren Shelbourne's father is going to hire a private detective."

With a long, exasperated sigh McKittrick opened a nearby file cabinet and picked out a slim folder. She placed it carefully and deliberately on her desk, then held Ingrid's gaze. "I need to visit the ladies'. You'll be OK waiting in here for me, will you?"

Ingrid glanced down at the file, saw Lauren Shelbourne's name printed on a neat label in the top right-hand corner, then nodded her understanding to McKittrick. Natasha was still in her corner after all.

"I won't be long." McKittrick left the room, opening the door wide on her way out, and made a point of leaving it open.

Ingrid checked the hallway outside. The coast appeared to be clear. She returned to the desk and flipped open the file, her back toward the door, obscuring what she was doing from anyone passing. There was no time to read the contents now. She opened the camera app on her phone and snapped a picture of the first page. The flash went off as she did.

Damn.

Ingrid disabled the auto-flash function and moved on to the second page. She had photographed all but the final sheet when she heard a noise behind her. She spun around and saw Mills standing in the doorway. Ingrid slumped heavily onto the edge of the desk, at the same time reaching an arm behind her back. She groped for the switch on the side of the phone and clicked it, hoping she'd captured an image of the last page.

"Hey! Ralph, isn't it?"

The detective nodded slowly.

"Natash—I mean DI McKittrick has slipped out for a moment." She smiled at him as innocently as she could.

He narrowed his eyes, tilting his head sideways to get a better view of the surface of the desk. "Everything OK?"

"Perfectly." In a single smooth movement she stood up, flipped the file closed and took a step toward him. "How are you?" He was still frowning at her, looking more and more like Clark Swanson from Middleton Junior High.

"Can I help you with anything?"

"No, I'm fine." She folded her arms.

"I'm glad we've got a few moments on our own." He closed the door behind him.

"You are?"

He glanced again at the desk. "I've been really interested in the FBI since I was a kid."

Ingrid's heart sank. "Don't tell me—*The X Files*, right?"

"Am I that much of a cliché?"

Ingrid threw her arms out wide. "Hey—it was a great show. I was a fan of it myself." *Geeks and weirdos.*

"Is that why you joined up?"

"Kinda." This was neither the time nor the place to reveal the real reason.

"I don't suppose you could tell me a bit about it? The training and all that? Maybe over a coffee or something?"

Was he actually hitting on her?

"I'm so busy these days. Work pretty much takes up all my time."

He shifted his position and stared pointedly at the desk. "Perhaps we could... pool our knowledge."

"Knowledge about what?"

"Any of our current cases you might be interested in."

Was he offering to keep her updated on the Shelbourne investigation? "I suppose I might be able to find some time in my calendar." She pulled a business card from her pocket and handed it to Mills. "We'll set something up. Call me."

He smiled at her, his cheeks showing just the hint of a blush. "Excellent." He turned and opened the door, but didn't leave. Instead he stood beside it and looked at her expectantly.

"It's all right. The inspector said I could wait for her in here."

"No. That's why I'm here. The boss specifically asked me to escort you from the building." He smiled and she was suddenly looking right at Clark Swanson.

"She did?" He knew exactly what she'd been doing in McKittrick's office, and now Natasha was giving him the nod to help her out. That's what friends are for.

Outside, Ingrid waved an awkward goodbye to Mills, already inventing excuses to turn down whatever date he suggested for their meet-up. She retrieved her cell phone from the back pocket of her pants and opened the photo gallery, enlarging specific parts of images that seemed relevant. Everything was more or less what she suspected until she reached the final page. The picture was a little blurred, and the left-hand side of the page cut off completely. But as she enlarged and brightened the image, the information she needed came into focus.

According to the Metropolitan Police toxicology report, at the time of her death, Lauren Shelbourne's bloodstream contained 'significant' amounts of LSD and methamphetamine.

15

Ingrid tied a double knot in the lace of her running shoe and scooted out of the embassy building, along Upper Brooke Street, across the eight-lane highway of Park Lane and finally into Hyde Park. Her second visit in as many days. Despite the soreness in her left ankle, she cruised along somewhere between a fast jog and a sprint. She eased up as soon as she saw the outline of her boss fifty yards away. Or rather her boss's boss. Amy Louden was further up the food chain than Sol. She was only forty-three years old, yet was already the Deputy Special Agent In Charge of the FBI's legal attaché program in the most prestigious US Embassy in the world. Ingrid was coming up to thirty-two. She was running out of time to have a meteoric rise of her own.

Louden had insisted their meeting take place in the park while she ran. Two birds with one stone, she'd said. "Let's show the boys how to multitask, shall we?"

Ingrid watched Louden's uneven gait as the woman ran holding a cell phone in one hand, a wire trailing out of the top. Ingrid stepped up her pace a little and effortlessly caught up with the DSAC, pulling in alongside and quickly mirroring her stride pattern. Louden glanced at her from the corner of her eye without turning her head. She finished up her call and navigated to an app on the phone without missing a stride. It seemed looking where she was going wasn't a priority for Louden.

"Steady at ten miles an hour; metabolic rate increased fifteen percent," she told Ingrid. "Three hundred forty-six calories burnt."

"Impressive."

"Three miles a day, rain or shine." Louden pointed a thumb toward her own chest. "For me it's just a part of my daily routine, like taking a shower. It's a matter of discipline. Like anything else."

Ingrid had decided long ago never to compete with a superior officer. She kept her five-mile minimum and parkour routines to herself. She was just glad Louden hadn't suggested racquetball: somehow Ingrid's hand-eye coordination got stuck on automatic, and she found it completely impossible to throw a game, no matter how hard she tried.

"We haven't had a chance to speak properly since you first joined us. How are you settling in? Enjoying London?"

"Yes, ma'am. One of the best postings I've had." It wasn't exactly true, but she knew it was what Louden wanted to hear.

"Good, good. We like to make new arrivals feel welcome."

Ingrid had to suppress a smile. Apart from Sol, no one had bothered to make much of an effort to extend a friendly hand.

"So, these assignments you're working on at the moment," Louden said while checking her running stats again. "Sol tells me you're not making much headway in the Brewster case."

So that was why Louden had ask to meet with her.

"The trail goes cold at the escort agency. I've been contacting other agencies with a description of the suspected perpetrator, but so far it seems he's simply disappeared. I'm sure I'd have better results if I knew more about the victim." Ingrid glanced briefly at the DSAC to check her reaction. Her boss kept her eyes front and center. "I take it there's a reason why you're asking me about it?"

Louden slowed slightly and inclined her head toward Ingrid for the first time. "Somebody leans on me, so I lean on you."

"Do you know who Greg Brewster is? Or what he does?"

Louden took several strides to answer. "I can tell you that's not his real name. But, no, I don't know what his legal name is, before you ask."

Ingrid was intrigued. "And this alias is approved by...?"

"I'm not entirely sure we should be discussing this."

"Due respect, ma'am, you want an update on a case I can't give you because I can't investigate it properly. Could you at least see if my security clearance could be raised?"

Louden didn't answer.

"Just for this one case?"

Still no response.

"I'll get you the answers you need if you let me know who Brewster is."

They rounded a corner of the path and found themselves running between flower beds alive with spring bulbs.

"I can't. I don't know. But I'm getting pressure from the Department of Defense, so I'm guessing it's military. That enough for you?"

It was a start.

"Thank you. I appreciate that." It was a lot less than she'd hoped for, and Ingrid felt a spike of anger erupt in her chest and travel to her legs. She wanted to take on a fast sprint or throw herself over a wall, burn away the fury, but neither of those two options was open to her in present company. She settled for clenching her teeth instead.

"Good. I hear the Shelbourne case is almost wrapped up. Such a tragedy."

"I've seen the toxicology report. She'd taken LSD and meth-amphetamine."

"She sounds like a very unfortunate individual." Louden was distracted by whatever her fitness app was telling her.

"Don't you think it's strange to find that combination of drugs in her system?" Ingrid skirted around a fresh pile of horse dung and landed heavily on her left foot. Fireworks of pain shot upward into her knee.

"She was obviously a young woman with serious problems."

"There's no record of previous drug offenses."

"That doesn't mean she was clean."

"I'm seeing her parents again later. I just want to be able to tell them it was a tragic accident."

"But you have reservations?"

They reached an enormous plane tree and Louden pulled up sharply. She tapped something into her smartphone and nodded with satisfaction. She looked at Ingrid. Ingrid hesitated.

"Well?"

"I have a few causes of concern. About the investigation. I want to make sure the Met hasn't missed anything before they release the body for repatriation."

"Tread carefully, agent. The Shelbournes have suffered enough. I don't want them upset needlessly." She tore her gaze away from a long list of 'missed call' alerts and turned to Ingrid. "Do I make myself clear?"

Ingrid suppressed a sigh. "Perfectly."

"Do everything you can to repatriate the body in the next few days."

"I'm not sure the inquest will happen that fast."

"Let's ensure it does, shall we?"

"It feels like we're rushing things when there's no need."

"You don't have children, do you, Ingrid?"

"No, ma'am."

Louden leveled a stare at her. "Try to imagine what those two souls are going through."

Ingrid only just managed to unclench her teeth to speak. "I'll do my best." She forced a smile and left her superior officer to continue with her carefully planned warm-down exercises. Ingrid sprinted back to the embassy as quickly as she could.

———

Showered and dressed, with a strong strapping of elastic bandage on her left ankle, Ingrid returned to her desk to collect her bag. She retrieved her cell and did something she should have done days ago.

Marshall picked up immediately. "Hey, sweetie. I was about to call your boss to find out what had happened to you."

"Sorry. It's been crazy here the last few weeks." Ingrid walked through the bull pen toward the elevators.

"I've been calling."

"I know. I got your messages."

"Why didn't you call back?"

Ingrid didn't have a good enough answer. Absence, it was turning out, wasn't making her heart grow fonder. She reached the elevators, then pushed through the doors to the emergency exit and took the stairs.

"I'm sorry, Marshall, but this isn't a social call. Can you see if you can find something out for me, on the down low?"

He sighed heavily.

"You're more senior than me; your clearance level is higher than mine. Can you run a search for me on someone called Greg Brewster?"

"You know I can't do that." He was such a stickler. Marshall Claybourne would never do anything that threatened to blemish his reputation and slow his progress up the Bureau's greasy pole. "How would I explain it? What if it raises a flag?"

You'd make something up. "Well then, can you do something else for me? Apparently my predecessor works in the DC office now. Dennis Mulroony."

"Never heard of him." The FBI's headquarters employed tens of thousands of people. Not even an uber-networker like Marshall could know everyone.

"Well, could you keep an eye out, and an ear out, for him? I'd like to swap notes, but don't want to alert anyone we're in contact. Can you find him for me?"

"Sure, but you've got to do something for me."

"Name it."

"Give me a date."

"We've been engaged for two years, Marshall. I think we're a bit beyond dating." She knew exactly what he'd meant, and she also knew how insincere she sounded.

"I mean a date for the wedding. My mom keeps asking."

Ingrid sucked on her teeth. "We discussed all this when I took the job. You agreed the posting will help with my promotion prospects. We can't all be highflyers like you." Her voice echoed in the stark, empty stairwell.

"Come on! Don't give me a hard time for getting lucky."

"You get lucky every time there's a vacancy."

"You don't resent me for that?"

Ingrid pulled the phone from her ear. *You bet your ass I do.* "Of course not! It's not like we're in a competition with one another." They always had been. Ever since Quantico.

"I want a date for our wedding. Can't we at least be working toward it?"

"We'll have to talk about this later. I have an appointment."

"What should I tell my mom?"

Tell her to butt the hell out of your business. "Tell her I was asking after her." She'd reached the lobby and decided to walk the short distance from the embassy to the Shelbournes' Mayfair hotel.

"But I miss you," Marshall said. "How about you come home for a couple of days? A long weekend?"

"I'm in the middle of two very important investigations."

"But you always are." An irritable whine had infected his tone, exaggerating his Southern drawl.

"We had an agreement."

"Sure, but an agreement needs an end date."

"I can't speak about this now. I'll call you back." She ended the call before he managed a rejoinder, then shoved her phone in a pocket. She puffed out her cheeks in frustration. He always made her feel this way. Always wound her up. Dating someone on the job had made so much sense in the beginning: a mutual understanding of the pressure of work, the sacrifices that had to be made, the last-minute cancelation of long-standing arrangements. They never needed to apologize, never needed to explain. Now that seemed all he ever wanted her to do. Her cell buzzed and she grabbed it, tempted to tell Marshall where he could shove his end date. But it wasn't him. It was a UK cell number she didn't recognize.

"Hello?"

"Ralph Mills here. I was wondering if you had a spare five minutes, maybe later today?"

When she'd given Mills her card, she'd wondered just how long it would take him to call her. She thought he'd take a little longer. If it came to it, she'd just throw Marshall into the conversation. He could still be good for something.

"Are you still there?"

"Hi, yes, I'm here."

"Mutually beneficial cup of coffee or glass of wine, I was thinking," Mills said, embarrassment detectable in his tone. Was he offering something on the Shelbourne investigation?

"Do you want to speak to me about the case?"

"Let's talk about that when we meet up, shall we?"

16

When she approached the five-star hotel, Ingrid was sure the BMW pulling away on the other side of the road contained McKittrick and Mills. He hadn't sounded like he'd been in a car when they'd spoken. Ingrid felt wrong-footed: if the Shelbournes had been briefed by the Met, they would know more about the case than she did, and she risked seeming a fool. Ingrid took the elevator up to the top floor with a certain amount of reticence. When she reached the family's suite, she heard raised voices coming from inside. Anthony and Lisa Shelbourne were shouting at one another. Ingrid leaned a little closer to the door.

"I never wanted her to leave the country in the first place," Mrs. Shelbourne said. "This would never have happened if you hadn't insisted that—"

The unmistakable trill of a cell phone cut her off.

"For God's sake. Ignore the goddamn phone for once, can't you?"

"I need to take this."

Ingrid stepped away from the door and raised her fist as if to knock, knowing from the loudness of his voice that Anthony Shelbourne was heading her way. The door swung open, Shelbourne took a moment to recognize her, then held up a silencing finger. His face was drawn, a dark shadow of stubble covered his chin, and his hair stuck out in cowlicks. He marched down the long, subtly lit hallway, shouting into his cell.

Ingrid tapped on the already open door and stuck her head inside. "Mrs Shelbourne, Agent Skyberg from the embassy."

"We only met a few hours ago. I'm hardly likely to forget. Despite appearances, I do still have some control over my faculties."

"I'm sorry, ma'am."

"Let's get this over with, shall we?" She ran a shaking hand through her hair. Her eye makeup had smudged beneath her eyes. Long dark trails of mascara slithered down her face.

Ingrid glanced around the room. There was no sign of Alex. Lisa Shelbourne dabbed at her eyes, making them even more of a mess.

"Please take a seat. I can order some fresh coffee if you'd like?"

Ingrid raised a hand. "Not on my account." There was a tray of dirty cups sitting on a low table between two formal chairs upholstered in maroon silk.

"The police were just here," Mrs. Shelbourne explained. "You've seen their report, I take it?"

"I realize it's been a very long day for you. I'll take up as little of your time as possible."

"How long have you been working here in London?"

Ingrid was taken aback by the change of subject. "Around four months, why?"

"And are you aware of a serious drug problem in the city?"

McKittrick must have disclosed the blood test results. No wonder Lisa Shelbourne looked so wrecked.

"Not in the course of my duties."

"I've never thought of England in that way before." She collapsed onto one of the silk-covered chairs, folding her stockinged feet beneath her. She grabbed a lilac angora sweater from the arm of the chair and clutched it to her breast. "I'm not naive. London is a major world city; I accept it must have a seedy side. But those aren't the circles I expected Lauren to move in. You've been to the college?"

Ingrid nodded.

"It has a good reputation. If I'd thought for a moment Lauren would be at risk from... undesirable influences while she was there—" She looked past Ingrid toward the door, an admonishing expression on her face. Ingrid turned to see Anthony Shelbourne standing in the doorway, his face paler and damper than it had been only moments before. "—I would never have let her go."

He quietly closed the door behind him and slipped his cell back into the breast pocket of his shirt. "You couldn't have stopped her," he told his wife.

"She may have listened to you. But you didn't even try to dissuade her."

"How many more times? She wanted to come. The research program here is one of the best in the world. Didn't she tell us that over and over?" He turned to Ingrid. "She wanted to be part of something important. I remember her face when she found out she'd been accepted in the course. It was the happiest I've ever seen her."

"There are colleges just as good at home. You should have made her stay." Lisa Shelbourne's voice was brittle.

Anthony Shelbourne started to speak but checked himself. His jaw muscles flexed. He began again. "We don't know what Lauren might have gotten into wherever she'd gone to study. We'll never know."

"Had Lauren..." Now it was Ingrid's turn to check herself. "Do you know if your daughter might have... experimented with drugs at home?"

"What?" Lisa Shelbourne leaped to her feet. "How dare you—"

Her husband grabbed her arm to stop her before she barreled straight into Ingrid. "Calm down, Lisa, the kid's just doing her job."

Kid?

Lisa Shelbourne snatched her arm away.

"The truth is we don't know," her husband admitted. "We've both been a little distracted the past couple of years. My business,

Lisa's charity work. I can't say for sure what Lauren may or may not have done, even when she was still living at home."

"Don't you dare lay any of the blame at my door." Their daughter's death had blown apart the cracks in their marriage. "I only started my work because I saw nothing of you."

A door opened behind Ingrid. She turned to see Alex Shelbourne hesitate on the threshold of the adjoining room. "I need some air," she announced.

"Don't stray too far," her mother told her.

Alex made a point of walking past Ingrid, rolling her eyes as she did, like a truculent teenager. Which, Ingrid supposed, was exactly what she was.

When the girl had left the room, Anthony Shelbourne cleared some space on an antique wooden bureau pushed up against the wall that divided the two rooms of the suite. "Let's just get this paperwork finalized, shall we?"

"Paperwork?"

"The inspector explained earlier—we need to complete the forms for the repatriation of… of…" He let out a long faltering sob.

"We can't do that yet," Ingrid said. "Then there's the inquest. And then the final coroner's report."

"Yes, I know. But the detective said the matter could be expedited. Fast-tracked somehow."

"I want to take my baby home," Lisa Shelbourne said. "She's lying in the morgue. In the dark and the cold."

"I can complete the appropriate forms with you when the time comes."

"If you don't have the paperwork now, why are you here?" Mr Shelbourne asked.

Ingrid looked from Anthony to Lisa Shelbourne. She cleared her throat. "In addition to the police investigation, the embassy has to complete its own report. I'm here to gather a little background information—"

"Why? Is there some doubt about what happened?" Mrs. Shelbourne got to her feet.

"It's just standard procedure, ma'am."

A phone rang. This time it was Lisa Shelbourne's. She answered and disappeared into the bedroom.

"That's her mother," Mr Shelbourne explained. "She'll be on that call for hours."

"They have a lot to discuss," Ingrid said.

His cell phone lit up in his pocket. "Excuse me," he said on his way out to the corridor.

Talking to grief-stricken parents was something Ingrid had plenty of experience with. In her four years in the Violent Crimes Against Children unit, she'd seen relatives behave in all sorts of ways from denial, to anger, to wailing and ululations: the Shelbournes' reaction to tragedy was not unusual. They were still trying to carry on with life as normal, not yet accepting that their lives would never be the same again.

She sat on the couch for a few minutes. When it was clear neither would be talking to her soon, Ingrid went in search of Alex. She passed Anthony Shelbourne in the corridor and said she would make contact to rearrange for a more convenient time, then opted for a swift jog down the twenty or so flights of stairs to ground level to shake some of the tension from her muscles. Her best guess was sixteen-year-old Alex would be walking in the direction of Oxford Street, but she found Alex Shelbourne standing by the main entrance, waiting for her.

The girl stubbed out her cigarette on the sidewalk, choosing to ignore the metal trash can right beside her. "You know it's bullshit, right?" Alex said, folding her arms across her chest.

"I'm sorry?"

"How can they swallow all that? Everything the policewoman said. They listened like a pair of morons, believing every line they were being fed."

"I'm not sure I understand—"

"The drugs? The drugs they say they found?"

"I've seen the toxicology report myself. I realize it must have come as a shock for you all, but the drugs were in your sister's bloodstream."

"Oh, cut the crap. Someone, somewhere is spinning you a line." She reached into her pocket and retrieved her pack of cigarettes. She waved them at Ingrid. "Lauren didn't even smoke. Not even a joint now and then, like any normal person. There is absolutely no way she would ever willingly take drugs."

17

Ingrid looked at Google Maps on her phone and selected a green space at random for her morning run. Twenty minutes later, she found herself on Hampstead Heath, breathing in the crisp spring air. From Parliament Hill, she looked down across the city and picked out all the landmarks she recognized, trying to assign a date and time she'd visited them.

Her ankle seemed completely healed, so she picked up her pace and focused on the Shelbourne investigation, attempting to untangle fact from fiction. She ran flat out for a solid forty minutes, which was enough to clear her lungs but not her mind. Too much about Lauren Shelbourne's death wasn't adding up. She thought about something Faber had said. When Ingrid had told her about losing her friend when she was fourteen, Faber had talked about the cops at the time leaving no stone unturned. Ingrid had been unable then, or since, to get closure for Megan and her family, but she could make amends by making sure Lauren's death was properly investigated.

When she arrived at Madison Faber's building later that morning, the student met her at the front door, grabbed Ingrid's hand and physically dragged her over the threshold. "Thank God! I thought you'd abandoned me." She led Ingrid into a wide hall then straight through an internal door and up a steep, narrow flight of stairs. The house was very similar to the one

where Lauren had lived, though with slightly grander propor-
tions. At the top, Faber guided her through another door into a
bright, cheerful apartment.

"Did you see anyone on the street outside when you arrived?
Anyone waiting?"

"Waiting? For what?"

"For me to come out." Faber scratched her arm. "I don't feel
safe. Not even here."

Ingrid walked Faber to a chair and pushed her gently into it.
"Has something else happened? Have you been threatened
again?"

Faber bit her lip. "Every time I close my eyes, I see that
fucking dead mouse."

Ingrid crouched down in front of her, choosing submissive
body language to help soothe Faber's anxiety. "Have you figured
out who left it there?"

"It has to be someone in the psychology department.
Someone with access to the laboratory." She paused, then locked
her imposing stare onto Ingrid. "You were going to look into it
for me."

"I plan to. I will. But you must have an idea who's threatening you?"

Faber pressed her lips together; her eyes darted left and right.
She dropped her voice to a whisper. "There is someone…"

"Then tell me."

Her eyes widened. "I can't give you a name." She sounded
manic, unhinged. "What if they find out I've spoken to you?"

Ingrid pulled a footstool over in front of the armchair and sat
down. She leaned forward, her elbows on her knees. "Tell me
exactly what you know. Everything."

Faber slumped back into the chair, putting distance between
her and Ingrid. "I can't believe the police are saying it was an
accident."

The pathologist's findings had been reported in the press. The
official line was accidental death caused by a fall while under the
influence of drugs.

"The pathologist's conclusions were reasonable, given the

drugs in Lauren's system. You know I share some of your concerns about what's been going on at Loriners, so if you want me to continue looking into things, you have to tell me why you think Lauren was killed." Ingrid grabbed a blanket from a couch and wrapped it across Faber's shaking shoulders. "Why would someone want to hurt Lauren?"

Faber rattled her head from side to side. "I'm so scared." Slowly, the movement changed and the girl began nodding.

"I want to get answers for you, Madison, but you have to give me more information."

A cell phone rang and Faber froze. "Every time it rings, my heart stops."

"Please, Madison. Tell me what you know."

"You promise you can protect me?" The girl was terrified.

Ingrid couldn't promise anything. The Met weren't treating it as a priority, the Shelbournes wanted things wrapped up so they could take their daughter home, and as far as Louden was concerned, Ingrid should be concentrating on finding Brewster's laptop.

"What I can promise you is that no one will ever find out where I got my information from. Whatever you tell me will never be repeated. Understand?"

For the first time, a tiny smile crept onto Faber's lips. "It's making sense to me now."

"What is?"

"Why Lauren moved out. That must have been when she started using drugs. She knew I would disapprove, so she had to hide it from me."

Ingrid thought about Alex Shelbourne's comments: she didn't know which young woman knew Lauren best. "Why is this making you scared, Madison? I don't understand."

"Don't you see?" Faber's voice was getting stronger.

"Join the dots for me."

"Well, I know who her dealer was, don't I? And if he was the killer, well…"

"What? He'll want to silence you?"

Faber nodded vigorously.

"Did you mention Lauren's habit when the police interviewed you?"

"No!" Her tone suggested she thought Ingrid was stupid. "I didn't know for sure she was using drugs until I heard about the postmortem."

"But you know who her dealer was?"

Another nod.

"You have to tell me a name. If I don't know who he is, I can't protect you from him."

"But what if he finds out I've been speaking to you?"

"The only way for that to happen is if you tell him." Ingrid felt like she was getting somewhere. "Come on, Madison. You can trust me."

"He's a student at Loriners. I don't really know him."

"A name is all I need."

"You promise me he'll never find out I told you?" Faber scratched her arm again, raking her fingernails hard across the skin.

How many more times did she have to tell her?

"I promise."

Faber closed her eyes for several seconds. "Timo Klaason." She spelled the name out for Ingrid. "When you find him, you should be careful. I don't know him, but I've heard he likes to hit girls."

18

The subdued atmosphere Ingrid had noticed on campus on her last visit seemed to have disappeared completely. Students hurried between buildings, chatting and laughing, heavy bags of books swinging from their shoulders. Although she looked carefully for it, Ingrid failed to spot any trace of graffiti on the wide gray concrete facades. She had sent the tissue with the paint sample on to the Bureau's lab in DC. Just because it was inadmissible in a court of law, it didn't mean it couldn't help identify who had labeled Lauren a whore.

She had called ahead and arranged to meet Madison Faber's research team leader after the first lecture of the afternoon session. The harassed tutor arrived late and insisted they talk on the way to her next meeting. She hugged an armful of files to her chest like a protective shield.

"I really appreciate your seeing me on such short notice, Ms—."

"Please, call me Rebecca. I'll feel a hundred years old otherwise." She nodded a greeting at a couple of students lounging on the grass next to the path. "You've seen Madison today?"

"I saw her this morning, as a matter of fact. She is extremely distressed."

"She must be taking it hard. Not something you get over easily."

"No—it was a traumatic experience for her."

"And to be accused of—"

"I don't think anyone was ever accusing her."

"No—no, of course not. Even so—to be in police custody. In a foreign country. Must have been terrifying." The woman checked her watch. "I really don't have long. You said you wanted to discuss her welfare. Doesn't sound like the sort of thing I'd expect the American embassy to take an interest in."

Ingrid slowed her pace, forcing the tutor to match her speed. Ingrid's assessment was that Faber was at more risk from self-harm than anything the mysterious Timo Klaason might do to her. She also knew how much support she had needed when her friend Megan had been abducted. "I just thought, after the suicide last week, after Lauren, the university might not want another young woman to come to harm. She was extremely agitated. How has she seemed to you?"

"Seemed?"

"Anxious? Depressed? Has she been getting along with other students in the psychology department?"

"Why wouldn't she?"

"There's been no evidence of… bullying, for example?"

"She's a postgraduate student, not a kindergarten pupil. Why would she want to bully anyone?" The lecturer lengthened her stride.

"I mean has Madison *been* bullied?"

"Of course not. That's just ridiculous."

"I take it she hasn't come to you with any problems?"

The tutor stopped abruptly. "I'm not the person she would come to."

"You aren't?"

"Madison has only been part of my research group for a short while. I really don't know the girl. Personally or academically." She squeezed the files tighter in her arms.

"I thought—"

A shrill whistle sounded at the other end of the path. Ingrid looked up to see Angela Tate with one hand to her mouth. She whistled again then gestured urgently to a man holding a long-lens camera. What the hell was Tate doing here?

"Madison Faber switched research groups just before the spring break," the tutor explained. "She was in Professor Younger's group before that."

"Are you sure?"

Tate whistled again. With some effort, her photographer jogged toward her. Ingrid scanned the wide piazza to see what the journalist was so interested in. She followed Tate's gaze upward and her breath stalled in her throat. Five stories above Tate's head, on the top floor of the main admin block, a girl stood at an open window, one foot resting on the window ledge, her arms braced against the window casement on either side. She threw back her head and let go with one hand. A collective gasp went up from the students gathered outside the building. The girl looked down at them and waved. A few hands waved back at her.

The girl let go with the other hand. She wobbled.

The crowd held its breath.

Behind the girl a figure approached the window. Tall, broad-shouldered. Definitely male. He reached a hand toward the girl. She half-turned her head. The man took another step forward and the girl tensed. The crowd gasped in unison.

Tate's photographer made long swooping arcs with his zoom lens, predicting the girl's downward trajectory.

Ingrid ran toward the crowd, not taking her eyes from the girl's slim frame in the window.

For God's sake, somebody grab her.

As if he'd read Ingrid's mind, the man hovering behind her lurched forward, grabbing her left shoulder and knocking her off balance. Her left foot swung out over the ledge. The man wrapped his other arm around the girl's waist and leaned away from the window. They both fell backward inside the room and dropped to the floor.

The crowd exhaled. Then a cheer went up.

Ingrid pushed into the building and threw herself up the stairs, leaping three, four steps with each stride. She reached the fifth floor to see the man and girl slumped against the wall, the man's arms wrapped tightly around her. He looked toward Ingrid, his face pale and sweating.

It took Ingrid a moment to get her breath back, then another moment to recognize him.

19

The waitress took their order and slowly returned to the kitchen. Ingrid leaned closer to Angela Tate. "If this is going to work, we need to trust one another."

The reporter raised her eyebrows and studied Ingrid from the other side of the table. They were sitting in a café that Tate had described as a 'greasy spoon' a couple of streets away from Loriners.

After the excitement in and around the admin building had subsided and the agitated student had been taken to the campus medical center, Ingrid had decided there was very little to be achieved by hanging around. Angela Tate had suggested they adjourn to the nearby establishment to 'compare notes.'

"Trust, yes. But you can't expect me to just hand over information without getting something from you in return," Tate said. "I'll show you mine if you show me yours."

Ingrid took a sip of coffee and quickly set her cup back down. Instant. It tasted like an infusion of pencil shavings. "We share the same goal, and if there is something fishy going on at Loriners, I will certainly help you expose it."

"So you do think something's going on?"

Ingrid pressed her hands against the table. "It's fair to say I wouldn't still be at the campus if I didn't think there was something that needed investigating." Ingrid waved to the woman behind the counter and ordered an orange juice, hopeful it would at least taste of oranges. "So what have you sniffed out about Professor Younger?"

"The hero of the hour? Quite dashing, wasn't he, in his tight shirt and designer pants? My photographer got some lovely shots as Younger helped the girl to the medical center. We'll probably run a feature tomorrow. Why are you interested in the good professor?"

"He was Lauren's research group leader. I'm following up on all her college contacts."

The waitress dumped a small carton of OJ on the table and wandered back to the counter. Ingrid stuck the plastic straw into the carton and took a tentative sip. The journalist arched an eyebrow. "And who else have you spoken to?"

"Mostly people outside the psychology department."

"Well, that's because the professor and his research are a closed shop." Tate wrinkled her nose. "There's a protective firewall around him and his inner circle that so far I haven't found a way of penetrating. And believe me, I've tried everything."

"And what have you found out?"

"You first."

"Excuse me?"

"You tell me what you've found out," Tate said, "and then I'll reveal all."

Ingrid had thought things had been going a little too well. She sucked on the plastic straw. "I take it you know about the drugs being taken on campus?"

"Students taking drugs is hardly news," Tate said, searching for something on her phone. "Lecturers taking drugs wouldn't even make it into the paper these days." The journalist pulled an irritated face. She placed her phone on the table and proceeded to scroll through her picture gallery. She stopped at a dark, blurry photograph. "It doesn't do you justice."

Ingrid caught a brief glimpse of herself, lying in an awkward heap on the walkway at Loriners, before Tate swiped a finger across the screen.

"Here we are." Tate tapped twice and an image of the graffiti symbols filled the screen. "I haven't had any luck trying to find reference to the symbols anywhere. I've had the paper's librarian dig into it, and she's come up with nothing. And believe me, if there was something out there, Rita would have sniffed it out." She tilted her head as she gazed at the image. "Have you found anything out?"

Ingrid hesitated. Feeding Tate a crumb couldn't do any harm. "I sent my own hand-drawn version of the symbol to Quantico. There was some excitement initially—an agent thought there might be some ancient hieroglyphic connection, but it came to nothing."

Tate narrowed her eyes, obviously trying to gauge whether or not Ingrid was telling her the truth. "I'm not surprised. As I said, Rita would have found something otherwise." She swiped at the screen again and stopped at a photo of two students, one male, one female, both sporting purple and green polo shirts. "Now this I find interesting," Tate said. "I've gone through all the clubs and societies listed at the college—even extended it to the rest of the University of London—and none of them uses this particular combination of colors." She shifted her gaze to Ingrid's face. "Don't you think that's peculiar?"

Ingrid shrugged.

"You must have noticed them, but have you also noticed they've disappeared from campus completely? Not a trace. The graffiti's miraculously vanished too."

Ingrid tried to recall when she'd last seen a student in one of the polo shirts.

"Take a look at these two." Tate tapped the screen, enlarging the image of the students.

"Let me see."

Tate handed her the phone. Ingrid scrolled through a selection of images. She spotted the student in Younger's tutorial group, but didn't know any of the others. But there was something striking about them. "Notice anything about them?" Ingrid asked.

Tate took the phone and peered at the images like a woman who needed reading specs. "What have you spotted?"

"It might be nothing." Ingrid slurped loudly as she reached the bottom of the carton. "Within a normal group, you'd expect a bit of… irregularity. Short, fat, spotty, ugly, older, balder. Some imperfection or other. These students are all perfect. Look at their hair. Their skin. Their smiles. All blemish-free and perfectly proportioned. They look like they've stepped out of a glossy brochure."

"And that means…?"

"I'm not—" Ingrid was cut short by her phone buzzing noisily on the table. "I need to take this call." She jumped up and ran out onto the sidewalk. "Jennifer, thanks for getting back to me so fast. What have you got on Timo Klaason?"

"I've got an address for you."

Ingrid clenched her fist. "Excellent. Well done."

"I'm texting it to you now."

Ingrid glanced through the window at wily old Tate. She hoped she'd get considerably more out of Timo Klaason.

20

Ingrid arrived at the pub early. After a brief survey of the exits, front and back, and the restrooms, she settled on a stool at the long bar. The bartender stopped wiping down the woodwork and stared at her quite openly. From the corner of her eye she could have sworn his mouth was gaping. He cleared his throat and ambled over to her.

"What's a nice girl like you—"

She cut him off with a wave of her hand. "Don't even think about finishing that sentence. I'll have a ginger ale. No ice."

"Only trying to be friendly. Jesus."

The glass was warm when he dumped it on the bar, fresh from the dishwasher. She saw no benefit in getting into a fight with him, so chose not to ask for a replacement.

Detective Constable Ralph Mills arrived ten minutes later. Right on time. So punctual, in fact, Ingrid suspected he'd been pacing up and down outside, just waiting for the big hand to hit twelve.

"Am I late? Have you been waiting long?" He slipped onto the stool next to hers. "Would you like another?"

"I'm fine." She gestured to a free table on the other side of the room. "Shall we?"

Mills ordered a pint of cider on draft and joined her, carefully tucking his long legs beneath the low table. "Cheers," he said and then proceeded to drink half his cider in three gulps. His nervousness was endearing. He wiped a hand across his mouth and attempted to suppress a belch. He almost succeeded. "So. This is nice. You found it all right?"

"Obviously."

"Sorry, stupid question." He looked so much like Clark Swanson, the motorcycle-riding bad boy of Middleton High, that Ingrid would swear they were related if they weren't so completely different in temperament. "I suppose you're wondering why I suggested getting together like this?"

Ingrid said nothing, preferring to watch Mills twisting himself further into his embarrassment.

He drank another quarter of his cider. "I don't want you getting the wrong impression. I mean, it's not as if I make a habit of this."

"It seems quite simple to me. You asked me out; I said yes. And here we both are." She smiled again, less fulsomely this time.

"But it wasn't as if this was my idea."

"It wasn't?"

"See? I knew I was right to clear things up straight off the bat."

Ingrid lifted her drink to her mouth, felt the warmth of the glass against her lip and put it down again. "Are you trying to tell me this isn't a date?" She couldn't decide if she was relieved.

"God, no. Is that really what you thought?" His face colored in an instant. A shade somewhere between crimson and beet.

"Ah," she said. "McKittrick."

His right eye twitched in reply. "Boss wanted to keep things strictly off the books."

And she also wanted to set us up.

"She said she'd liaise with you herself, but"—he lowered his voice—"she asked me to speak to you because she's under a lot of pressure at the moment. From high up. Plus she's being scrutinized." He pulled a face.

"Scrutinized how?"

"Can't say exactly—it's not really my place to. There's stuff going on."

"What kind of stuff?"

"All kinds. Thing is, she can't throw resources at the Shelbourne case because, well, the scrutiny."

"But?"

"But she isn't happy about the situation."

"She didn't seem to have a problem with the accidental death verdict when I spoke to her about it."

"See." He inched in further. "She's being leaned on… and well… that's made her curious. Now she wants to probe a little more."

"I still don't see how I fit in."

He ran a pale hand through his thick brown hair. "The boss was hoping you'd share anything about the case that you happen to dig up. She can't be seen to do it herself."

"And in return?"

"I help you out on the QT."

"QT?"

"The down low." He smiled shyly at his use of teenspeak, lifting the corners of his mouth a fraction. He had never looked more like Clark Swanson, and Ingrid's cheeks prickled with heat. *You're engaged*, she told herself. *To be married*.

Mills's smile disappeared. He furrowed his brow, a knot of tension forming between his eyebrows. "It's just occurred to me… you thought I'd actually asked you out on a date… yet you still agreed to come."

"'Mutually beneficial' you said." She was smiling at him.

His frown deepened. "So, how can I help?"

She told him about the paint sample that she had sent for analysis, and he told her from now on he would help with that sort of thing. When she got the results, he could run it on their database to see if the same paint had been used by known graffiti artists, though whoever wrote *lauren shelbourne = whore* wasn't exactly Banksy. But it was a start.

"There is something else you could do for me," Ingrid said.

"Of course."

Ingrid wasn't at all sure that what she was about to suggest was a good idea. "Can you run a name through your databases for me?"

"Sure."

"Greg Brewster." A chill spread over her skin. She wasn't used to flagrantly breaking the rules.

"You think he's a suspect?"

Ingrid took a long mouthful, giving herself time to think. "I don't even know if it's his real name. All I know is he's from Tulsa, Oklahoma, and fifty-one years old. Though both those pieces of information could be as fake as the name."

"And you're interested in him because?"

She'd played everything by the book for so long this minor transgression felt like treason. She was terrible at lying. "It may be nothing."

"Is he related to Lauren Shelbourne or something?"

"Not exactly." Ingrid rummaged around in her bag for the printout of Barry Cline's photograph. "And if you can, see if any of your colleagues recognize this guy."

Mills looked at the already tattered sheet of A4.

"His name may or may not be Barry Cline."

"Same drill? Trawl the databases?"

"Not for this guy—I've done that much myself. I'm figuring he's a petty criminal, working over vulnerable tourists, and hoping he's known to the Met."

"Tourists from Tulsa, Oklahoma, for instance?"

"That's the idea. Now… let me get you another drink."

21

The GPS guided Ingrid and her Triumph Tiger 800 to a dark little side street in Deptford, a district of south London not far from Loriners college. She climbed off the bike, stowed her helmet and gloves, and pulled a dark blue beanie over her head, tucking her short blond hair inside.

The narrow street was lined on both sides by seven-story black-brick warehouses, the facades looking like ominous cliff faces in the dark. The road was paved with smooth, rounded cobblestones, slick with rain from a recent downpour. It was like stepping into another century. The buildings were run-down with broken windows and rusting ironwork. Surely it wouldn't be long before they were converted into luxury apartments, like the rest of the old buildings in the city. She checked the address Jennifer had given her for Timo Klaason, as these buildings were so dilapidated it didn't seem possible anyone could actually live inside.

She'd already tried calling the cell number Jennifer had provided. The line was dead, her call not even diverting to voice-mail. Timo Klaason was a hard man to pin down.

Ingrid peered up and down the street. A single streetlamp at the far end emitted a weak yellow glow, illuminating no more than a circle beneath it ten feet in diameter. She pulled a Maglite flashlight from a pocket in her vest and flipped on the bright beam, tracing it up the buildings on both sides of the street. She walked slowly toward the streetlamp, stopping regularly to listen. Despite the busy main street just a hundred yards away, the noise of the traffic was no more than a distant hum. She aimed the flashlight in the direction of a scuttling, rustling noise, letting out an involuntary gasp when she saw what was making it. A rat the size of a cat, sitting on its hind legs, was watching her with beady eyes. It sniffed the air. Two more rats appeared, even bigger than the first. Ingrid feinted a step toward them, jabbing the flashlight in their direction, her arm extended. Unafraid, they continued to regard her with something approaching curiosity. A shiver crept up her spine. She was just a few hundred yards from a small creek that emptied into the Thames: this close to water, there were probably dozens of rats. She rolled her shoulders to shake some of the tension from her arms, then carried on walking along the street. She trained the light beam onto the warehouses on either side, looking for an entrance.

Painted in untidy, whitewashed brushstrokes on the wall of a building were the same symbols she'd seen on campus. Three zigzagging lines. She aimed the beam immediately below the graffiti and discovered a doorway set inside a twelve-inch-deep recess. Attached to the side wall of the recess was a broken intercom buzzer hanging from a single screw. Stuck to the intercom was a yellowing scrap of paper with the number 32 printed on it in faded black marker. This was the property she was looking for. She tried the handle. The door was locked. The frame was made of steel, the door opening outward. There was no way to kick or shoulder it open.

There was more scuttling and scraping. Expecting to see another half-dozen giant rats, Ingrid poked her head out of the recess. Two figures were standing by a dumpster, one holding open the lid, the other throwing an armful of rectangular packets inside. It was close to midnight: far too late for putting out the garbage. She stepped into the street, shining her torch toward them.

"Hey! Can you help me?"

Two men, early twenties, tall and trim, spun around, holding up their hands against the glare of the flashlight. The metal lid of the dumpster clanged shut.

"Hi. I'd like to speak to you for a minute. I'm looking for somebody who lives here. You might know him. His name's Timo Klaason."

They looked at one another, then turned and ran. Ingrid shoved the flashlight into her waistband and gave chase, pumping her arms and stretching her legs. "Hey! Mr. Klaason? I only want to talk to you!" she hollered.

After a few strides she was gaining on them, but a third man suddenly appeared from the other side of the dumpster. He dropped his head low and ran toward her. She checked right and left, looking for somewhere to go. Her momentum continued to take her forward, but still he kept coming straight toward her like a freight train.

She grabbed for the flashlight, ready to jab it into his face, but before she could retrieve it, the running man slammed into her, knocking her off her feet. She fell hard on the cobbles, and her attacker drew back his leg before driving his foot into her ribs. Intense pain radiated around her back one way and into her chest the other. He drew back his foot again and kicked hard. Her head buzzed; darkness crept into her vision. He lifted his leg a third time, and this time she rolled out of the way.

"Come on, man!" A shout from one of the other two. "We have to get out of here."

Breathing hard, she watched them run off. She lay on the ground for what seemed like minutes before she felt able to roll onto her side. *This*, she said to herself, *is why cops in the States carry firearms.* No one else about, she could have put a slug in his thigh and stopped him.

Eventually, the pain eased slightly and she could draw a deeper breath. Then another. Ingrid pressed a hand against the wet cobbles and levered herself into a sitting position. Then, inch by excruciating inch, she got to her feet and staggered down the road toward the dumpster. She leaned against it, steadying herself before she attempted to move again. With one hand flat against the body of the big metal cube, she used all her strength to lift the lid, flipping it right over. She peered inside and retrieved one of the rectangular packets the men had discarded.

Within the transparent plastic wrapper, she could see, even in the faint glow from the distant streetlight, a perfectly folded purple and green polo shirt.

22

Aware she was listing to one side, Ingrid adjusted her posture. Each time her foot hit the ground, an electric shock of pain jolted around her ribs. The embassy MD had prescribed nothing stronger than Tylenol. No strapping, no binding, just a handful of over-the-counter painkillers and the unhelpful suggestion she 'take it easy' for a few days.

Sure.

Ingrid made her way slowly across the main piazza at Loriners, carefully avoiding groups of students not looking where they were going or anyone who appeared to be in a hurry. Another blow had the potential to bring tears to her eyes.

She hadn't reported the incident the night before to the local cops. She hadn't seen any of the men well enough to give the police a helpful description, so it would have been a futile exercise. She suspected one of the three men was Timo Klaason, but she had absolutely no way of proving it. Her presence in the deserted street close to midnight would have taken some explaining too. No need for that to get back to Sol or Louden.

Jennifer hadn't been able to dig up much about Klaason, but Faber had said he was a student at Loriners. She had visited the registrar's office and wasn't entirely surprised to find out Timo Klaason had been studying under Professor Younger. Unfortunately, the staff in the office also told her he'd left college the previous semester. Armed with directions, Ingrid set out to find the lecture theater where Younger was teaching: there was an outside chance he would be able to guide her toward Klaason's friends and acquaintances at college. One of them might know where to find him.

Ingrid slipped quietly into the cavernous space, taking a seat right at the back. On stage, Younger leaned on a lectern, looking up at a young student who was standing to attention on top of a table.

"OK, you can come down now." Younger snapped his fingers.

The young man on the table staggered slightly to one side and an 'ahhh' erupted from the audience of rapt students.

"And that, ladies and gents, is the power of suggestion." Younger stepped toward the table and held out a hand. The student ignored it and clambered down unaided. He patted down his clothes as if he was half expecting a vital garment to be missing.

Younger took a bow and was rewarded with a round of enthusiastic applause. He held up both hands and turned his head to one side, feigning embarrassment. He was enjoying every moment. When the applause died down, the students got to their feet and shuffled toward the exits. Ingrid fought her way to the front against the tide of chattering young men and women, taking care to skirt around the gesticulating arms as she went. She reached the lectern as Younger packed the last of his notes into a battered leather satchel. He glanced up, frowned at her for a beat, then smiled. He looked more youthful without his beard. But his eyes were still bloodshot, his forehead crisscrossed with deep lines. Something was keeping him up at night.

"Agent Skyberg." He drew down the corners of his mouth.

"Do you have a moment?"

"Ten whole minutes before my next... performance." His shoulders slumped. "I do sometimes feel like a vaudeville entertainer. But it's just the sort of thing that keeps the students interested. Stops them switching courses. Got to keep the faculty full of fee payers."

Ingrid pointed to the first row of seats. "Can we sit down?" Her aching ribs were affecting her energy levels more than she'd expected.

"If the sun is still shining, I think we should take full advantage, don't you?" Younger headed toward the exit.

Outside, the professor dropped onto the verdant lawned quadrangle, his long legs splaying out in front of him. Ingrid lowered herself to the ground, her ribs screaming in protest every inch of the way.

"Are you all right?"

She forced a pinched smile. "Perfectly." She blinked, conscious her eyes were prickling. "That was an impressive performance."

"A cheap end-of-pier hypnotist's trick, believe me."

"No, I meant what you did yesterday." Ingrid gestured to the roof of the tall administration building. "Quite a feat of strength. And fast thinking."

"Ah. I did what anyone would have done in the circumstances. Right place, right time."

"Is the girl a student of yours?"

"Emily? No—she's a medic."

"Where is she now?"

"Gone home to her parents, I believe. Best place for her. Seems end-of-year exams stress really got to her." He picked a stalk of grass from the knee of his pants.

"Will the college offer her counseling?"

"Most definitely."

"And have you arranged a counselor for Madison Faber yet?"

He froze. "Not really my job."

"Oh. Sorry." Ingrid observed him for telltale micro-expressions. "I'm sure Madison said that was why she was coming to see you the other day."

Younger said nothing.

"You remember, when we were talking in your office?"

His Adam's apple plunged and rose in his newly shaved neck. "Yes, of course I remember. I should check with the office.

Make sure she's getting support. Is that what you wanted to speak to me about?"

Ingrid shifted her weight so she could straighten her spine and put less strain on her bruised ribs. "I actually wanted to speak to you about another student of yours."

He narrowed his eyes. "Who?"

Ingrid stared into his face, not wanting to miss the merest flicker of emotion. "Timo Klaason."

There it was—a definite tightening around the eyes.

"Timo?" He scratched his head. "It's not ringing any bells. You'd think it would—an unusual name like that." He screwed up his eyes. "Are you sure he's one of my students?"

"I just checked with the registrar's office."

"I hate to be disloyal, but they do operate on a skeleton staff over there. It wouldn't be the first time they've made a mistake. It's not their fault; budget cuts, I'm afraid."

"The staff were very thorough. They showed me the paperwork."

"Ah. Well… I shall have to put on my thinking cap. Clarkson, you say?"

"Klaason. He's Dutch. I'm supposing you don't have too many Dutch students here."

"It's quite a mixed bunch, actually. Budgets again, of course. Overseas students are our bread and butter." He pursed his lips and patted an index finger against his chin. Another performance, Ingrid suspected. "Timo… Do you know what he looks like? So many students pass through this place."

Ingrid pulled out a printout the registrar's office had given her, a blurry black-and-white version of Klaason's passport picture. Younger squinted at the image.

"Perhaps," he said eventually. "He's not in the faculty now; I'd definitely know him otherwise."

"He left just before the spring break."

He nodded and handed the sheet back. "Well, there you are."

"Can you tell me anything about him? What kind of student he was? How he got along with his classmates? Who he hung around with?"

Younger shrugged. "I know he can't have excelled academically. Or indeed been struggling terribly. In either case he would have come to my attention."

"You're absolutely sure you don't know him?"

Younger got to his feet. "One hundred percent. I'm really sorry I can't shed any light." He held out his hand. "Would you like some help getting up?"

Ingrid ignored his hand and did her best to stand without grimacing.

"My audience awaits. Another two hours of spinning plates and fire-eating. Please excuse me." He smiled at her then strolled toward the lecture theater. A moment later he stopped and turned back. "If you happen to... I mean..." He puffed out a breath. "If you see Lauren's parents, would you tell them all of us here at Loriners—staff and students alike—miss her terribly. She's a great loss to the field. She really might have made a difference."

Ingrid watched his loping gait until he disappeared inside the building. She wasn't sure what to make of Stuart Younger. Her research revealed a man who appeared to have led a blameless existence. He didn't even have a record for weed possession when he was at college himself. Or a speeding violation in the two decades since. He was squeaky clean. Too damn clean for comfort.

"Hello!"

The voice in her ear made Ingrid jump. She stepped back and found herself staring into the eager face of the medical student she'd met on Tuesday morning.

"So you must be *seriously* considering coming here to study, then?"

Ingrid quickly tucked her visitor's badge into her jacket.

"Second visit in four days. That's keen," Mohammed said. "You got over the whole 'serial killer' thing?"

"I, um, haven't made a final decision yet."

"Good job you weren't here yesterday. That would've put you right off."

"Why?" she said innocently. "What happened?"

"We almost had another jumper splatted across the square." He shook his head. "I thought Emily would have more sense than to get herself mixed up in all that crap."

"Emily?" Ingrid walked him away from the lecture theater building, concerned Younger might come back out and blow her cover.

Mohammed fell into step with her. "The girl who nearly jumped."

"You know her?"

He nodded. "She's in my year. Studying medicine, like me."

"What 'crap' is she mixed up in?"

"If I tell you, you might decide not to come here. Like I said before, you improve the scenery round here, innit?"

"What if I promise you right now that anything you tell me won't affect my decision one way or the other?"

"OK. You swear, yeah?"

"Cross my heart."

Mohammed stared at her finger as she dragged it across her chest.

"Emily was a volunteer. I was telling you about the experiments when I spoke to you before. She was a guinea pig in the psycho department. I reckon whatever twisted shit they did to her must have pushed her over the edge."

"You think the research program had something to do with what happened yesterday?"

"Emily's sound. Not my type, like." He smiled slyly at Ingrid. "But she's a good sort, you know? Maybe too good. Maybe that's why she agreed to take part in the research; she was too nice to say no."

Ingrid frowned at him.

"What I'm trying to say... Emily's solid. Smart. Sensible. She wouldn't try to throw herself out of a window without someone or something influencing her."

"Someone?"

Mohammed shrugged. "There's a bunch of them running the experiments."

"You're sure about Emily's involvement in the research?" she said.

Mohammed nodded vigorously. "I told you it was twisted."

23

Madison Faber yanked hard on the black Labrador's leash and the dog immediately stopped pulling.

Ingrid gingerly bent down and squeezed the dog's ears. "You're quite the disciplinarian."

"You have to be firm with him, or he'll take advantage. Sorry about just now, but I needed to get out of the apartment. Miriam, my mom's college friend, is driving me crazy. Fussing over me, wanting to talk about anything that happens to pop into her head. Walking the dog gets me a break from her. Though I'm actually quite allergic to his fur." She gave a little sniff as if to prove it.

Ingrid had been wondering how Faber was managing to resist petting such a cute canine specimen. "But you feel safer now you've moved out of your apartment?"

"A little, I guess."

"Good. And your mom's friend is happy to let you stay for as long as you want to?"

"She is. If I don't wring her neck first."

Ingrid smiled. She was pleased Faber was up to making a joke. The girl was much calmer than their previous meeting. "You've got to admit Hampstead is a nicer suburb than New Cross."

"I feel like I'm on the set of a Hugh Grant movie."

"And having access to the Heath"—Ingrid gestured to the almost rural landscape surrounding them—"is great for clearing your mind."

Faber pulled the dog away from a French poodle he'd taken a shine to. "So, what did you want to talk about? Did you speak to Klaason?"

"Not yet. I'm having some… issues tracking him down. I was hoping you could tell me a little more about him."

Faber inhaled sharply. She was marching up the same hill Ingrid had run up two days previously. "Like I said before, I don't really know him. Not personally." Her voice sounded strained. She lengthened her stride, and the dog trotted along obediently beside her. Then she suddenly pulled up and did a three-sixty turn, scanning the horizon in all directions. "You're sure no one knows you're meeting me here?"

"No, nobody. You're quite safe."

"You can't guarantee that."

Ingrid held onto the young woman's arm. "I'm not going to let anyone hurt you."

The dog barked once and buried its nose into Faber's thigh.

"And you've got this guy looking out for you too." Ingrid held Faber's gaze.

Faber pulled away, changing direction toward a lake at the bottom of the hill. The dog's tail wagged in anticipation. "No!" Faber told him. "No swimming for you." She turned to Ingrid. "He got me drenched when I let him in the pond yesterday. Scared the shit out of the ducks too."

They walked several yards in silence as Ingrid tried to find the right words to get what she wanted out of Faber. "Do you know why Klaason left Loriners last semester?"

"Left?"

"Just before the spring break."

"He hasn't left."

"He has, according to the registrar."

A gaggle of schoolgirls in dishevelled school uniforms pushed past them, teasing one another and shouting and giggling as they went. Faber tensed at the noise. When they were gone, she bent her head close to Ingrid's, as if she wanted to make sure their conversation wasn't overheard. "The registrar's office must have made a mistake. Klaason is a psychology undergrad though he spends more time partying than studying. Somehow he still manages to pass all his assignments."

"And he's running a drug-dealing operation on the side."

"I never said he was a drug *dealer*. I get the impression he's more of an *enabler*. Though he did try to sell me some coke once at a party. He got really angry when I refused."

"You should tell the police."

Faber shuddered, then said softly, "I shouldn't even be talking to you about him. There's no way I'm going to the police." She grabbed Ingrid's arm. "And you promised me you wouldn't tell anyone."

Ingrid patted her hand. "I know. I won't." They started walking again. "How well did Lauren know Klaason?"

"Um. I'm not really sure. But they were in the same research group."

This time it was Ingrid's turn to grab Faber's arm. "Wait a minute. Professor Younger's research group? *Your* research group right up until the spring break?"

Faber's expression remained fixed.

"You were all in the same group together?"

"It's a big group. Around thirty people or so."

"I thought Klaason was an undergrad."

"He is. But…" Faber's right eye twitched as she surveyed the distant horizons again. "I don't know if I should tell you this."

"Haven't we moved beyond that by now?"

"Klaason's useful to the professor, so Younger lets him assist in the research. Klaason's practically his right-hand man."

"Younger knows him that well?" Ingrid was careful to keep the tone of her voice neutral.

Faber wriggled her arm free of Ingrid's grasp and walked ahead. "I've just said, haven't I?"

Ingrid pushed her hands deep into her jacket pockets. Faber was too relaxed about contradicting herself, and this wasn't the first time she'd remembered a fact when it was convenient to do so. She caught up with her. "Why didn't you tell me you were part of Lauren's research group before? Working with Younger."

"I'm sure I did. I definitely told you I don't agree with his methods, and that was why I left his group."

That was true, but it still felt like a lie. "Yes, I remember. So does that mean you have some mutual friends? People who can help me track him down."

Faber stood a little straighter. "I can give you one or two addresses. Friends of friends of friends. But you didn't get them from me—is that clear?"

"Crystal." What was less clear, however, was why Madison Faber was suddenly trying to be more helpful.

24

After a fruitless night keeping vigil outside one of the addresses Madison Faber had given her, Ingrid was not in the best shape to handle an early morning meeting with Louden and the Shelbournes. Two double espressos and a couple of Tylenol weren't enough to deal with the pain in her side and the intense fatigue fogging her head like a thick wad of cotton.

At least a dozen CIA field officers and their superiors huddled in groups of twos and threes in the bull pen outside her office. There were faces she didn't recognize. They lowered their voices or stopped conversations altogether as she approached. It was as if someone had called a crisis meeting at the embassy and hadn't bothered to mention it to her. Sol was waiting for her outside Louden's office when Ingrid arrived, pacing up and down, his face grave.

"Hey—I thought Saturdays were sacrosanct for you. What're you doing here?" Ingrid's smile wasn't returned. She lowered her voice. "Is it something to do with whatever the hell is going on around here?"

He said nothing.

"Imminent invasion? National emergency? Help me out here. I've never seen so many spooks outside Langley."

Sol gnawed his bottom lip.

"You're scaring me now. What is going on?"

"It's nothing that concerns you. Or me, really, just some high-level CIA stuff."

Ingrid folded her arms. "You mean you can't tell me because my security clearance is too low."

"Something like that."

"Should I be buying canned goods and a year's supply of batteries?"

Sol ignored her flippancy. "I'm looking into it, by the way. Raising your clearance."

Well, that was a surprise.

"But there are issues."

"Such as?" she asked, suspecting he was giving her the brush-off.

"It's nothing to do with you."

"Then who is it to do with?"

He bit his lip, then leaned in. "Your predecessor."

"Mulroony?"

Before he could elaborate, the elevator doors opposite Louden's office opened and the Shelbournes emerged.

Ingrid set her face in what she hoped was compassionate understanding, doing her best not to tilt her head to one side. Lauren Shelbourne's parents stepped into the corridor and both acknowledged her with a nod. They didn't look at one another. There was no supporting arm from Anthony Shelbourne for his wife to lean on today.

"Have you met my colleague, Sol Franklin?" Ingrid asked.

Sol stretched out his hand. "I am so sorry for your loss."

The Shelbournes nodded mutely. Alex Shelbourne curled her lip, tired of the platitudes.

"I hope you've got some news for us," Anthony Shelbourne said.

"It's this way," Ingrid said, guiding them toward Louden's office.

Alex didn't move. "I need the bathroom."

"Yes, of course," Ingrid said, "it's just along there." She pointed out a door a short distance down the corridor, and when Alex brushed past her, she pressed a folded square of paper into her hand. Ingrid slipped it into her pocket, glancing uncertainly at the girl's parents.

Alex emerged a few moments later, her face glistening with moisture. "Just needed to freshen up," she said pointedly.

They knocked on Louden's door. Alex Shelbourne glowered at Ingrid as they waited for the DSAC to open it.

"Mr. and Mrs. Shelbourne." Amy Louden outstretched her hand. "I'm so sorry we're meeting under such sad circumstances. You must be Alexandra. Won't you all come in."

Louden ushered them toward two couches facing each other across a low mahogany coffee table laden with a selection of international newspapers and huge photo books about America. *New York From The Air. A Journey Through Yellowstone.*

"Thank you for agreeing to meet with us on the weekend," Lisa Shelbourne said, still studiously ignoring her husband.

"It's the least I can do."

For the next fifteen minutes, Louden painstakingly went through the police report with them, patiently answering the Shelbournes' questions whenever they needed something clarified. Alex Shelbourne remained silent throughout, occasionally throwing Ingrid a look. Something was preying on the girl's mind.

"Is there anything else you need to know? Any ground I haven't covered?" Louden said as she closed the file on her desk.

"You've been very thorough," Anthony Shelbourne assured her. "Thank you for taking the time to go through the report. The police offered to do it themselves, but I feel... more reassured hearing the details from you."

Alex shifted in her seat, cleared her throat, then said, "Is it possible they've made a mistake?"

Immediately her parents turned in their seats and the temperature in the room dropped. Louden did no more than raise her perfectly threaded eyebrows.

"Alex?" her mother said, "where has that come from?"

"I'm just saying..." She leaned forward in her seat, ignoring both her parents and Ingrid, and leveled her gaze at the DSAC.

"Do you really trust that the local cops know what they're doing?"

"I can understand your feelings, I can, really," Louden said in a voice so gentle Ingrid couldn't quite believe the words were coming out of her mouth. "You want to know nothing has been overlooked, no piece of evidence, however small, has been missed. Rest assured, the Metropolitan Police Service is one of the best in the world." She patted the file to reinforce her point. "But, as you know, we have our own officer carrying out an independent investigation." She turned to Ingrid. "Agent Skyberg, what's your opinion?"

Ingrid thought about the note Alex had slipped her. What did the girl know? Was she about to drop a bombshell? She glanced at Sol, who was pulling his gravest face, his eyes urging her not to cause the Shelbournes any unnecessary pain, and mostly not to contradict her DSAC. Louden steepled her hands and leaned her chin on the tips of her fingers. The Shelbournes leaned forward expectantly. The room was painfully silent.

"I have full confidence in the Met." Ingrid's stomach muscles tightened. She watched as Mr and Mrs Shelbourne slumped back in their chairs, relieved. Everyone seemed to exhale at once. "There was no evidence of a break-in at Lauren's apartment, no evidence of a visitor, and given the level of drugs in your daughter's body and the lack of other wounds, I wouldn't expect the inquest next week to alter the preliminary findings of accidental death."

"I'm sensing a but," Louden said, her face sour with frustration.

"But…" She stopped herself. "I don't want to cause you any more pain, but I do think there may be some scope for accusing the university of being negligent in their duty of care to your daughter."

Lisa Shelbourne stiffened.

"I've been spending some time on campus," Ingrid said, "and I'm hearing things about drug dealing and also extreme pressure being put on students." She told them about the most recent suicide attempt. Sol's expression collapsed: he really didn't want his lone criminal investigator wasting her time on this. "I think, until the inquest has taken place, there are a few enquiries I can make. They will not, of course, bring your daughter back, but they may begin to answer why Lauren's life unraveled so quickly."

"See, I told you," Alex said. Neither of her parents looked at her.

Ingrid remembered something Faber had said, about Lauren being the happiest she had ever seen the day before she died. It wasn't the behavior of someone whose addiction had gotten so out of control they lose consciousness the next day. She wanted an explanation. She looked at the Shelbournes' ashen faces and was momentarily floored by their loss.

"And might," Anthony Shelbourne began, "might this lead to charges? To a prosecution of some sort?" He had balled his fists so tight his knuckles were white.

Louden intervened. "I wouldn't want you to get your hopes up."

"But it might?" Lisa Shelbourne asked.

Ingrid scratched her forearms. "A slim chance, yes, depending what I find out."

"It sounds more like," Sol said, his eyes boring into Ingrid, "the basis for a civil case against the college."

She understood the subtext: this is not a criminal matter, move on, agent, and don't waste the Bureau's time. She nodded at Sol, then turned to the Shelbournes. "With your blessing, I'd like to use the next few days before the inquest to gather more evidence. But you should know that if I do find something, and the coroner accepts it, it may mean Lauren's body is not released for—"

Lisa Shelbourne gasped before Ingrid could say the word *repatriation*.

A smile stretched Alex Shelbourne's lips. Anthony's hand—finally—reached for his wife's arm. "Yes, please, Agent Skyberg, please continue your work."

Ingrid tried hard to keep the satisfaction from her expression: Louden and Sol wouldn't stop her now the Shelbournes had endorsed her plan. "I will let you know what I find out," she said.

"Thank you," Lisa Shelbourne said. She had not responded to her husband's timid show of affection.

"If that's it..." Anthony Shelbourne shuffled forward in his seat.

"I'm sorry we don't have more for you at this stage," Louden said, "but Agent Skyberg will keep you up to date."

Shelbourne got to his feet and stuck a hand out toward Sol. He shook it, encasing Sol's hand in both of his. Then he extended the gesture to Louden. He turned to Ingrid. "We really do appreciate everything you're doing."

Lisa Shelbourne grabbed Ingrid's arm on the way to the door and gripped it firmly. She went to say something, but she didn't need to: her eloquent eyes expressed more than words. Find who did this. Ingrid nodded that she understood.

"I'll show you out," Ingrid said.

"Actually," Louden said, walking back to her desk, "Sol, would you please escort the Shelbourne family to the lobby."

He raised an eyebrow but said, "Of course."

He held the door for Lauren's family, then followed them out of the room.

"Ma'am?" Ingrid turned to Louden.

Louden looked at something on her monitor, then at Ingrid. "I was just wondering what progress you've made in the Brewster case? Any closer to that laptop?"

Ingrid took a moment before answering. "Ah. Not much." What was Louden's interest in Brewster? "Without knowing the victim's real identity, or the likely thief's, I'm at a serious disadvantage."

Louden frowned.

"But I have a meeting later today." It was a weak lie, and if interrogated further, she'd have nothing to reinforce it.

"With whom?" The words shot out of Louden's mouth with the force of a bullet.

"A... another escort agency. And I'm interrogating other databases." Or rather, the pliable Ralph Mills was.

"Good... good." Louden was distracted by whatever was on her screen.

"Sol mentioned my clearance level was being looked at." Ingrid stood a little straighter, sending a spasm of pain across her ribs. "If it's going to take a long time, perhaps you want to assign this investigation to an agent with the appropriate authority?"

Louden looked at her as if she hadn't understood. "I'm sorry. I really have to deal with this."

Ingrid nodded. "Of course. I'll keep you updated."

Louden had already picked up the phone and wasn't listening. Outside in the hallway, Ingrid exhaled very slowly and shoved her balled fists into her pockets. She felt the folded piece of paper Alex Shelbourne had given her and quickly retrieved it.

There's something you need to know about Lauren.

25

Ingrid stabbed the 'B' button inside the elevator and willed the metal doors to close. But by the time she reached the parking lot in the basement, there was no sign of the Shelbournes' car. She considered racing to the exit at street level, but the car was probably long gone. She had no means of contacting Alex Shelbourne short of turning up at the hotel. Not something she wanted to do unless she knew Lisa and Anthony Shelbourne were elsewhere. Whatever it was, Alex didn't feel she could reveal it in her parents' presence.

She returned to her desk and checked her emails. Brewster's laptop hadn't shown up on any of the registers of secondhand computers. She entered the make and model into eBay but didn't find a match. Just about the only thing she knew for sure about the theft was that whoever had stolen the laptop was interested in its contents, not in blackmailing Brewster. In any normal investigation, knowing the motive would make it easier to identify potential suspects. But unless someone told her what was so valuable, she was fighting blind. Hopefully Marshall would track down Dennis Mulroony and she could swap notes.

Mulroony. Sol had been about to say something, hadn't he?

Energized, Ingrid leaped up and hurried to Sol's office, her bruises rubbing painfully against her pullover. His door was locked. She tried his phone. Voicemail. She wondered how long it would take him to call her back.

With a renewed sense of purpose, Ingrid called the embassy garage and requested a car. They only had limousines, which weren't the incognito vehicle she was hoping for. So she found a local car-hire company and picked up a dinky Chevy Spark that she drove to one of the addresses Faber had given her, not far from the warehouse she'd visited two nights previously. Feeling decidedly conspicuous in a quiet residential street, she wriggled further down in the driver's seat. She'd promised Madison Faber she'd do everything she could to find out what really happened, and now she had made the same pledge to Lauren's family. She had a snowball's chance of finding Brewster's laptop, but was confident a little diligent police work could explain Lauren's death. She might not be able to get the Shelbournes justice, but she could damn well get them answers.

Memories from the past surged, thrusting painful images to the fore. *Not here. Not now.* If there was one thing the experience of losing Megan had taught her, it was that without answers, you remain lost. It had been eighteen years since Ingrid's best friend had been abducted in front of her, never to be seen again. When the local police closed Megan's case without a conviction and without finding her, Ingrid had vowed to uncover the truth about her friend's disappearance. It was why she joined the sheriff's department. It was the reason she had gone on to become an FBI agent. But she was no closer to finding Megan, and she was still living with the void that might have been healed had the original investigation turned over every stone.

So far, every lead she'd followed had led her back to Loriners, the psychology department and Professor Younger. Maybe Timo Klaason had nothing to do with Lauren Shelbourne's death, but if he was dealing drugs, and he was connected to the polo shirt wearers within the psychology faculty, she was going to pay him a visit.

She focused her attention on the blue door of the two-story house. The drapes were drawn at all the windows, even though it was well after midday. She was hopeful Klaason was yet to crawl out of his bed. Assuming, of course, he was even inside. She shook another couple of painkillers from the bottle and swallowed them dry.

Two hours later, as the effect of the pills was beginning to wear off, she considered getting out of the car to stretch her legs. She had just popped the lock when the drapes fluttered in the downstairs window. She sat very still and held her breath, but there was no further activity for another five minutes. Her patience was finally rewarded when the blue door opened and a tall, slim white man, early to mid-twenties, closed it behind him and stood for a moment on the low stoop. Ingrid slipped further down in her seat. The man placed a pair of headphones on his shaved head, fiddled with his iPhone, then set off at speed, striding out of the front yard and down the street, heading north toward a network of equally respectable residential streets.

Ingrid quickly checked the passport-sized portrait of Klaason she had on her phone. It had to be him. It was also possible it was the man from the warehouse who'd played football with her ribs. She eased herself gently out of the car, and by the time she'd locked the door, Klaason was already nearing the end of the street. A good distance for a tail. She reached the corner and spotted him heading west. Then he stopped abruptly and started patting his pockets. He had forgotten something.

Crap.

Ingrid looked around for some place to hide, but short of launching herself over a wall into somebody's front yard, she had few options. She tensed, waiting for Klaason to turn around and look straight at her. She jammed her cell phone to her ear and angled her body away from him, keeping her head half-turned. A moment later, he retrieved a small packet from the rear pocket of his pants. He lit up a cigarette and Ingrid exhaled. He was on the move again, stretching his long legs, forcing her to trot along behind in order to keep up.

A half mile later, he turned into the cobbled street where she had been kicked the night before last. In daylight, she could see the businesses that plied their trade from the ramshackle collection of buildings and derelict warehouses: a health food wholesaler, a vehicle repair shop and a clothing recycling business. Only the clothing operation was in operation on a Saturday afternoon. A large truck pulled through a set of metal gates, which clanged shut behind it.

Klaason stopped at a building immediately beyond the clothing business and reached into a pocket. He pulled out a key and unlocked the door. Ingrid crept closer, hiding behind a truck. The door opened and Klaason stepped inside. Ingrid raced across the street, toward the closing door, and just managed to shove a foot between it and the frame before it shut. Three painted zigzags told her she was in the right place. She got her breath back and tried to ignore the nagging pain in her side, then ventured inside.

26

At the end of a long corridor, Klaason turned right. Ingrid traced his steps, reaching the corner just as the doors of an old-fashioned industrial elevator cage clanged shut. The elevator ascended, and she watched the numbers above the door light up one after the other, finally stopping when it reached number 7.

Not wanting to alert anyone to her presence, Ingrid made her way up a narrow staircase as quickly as she could, stopping on each landing to draw painful breaths. At the top, she pulled open the heavy spring-loaded door that led to the corridor. She counted a half dozen doorways, three on each side, though she couldn't see the doors themselves, as they lay in shadowy recesses set back from the hallway. She listened for a moment, heard nothing beyond the low hum of the fluorescent strip lights, and moved out into the corridor. The first door she came to was padlocked with three solid steel locks. She checked the opposite door, and again it was padlocked. More businesses that didn't open on the weekend. She ventured slowly down the corridor.

She froze at the sound of distant voices. Ahead, the elevator door slid noisily across its rail. Ingrid was in no-man's-land between doorways. She retreated, running backward, keeping her eyes on the elevator. A man stepped out, his head turned away from her. He laughed, throwing back his head. He was wearing combat pants tucked into black boots and a purple and green polo shirt.

Ingrid's heart thumped hard against her ribs.

Another man pushed past the first one, knocking a hand against his shoulder.

"Later. There's plenty of time for that," the second man said.

She pressed herself into a recess just as they turned her way.

"Did you see the look on his face?" one voice said.

"He's all right. He knows what he's doing."

There was a loud bang, fist against wood. A door creaked open. Another voice, deeper than the first two, mumbled something indistinct. Ingrid risked a glance into the corridor in time to see the two men disappearing inside the door furthest on the left, nearest the elevator. It had to be where Klaason was. She waited for a minute before making her way stealthily down the hallway. There was no name plate or number on the door, just the three symbols she'd seen before scratched into the paintwork. She could hear voices on the other side of the door, but wasn't able to pick out specific words. A light flickered in the corridor, a warmer glow than the fluorescent glare. She looked up to see narrow windows set high into the wall, just below the ceiling. Klaason or his new visitors had switched on more lights inside the room. She stared at the high windows, knowing the only way to get a glimpse inside the room would be through one of them. She stepped back to inspect the wall. It was rendered in smooth concrete. A few feet from where she was standing, she spotted a pipe running from floor to ceiling. It was three inches in diameter and attached to the wall with metal brackets large enough to use as climbing toeholds. The big question was whether it was strong enough to take her weight.

There was only one way to find out.

Ingrid stood with a foot on either side of the pipe. She reached up and clamped her left hand around it, braced herself for the inevitable surge of pain in her ribs, and lifted her right leg. She rested the toe of her boot on the first bracket, grabbed the pipe with her right hand and heaved herself up.

The pipe was solid.

She repeated the process the other way, right hand grab, left foot against the next bracket. Again she hauled herself up. Took a breath. Listened. If anyone chose that moment to open the door, she would be completely exposed with nowhere to go and no possible explanation. She stretched up with her left hand and saw the next bracket had only one loose screw attaching it to the wall. It was doing nothing to secure the pipe to the wall, and the smallest amount of force would wrench it from its moorings and send the metal ring and screws, and quite possibly her, clattering to the ground. She reached as far as she could, her fingertips finding the edge of the nearest window ledge. She tried to pull herself up, her hand grabbing tightly on the ledge, but the throbbing in her ribs was too great. She blew out an agonizing breath.

She needed to get a look inside the room. Maybe she could wait for Klaason and his two visitors to exit the premises. But she had no idea how many other people might be inside. She risked walking into a situation she would be unable to extricate herself from. She reached for her pocket for her phone. If she stretched enough, she might be able to get a photograph of the interior of the room. She disabled the flash function and, holding the phone by its bottom edge, reached up again. The pain in her side made her head buzz. She bit into her bottom lip. With effort, she positioned the phone higher than the window ledge. She squeezed the button on the side of the phone, but heard no reassuring shutter click.

Damn.

She reached up higher and squeezed again. This time a bright white flash reflected off the windowpane.

27

Ingrid dropped from her perch like a stone, landing hard, both ankles taking the full force of her weight, her knees bending a fraction too late to distribute the shock wave. Despite the pain, she gathered herself quickly and ran for the stairway, the shouting voices inside the room getting louder as the occupants approached the door.

Shit.

She flung open the door to the stairwell and started to head downward. *No. Mistake. They'll head down too.* She turned quickly and bounded upwards, her head spinning from the pain in her ribs. She reached the next landing and heard the door below being yanked open. She waited till she heard their footsteps going down, then dragged herself up another two flights until she was out of steps. She had two options. The first was waiting for them to leave the building.

"Where are you, bitch?"

"She must have gone up!"

The second option was a fire exit that she guessed led onto the roof. She tried the handle. It turned, but when she leaned her weight against it, the door wouldn't budge. The door frame was damp and swollen.

Footsteps thundered up from below.

Ingrid leaned harder against the door, stifling a scream as her ribs slammed into the wood. The door burst open, sending her flying out onto the roof. It was empty apart from another door on the opposite side, identical to the one she'd just come through, about forty yards away. There was nowhere else to go, so she headed for it as quickly as she could. She pumped her arms and drove her feet into the ground, pushing herself forward.

"There she is!"

She threw a glance over her shoulder. Klaason stormed out of the doorway and ran toward her. She gasped for every breath as she ran for the other door. She was ten feet away when it flew open.

Shit, shit, shit.

Two men, both wearing the signature polo shirts, bundled through the doorway and ran toward her. She couldn't go forward. She couldn't go back. She checked left and right. The rooftops of the neighboring buildings were a good fifteen feet away. Too far to jump with her injuries. But she had no choice. She swung left and drove herself forward, picking up momentum. She gripped the cell phone, which was still in her fist.

There was a low wall at the edge of the roof. She aimed for it, adjusting her stride so she could launch herself from it and clear the sixty-foot drop. Anything other than a clean jump down onto the next rooftop and she was finished.

She lengthened her stride. The edge was coming up fast. She kept her head up, her gaze focused on the perimeter wall. She gritted her teeth. Her right foot hit the top of the wall perfectly; she threw out her arms and thrust both legs in front. There was nothing beneath her but air. She swung her arms backward, propelling her hips forward.

Her feet hit the roof, but her weight fell backward, away from safety, toward the drop. She curled her torso, and her buttocks hit the asphalt, followed quickly by her upper back and shoulders. Her cell phone flew right out of her hand. She watched as it somersaulted through the air.

"Get over there!" Klaason yelled.

Ingrid scrambled onto her side and looked at him. He couldn't believe what she had done, and his face was a picture.

"Five years of parkour," she shouted, her chest heaving with deep, heavy breaths.

His companions peered over the rooftop edge at the sheer drop. Ingrid tried to get to her feet, but the soreness in her ribs forced her back down. One of the polo-shirted men jogged back across the roof to the far side then turned. He started to run toward the edge, his speed nowhere near fast enough to carry him over.

"Go on!"

"Get her!"

Ingrid tried to get up again and made it onto her hands and knees. She watched in horror as the man on the opposite building hurtled toward the edge.

"No!" she shouted, her voice getting lost on the wind.

He pulled up. Just a few yards from the drop, his arms swinging wildly to stop his momentum. In slow motion, Ingrid saw him slide toward the low wall hemming the roof, his feet slamming into the bricks. He dropped backward.

Klaason shouted something in Dutch. He grabbed the prostrate man by the collar and hauled him to his feet. Then he shoved him at the rooftop door.

"Get over there!" he yelled.

Ingrid had to get moving. Little by little, she pulled herself vertical, her head spinning as soon as she was upright. She blinked, then staggered. She scanned the roof for her phone, praying it hadn't gone over the edge. She spotted its cover first. A moment later she located the phone. She bent down, letting out a yelp, and scooped it up. There was no door on this roof, no obvious way down. She limped to the edge of the building and peered down at the street. A rusting metal fire escape zigzagged down as far as the second floor. Klaason's henchmen burst out of the warehouse next door and ran toward her only obvious means of escape. One of them jumped up, grasping for the bottom rung. Ingrid crossed to the other side of the roof. The rear of the building looked out onto a goods yard, a tall metal fence protecting it from the street beyond. There was no way down. No access hatch. No roof ladder.

Directly beneath her, a truck belonging to the recycled clothing business was parked in a loading bay. It was piled high with rags and old clothes. Not a bad option. She stood on the edge, pressed her elbows into her sides, laid her forearms across her chest and stepped off.

She hit the clothes, rolled sideways and tucked her knees into her chest. Then she lay completely still, assessing the damage. Nothing seemed to hurt more than it had before.

She pulled her cell from her pocket and found the picture she'd taken of Klaason's premises. The image was blurry and dark. She stared at it until she could make sense of the strange shapes. She'd seen those shapes before. But not for years. Not since she was a rookie agent working out of a field office in Cleveland. It had been her first big bust: a methamphetamine factory.

28

The crime scene investigators removed the last of the meth-making equipment from Klaason's makeshift laboratory: a large set of kitchen scales wrapped in a huge plastic evidence bag. Ingrid had been interviewed by the senior investigating officer from the London Crime Squad at length and had arranged to make a formal statement in the station on Monday morning. From what the SIO had told her, the squad was responsible for most of the drug busts across the whole of London.

"You look like you just crawled here from a war zone."

Ingrid turned slowly to see Natasha McKittrick, burger in one hand, can of soda in the other, hurrying toward her.

"Jeez, what is that?" The aroma of the beef fat and burned onions had Ingrid's stomach roiling. "It smells like yesterday's garbage."

McKittrick tipped her head to one side. "If I'd known you were going to nag me about my eating habits, I wouldn't have come." She took another bite. "I can't walk past a burger van without buying something. It's the onions." She waved the offending meat sandwich under Ingrid's nose. "Want a bite?"

"I'll pass."

McKittrick shrugged, took another mouthful and tossed what was left in a nearby trash can. She took a swig of soda. "Takes me back to my childhood."

It did the same for Ingrid, which was why she never drank the stuff.

McKittrick wiped her hands on a paper napkin. "So... what was so important you couldn't tell me about it over the phone?" She dabbed some ketchup from the corner of her mouth. Ingrid took a moment to study the off-duty detective. In the four months she'd known her, she'd only ever seen her this upbeat on tequila.

"Are you OK?" Ingrid inquired.

"You're asking *me* that?" She stepped back and looked Ingrid up and down. "You need to get yourself down to the nearest A&E department."

"I'll be fine." A CSI closed the doors of a nearby truck, making Ingrid flinch.

"Some people go to the cinema on a Saturday afternoon, you know, settle down with a big box of popcorn and while away a couple of hours. Are you auditioning for the part of a superhero?"

"I thought you'd want to be updated if I discovered new evidence connected to the Shelbourne investigation."

McKittrick's face sank.

"Why else did you think I'd get you here on your day off?"

"I dunno, maybe you wanted to see a friendly face, a shoulder to lean on? Instead I see you've added to my workload."

McKittrick blinked, her eyes swimming slightly as she stared at the front of the building. "I take it you think this meth factory supplied the drugs Lauren Shelbourne took?"

"It's run by a student in Shelbourne's study group. Timo Klaason, the man responsible for this... enterprise, was, or is, in Professor Younger's research program at Loriners."

"He was Lauren's supplier?"

"According to Madison Faber."

McKittrick's eyebrows shot up. "Didn't know you were still in contact with her." She licked the last of the ketchup off her fingers. "I'm sure I don't need to remind you the cause of death wasn't an overdose. The girl hit her head. That's what killed her."

"I thought you weren't happy with the findings."

"Never said that."

"I thought that's why you sent Mills to help—"

"I'm not happy being leaned on. Being told what I should be delivering and by when, especially when you're not my boss, and extra especially when it makes me look bad."

Ingrid let out a sigh. "That's why I figured you'd want to see it. This way you can let your Crime Squad colleagues take the bust, or you can send in your CSIs and see if there's anything that relates to Lauren."

McKittrick tapped her foot rhythmically. She didn't seem to be concentrating. She was hyper. "Jesus, Natasha, are you high?"

McKittrick whipped round so fast Ingrid took a step back, fearing she might actually slap her. McKittrick nodded at her Met colleagues, all of whom were out of earshot. "What did you say?"

Ingrid was in no mood for another fight. "Nothing."

"Good. Because it is my day off. Or at least it was meant to be."

She didn't know Natasha that well. She liked her. They'd been out for a few drinks, but Ingrid realized she knew very little about her friend. And she had enough experience with addicts and users to think McKittrick wouldn't pass a blood test. Her cell phone bleeped twice. The vibrate function hadn't survived being dropped. She retrieved it from a pocket and scanned the text message. It was from Mills, suggesting they meet. He had 'discovered something' about their 'American friend.'

"Anyone I know?" McKittrick asked.

Ingrid glowered at McKittrick, suddenly very unsure where she stood with the inspector. "It's personal."

McKittrick raised her hands and took a step backward. "Sorry I asked. You said Faber put you onto this Timo fella?"

Ingrid nodded.

"Why?"

"She said she was scared. Scared that Lauren's dealer would seek to silence her." Ingrid thought better of mentioning the mouse.

McKittrick rubbed her chin. "She called the station yesterday, wanting to know if we'd found Lauren's laptop and mobile."

"You seem to be implying there's something wrong with that. What am I missing?"

"I thought she was smarter than that."

Ingrid wasn't catching Natasha's drift. "What point are you making?"

"Faber's pushing you; she's nagging us—doesn't she realize she could be putting herself back in the frame? She was covered in Shelbourne's blood when we found her."

"That doesn't make sense," Ingrid said. "Why would she be so insistent we look into her friend's death if it could backfire on her?"

McKittrick shrugged. "Don't you think there's something odd about that girl?"

Ingrid was exasperated. "She just found her best friend in the country dead in a pool of blood. Trust me, none of us know how we'll behave in those circum—" She was cut off by sudden shouting on the other side of the police cordon.

McKittrick's lip curled. "Christ, not her."

Running toward them, pursued by a uniformed policeman, was Angela Tate. "Just a brief statement," Tate shouted. "The people of Lewisham have a right to know what's happening on their streets." She reached McKittrick and Ingrid just as the constable caught up with her. "Don't even think about laying one of those fat-fingered paws on me." She scrutinized McKittrick, a sudden sparkle in her eyes. "What are you doing here? Do we have a homicide to report as well as a drug bust?"

"How did you find out about this so quickly?" McKittrick asked her. "Does the *Evening News* have spies on every corner?"

Tate caught Ingrid's eye. Ingrid tensed. She'd called the journalist right after dialing nine nine nine. She'd decided she needed to keep Tate on side, in case she needed a favor later. With only three days before the Shelbournes were due to return home with their daughter's body, Ingrid needed all the help she could get.

"Spies on every corner? Hardly. But keen-eyed members of the public with camera phones at the ready are happy to tell us what's going on," Tate said, still looking at Ingrid. "So—*have* you found a dead body in there?"

"Detective Inspector McKittrick isn't here in a professional capacity," Ingrid told her.

Tate raised her eyebrows. "What? Is this what you do at the weekend for kicks?"

"Something like that." McKittrick pulled Ingrid to one side. "Anything new, let me know. Else my hands are tied."

"Ma'am?" The uniformed police officer was still hovering nearby. He nodded toward Tate.

"Oh, leave her be. Just don't let her get inside the building."

Ingrid and Tate watched McKittrick leave. "What do you make of her?" Tate said when the detective was far enough away.

"What do you mean?"

"There's something... not quite... I don't know. Journalist's nose. Something about her doesn't smell right."

"Can't say I've noticed." There was definitely something up with McKittrick—Mills had said as much—but Ingrid was far too faithful a friend to voice her concerns to a reporter. Especially this one.

29

Ingrid ordered an orange juice. When she put her change back in her wallet, she saw the photograph of Marshall. She found a table with a view of Greenwich Market and considered giving her fiancé a call.

We look so young.

The photo had been taken at the finish line of a half marathon. They looked exhausted but elated, covered in mud. Ingrid remembered the day well. Marshall had said he would run with her for the first few miles but intended to push himself. He hadn't reckoned on Ingrid's extra hours of preparation and her absolute determination not to be beaten. When they'd crossed the line together, everyone said how well matched they were. And for a couple of years she had believed them. She stared down at the photo, unable to unsee the indignation behind Marshall's smile. The hand that held the photo wasn't wearing an engagement ring. It hadn't left her hotel safe for months.

She didn't even reach into her bag for her cell. An impromptu conversation with Marshall was likely to make her feel even more unsettled. He'd only ask her again about a date for the wedding. Instead she fished out a packet of painkillers and administered two more pills. She closed her eyes and relived her jump onto the roof. The rush was electric. She would never forget the look of astonishment on Klaason's face. She opened her eyes to see the tall, slim figure of Ralph Mills standing in front of her.

"I've kept you waiting again. I'm so sorry." Mills grabbed her shoulder. She winced and he pulled back his hand as if he'd been electrocuted. "What did I do?"

"I'm a little worse for wear. I'll get over it."

He pointed to her orange juice. "Can I get you something stronger?"

"I'm driving. I've got a rental car to deliver back to Mayfair."

An expression of intense disappointment cast a shadow over his face. He had hoped this might be more of a social meeting. "Oh, OK. I'll just get myself something."

Ingrid heard him charming the woman behind the bar with his schoolboy banter. He was the polar opposite of Marshall. It took her a while to realize she was gawping at his skinny ass and admiring his slender torso. No preening muscles. No tight tee shirt. There was a modesty to Mills she was finding attractive.

You're engaged.

She turned in her seat, sending a wave of pain from her hip to her shoulder. Maybe McKittrick had been right; perhaps she should go to the hospital. Mills returned with a pint of Guinness. His first sip left him with a white mustache.

"That's the trouble with these things," he said, producing a handkerchief and dabbing his mouth.

The silence that followed was awkward.

"Ah. Um. You had some information, I think, that you wanted to share?" Ingrid prompted.

"Oh yes. Of course. The whole reason you're here."

Not entirely. The logo on his tee shirt was for a band she'd never heard of. It had been years since she'd been to a gig. Damn, now she was staring at his chest. "So, you got something on Greg Brewster?"

He smiled one of the Clark Swanson smiles. "He's an arms dealer."

"Really?"

"Honestly. All above board and everything. Works for a major arms manufacturer in Florida. I wrote the name of the company down somewhere…" He patted his pockets.

"It's OK—that can wait. What else did you find out?"

"It seems his… entertainment preferences… I mean…" He pulled a face. "I'm not really sure how to say this in the right way."

"I know about his taste in men."

"Right. OK. Good. Well, it turns out the company he keeps when he's over here isn't the most… wholesome."

"How d'you know that?"

"He's been robbed before."

Ingrid said nothing. She'd expected as much by the casual way Brewster had reacted to the loss of his laptop.

"Less than twelve months ago he was over here for some big trade show—an arms fair. Can you believe that? They actually have shows at conference centers where regular punters can just wander round and gawp at automatic machine guns and ground-to-air missiles." He frowned, staring right into Ingrid's face. The frown disappeared and his face softened. "Where was I?"

"Brewster was robbed last year."

"Yes. His wallet. Cash, credit cards, everything. He reported it to the local borough force—the Belgravia uniforms dealt with it. I was a uniform there once. Seems like a million years ago now." He stared out the window at the bargain hunters and tourists browsing the market stalls.

"Ralph?"

"Hmm?"

"You got distracted again."

"Sorry. Anyway, one day he gets his wallet taken—mugged in St James's Park two o'clock in the morning—the next day he's withdrawn his statement. Said he was mistaken. The wallet wasn't missing after all. My ex-colleague at Belgravia said he wasn't that surprised, given the circumstances."

"He was with a guy in the park?"

"That's what he'd said originally. Then he said he'd been mistaken about that too." He took a sip of his pint and managed to avoid a frothy upper lip this time. "You'd expect he'd be more careful. I mean in this day and age, there's no need to be skulking around public lavatories and parks after dark. There are apps for that kind of thing now. You can just tap something into your phone and Bob's your uncle, or... whoever you want him to be."

"You seem to know a lot about it." Ingrid decided to distract herself from the pain in her back by teasing him. He didn't rise to the bait. Another way in which he was so very different to Marshall.

"Me? I'm an expert. Another ex-colleague of mine keeps me up-to-date on all that stuff." He smiled to himself. "You should meet Cath. You'd like her."

Was he so easily distracted because he was nervous?

"Brewster obviously thought he was being careful this time," Ingrid said, yanking the conversation back to Brewster. "He went to the trouble of using an escort agency."

"But they're not exactly... reputable, are they? They can't afford to ask too many questions in their line of business."

"Did your friend at Belgravia have anything else to say?"

"It wasn't the incident itself that he said was interesting, which is why it stuck in his mind so much. It was the way Brewster withdrew his statement. My mate said he seemed really twitchy when he saw him the second time. Anxious, like he was looking over his shoulder constantly. You'd think he would have been more anxious straight after being mugged by the strange bloke he'd picked up in the park. But apparently he was quite defiant about the incident just after it happened. Throwing his weight around. Not embarrassed in the slightest. He was a different man the second time my mate saw him. Meek as a lamb."

"Did your friend have a theory why Brewster had changed his attitude so much?"

"No, he just thought it was strange. What do you make of it?"

"Not sure. Did you have any luck tracking down information about the escort?"

"Didn't really have much to go on. False name. False address. Throwaway phone."

It had been a long shot asking Mills for help, but he'd delivered. "Talking about phones... did you ever find Lauren Shelbourne's cell phone and laptop?"

"No. We've not managed to track them down. We've checked the phone company records, obviously, but her phone hasn't been switched on since she died. We're still monitoring it." Mills took a long drink of his Guinness and sat quietly for a moment. "The thing I mentioned before, about our meeting being mutually beneficial?"

Ingrid shifted in her seat. What was he going to suggest?

Mills swallowed noisily. "I'd be really grateful if you could do me a favor."

"Name it." She braced herself.

"I'm worried about the boss."

"Natasha?"

"She's going through a tough time at the moment. She's not been in London that long. I'm not sure how much support she has in this part of the country. She worked out west before— Bristol. I'm doing my best to keep an eye out for her, but I think she might need a mate, you know? Someone to confide in."

Ingrid considered her erratic behavior at the meth bust. "You think she'd confide in me?"

"I know she respects you."

Didn't seem that way earlier.

"I just saw her, actually."

"You did?"

She filled him in on the afternoon's action. "She wasn't in much of a confessional mood. She certainly didn't seem to relish the prospect of reopening the Shelbourne case."

He screwed his face up. "There's a lot of stuff going on at work at the moment."

"You mentioned as much before. What kind of stuff?"

"I can't say what." He pushed away his glass. "Maybe you could go out with her? Let her know she can speak freely to you."

"I can try. But Natasha isn't really the talking kind." She

wondered if McKittrick thought exactly the same thing about her. Perhaps they should go out and sink a few tequilas.

"My hunch is she puts on a good front."

Jeez, you're a nice guy, Ralph Mills.

"I'll call her. I promise."

Ingrid's phone buzzed and she glanced at the screen. "I should take this."

"Sure. I'll get us another drink."

Ingrid turned away to answer the call. "Madison, how are you?"

"I have to see you. Now. I'm at my apartment." She hung up.

30

Ingrid slammed the car door. She turned toward Madison Faber's building and froze. Painted across the front door in wide brushstrokes were the words *faber* □□*whore*. The bright yellow paint had dripped messily down the door and onto the step.

Ingrid looked up and saw a twitch in the wooden window shade at the second-floor window, then glimpsed Faber's face at the glass. A moment later the face disappeared and the buzzer sounded on the door. Ingrid hurried up the steps, doing her best to ignore the grinding pain in her side and back.

Inside, Faber was waiting for her at the top of the flight of stairs within her apartment.

"What took you so long? I've been going out of my mind."

"I came right away."

"You've seen what they've done to the door?"

"Did you call the police?"

Faber marched into the living room and Ingrid followed.

"Sit down, Madison. Big, slow breaths."

"Don't patronize me!"

"Did you call the police?"

"I can't speak to them. I've got to get out of here. I only hung around because I need to show you something." She stopped abruptly and studied Ingrid's face. "What happened to your cheek?"

Ingrid lifted a hand to her face, lightly tracing her bruised cheekbone with her fingertips. "It's nothing. Madison, listen. We need to tell the police. They need to take a sample of the paint. They need to take prints. You understand?"

Faber got up and paced the room. "I should never have told you about Klaason. My God. What if I'd been here when he did that to the door?" She shivered.

Ingrid held up her hands, only just managing to stop herself telling Faber to calm down. "Why did you come back?"

"I needed fresh clothes."

"And the door onto the street was already vandalized when you arrived?"

"Yes."

"Do you know when it might have happened?"

"The woman downstairs told me it wasn't there last night when she came in around eleven. She asked me what I was going to do about it? As if it were my fault. My mess to clear up." She started shaking her head and biting her lip. "Stupid bitch."

"And you think Klaason is responsible?"

"Who else would do that?" She was squeezing her hands together, the knuckle bones straining her delicate skin. Faber's fingers looked raw, as if she'd been scrubbing them obsessively.

Ingrid sat down, hoping to set an example for Faber. "There is no way Timo Klaason knows you've spoken to me."

"I tell you where you might be able to find him, and less than twenty-four hours later, that message gets painted on my door." Her head turned at whiplash speed, her fierce eyes locking onto Ingrid. "That's one hell of a coincidence, wouldn't you say?"

Ingrid sat back, attempting to look as nonconfrontational as possible.

"Please tell me you've found him," Faber said, still pacing.

"Klaason hasn't been apprehended yet. But I did find his meth factory."

Faber didn't appear to have heard her. "I've got to leave." Her voice was jittery.

"I'm confident the police will track Klaason down soon."

"I told you not to go to the police!" Faber flung her arms in the air. "Jesus."

"I didn't have much choice in the matter. I discovered his laboratory."

"His what?"

"He was manufacturing methamphetamine."

"Manufacturing? Jesus—no wonder he's so fucking angry with me. I really need to get out of here now."

"Are you still staying with your mom's friend in Hampstead?" She had the car for another twelve hours at least: she could give the girl a lift.

A sob escaped from Faber's mouth. "I only wanted justice for Lauren, and all I've done is make myself even more vulnerable. I've put myself at greater risk and for what?" She looked at Ingrid, an accusing glint in her eye. "The police have no intention of reopening their investigation. Why haven't you convinced them?"

"How do you know I haven't?"

"I know Lauren's parents are taking her body home in three days."

Where was she getting her facts?

"When were you going to share that particular piece of information with me?" Faber said. "After she'd arrived back on American soil?"

"Who told you about—"

"I went to see her parents."

"When? How did you even know where to find them?" She remembered the note Alex Shelbourne had passed her. She still hadn't managed to follow it up.

"It wasn't that much of a challenge. I called every five-star hotel in central London until I got lucky."

The prospect of a distraught and paranoid Faber trampling over their grief, telling them things they didn't need to know about how much blood their daughter had lost, alarmed Ingrid. "What did you say to them?" she said warily.

"What did I say? My God, I wanted to scream at them to open their eyes. They've just accepted everything the police have been feeding them." Spittle collected at the corners of her mouth. She dabbed it with the back of a hand. "Poor bastards." She sniffed loudly.

"When did you see them, Madison?" Ingrid needed an answer.

"Oh? Yesterday," she said offhandedly. "But anyone could see they were hurting too much for me to tell them that their daughter was murdered."

Ingrid exhaled, relieved Faber hadn't seen them since her meeting with them. "There's no proof she was murdered, Madison. You're right to keep your suspicions to yourself." She reached for Faber's arm and pulled her down onto the couch.

"You saw her body, Ingrid."

An image of the crime scene thrust its way into Ingrid's vision.

"And her laptop is still missing! Why am I the only one who thinks she was murdered?" Faber stared wide-eyed at Ingrid. "Will it take them killing me for you to believe me?"

Ingrid was starting to feel no amount of effort would be good enough for Madison. The girl needed counseling. She needed support. It was surprising her parents hadn't flown over to take care of her, or insist she recuperate at home; it was no wonder the girl was falling apart.

Ingrid took a deep breath. "If you tell the cops about the graffiti on your door, maybe they would offer you some protection."

Faber's gaze hadn't wavered. "I am done with the Metropolitan Police."

"If you don't tell them, they can't help you."

The girl finally blinked. "I have no faith in them. They're all useless."

Ingrid wasn't going to respond. She felt responsible for Faber, she shared some of her concerns, but she couldn't let herself be drawn any further into her delusions. Ingrid spread her hands into stars and pressed them against her thighs. "Was the graffiti why you called me, Madison?" She made an effort for her voice to sound level, reasonable.

The girl leaped up. "Gosh! No!" She was smiling.

"What is it?"

"I found something!" Her voice had become girlish, almost squeaky. "Come with me!"

Wary, Ingrid followed the increasingly unstable Faber down the hallway and into Lauren's old room. The window was wide open, a light voile drape billowing in the breeze. Beneath the window was a black trash sack. Faber saw Ingrid looking at it.

"A few of Lauren's clothes. She left them behind when she moved out. I thought I'd give them to her mother. I don't know how much of Lauren's things the police have given to her parents." She picked up a ragged sheet of paper from the dresser opposite the window and held it up to Ingrid. It looked as if it had been folded and unfolded several times. There was a brown stain in the middle where it must have gotten damp and dried out again, leaving an inch-long hole near one edge. Untidy block capitals were scrawled across the page. A dozen or so lines of what Ingrid supposed was poetry.

"What is it?" Ingrid asked.

"I opened the window when I came in here—the room smelled musty—I thought it needed airing. This was folded and wedged between the window and the frame. To stop it rattling in the wind, I suppose."

"I don't see how it's relevant."

"It's Lauren's handwriting."

"Really? How can you tell?"

"Believe me, it is. Besides, the content proves she wrote it."

Ingrid looked more closely at the sloping scrawl. "A poem?"

"It's a sonnet. A love poem."

Ingrid scanned the text. English lit had been her worst subject at high school.

"It's based on an Emily Dickinson poem. You must recognize it."

Ingrid shrugged an apology. "You still haven't explained how this is relevant to Lauren's death."

"Don't you see? It's a *love* poem. Written to her lover."

"So?"

Faber jabbed a finger at the end of one line where three capital letters had been made to rhyme with 'lie.' "Look at that."

"S-M-Y?"

"Stuart McKenzie Younger. Don't you see! She was having an affair with Younger. With her *tutor*, for God's sake. There's the proof you need to reopen the case."

Ingrid took a moment to work through the implications. Even if this were a poem to Younger, and even if they were having an affair, it didn't prove he had anything to do with Lauren's death. She hesitated, not wanting to voice her misgivings to Faber. She was close enough to hysteria already.

"You can take that to the police." Faber pressed the piece of paper into Ingrid's hands. "They wanted to know who she was seeing, didn't they?" Faber's eyes were shining with tears. "Because, you know, nine times out of ten, the boyfriend is the killer." She looked expectantly at Ingrid. "Stuart Younger murdered Lauren."

31

Ingrid thought long and hard about involving Natasha. If she had been drinking at three in the afternoon, she didn't hold out much hope of an enthusiastic response to Faber's revelation at eight o'clock in the evening. Like the tissue in the candy wrapper, the poem's forensics value was minimal. And the mistrust on both sides between Faber and the Met had reached such a level she decided to take a different approach.

She drove Madison to Hampstead, returned the rental car, then installed herself in a quiet pub not far from her hotel in Marylebone. She then called the one person who was very interested in Stuart Younger: Angela Tate. The journalist pushed open the door, and Ingrid plastered a friendly smile on her face.

"Wow, the bruising has really come out since this afternoon," Tate said.

You should see my ribs.

"What can I get you?" Ingrid offered.

"Oh, um, just a ginger ale, thanks."

Angela Tate not drinking? That was a surprise.

Ingrid got up carefully; the effects of the painkillers she'd taken had long worn off.

"My God, you really are in the wars."

Ingrid returned with a ginger ale for Tate and a neat double vodka for herself. The moment she put the drinks on the table,

Tate pulled out a silver flask from her coat pocket and slipped a brazen measure of whisky into her drink.

"No point you paying for what I've already got," she said. The pub—pastel colors, uniformed staff and blackboard menus—was part of a national chain. During the week, it would be busy with after-work drinkers, but on the weekend it had a lackluster, insipid corporate vibe. "I think the shareholders will survive without my contribution. To be honest, when you suggested this place, I thought about not coming." Tate slipped the flask back into her purse. "I've got principles."

"You said it was urgent on the phone."

"Well, I wanted to make sure you had all the information before you go to print."

"All the information on what?" Tate asked.

Ingrid leaned in. "Stuart Younger."

Tate's eyebrows did a high jump. "You have my attention."

"And you have mine. You tell me what you've dug up about the esteemed professor, and I'll give you a killer final paragraph." Ingrid regretted her choice of language the moment the words left her lips.

"Killer, eh?"

Ingrid left her hanging.

"OK, I'll go first, but if I say anything you know not to be true, you have to correct me, understood?"

"Completely."

Tate shuffled her chair closer to Ingrid and took a theatrically deep breath. "I finally managed to get through the force field Younger has constructed around his research. It's genius, really, what he's done."

Ingrid took a long sip of her vodka and prayed the journalist would get to the point soon.

"So are you sitting comfortably? It might take a while."

Ingrid shifted in her seat. She doubted she'd sit comfortably for weeks.

"How familiar are you with CIA history?" Tate asked her.

Ingrid had the feeling a good night's sleep was a little further away than she had hoped.

"The Agency? Can't help you. But feel free to ask me anything about the FBI."

"How very loyal of you." Tate pushed her glass out of the way and set a file in front of them. "Do you know about the psychological experiments the CIA undertook in the fifties?"

"A little before my time."

"Mine too—believe it or not." Tate removed a sheet from the file. "MKUltra—ring any bells?"

It did. "Keep talking."

"From as early as 1953, the CIA conducted experiments in mind control, using electroconvulsive therapy, torture, hypnosis… and… wait for it—"

"The administration of LSD."

"Go on, steal my punch line."

"What's this got to do with Younger's research program?"

Tate raised her eyebrows. "Everything."

"You're not seriously suggesting he's been using MKUltra techniques at Loriners? That would be totally unethical."

"I'd wager a year's salary on it."

"Drugs? Hypnosis?"

"I don't know exactly how many of the techniques Younger has decided to employ. As I said, he's been quite rigorous in covering his tracks. Though I would imagine even he would draw the line at strapping electrodes to students' temples."

Ingrid remembered the claims of torture Mohammed had made. Maybe they weren't so far from the truth after all.

"The girl who supposedly jumped to her death last week?" Tate continued. "She was a participant in the program. And the near miss two days ago? Same with her. Strange how Younger was right there to save the girl from jumping, don't you think?"

Ingrid didn't answer. She sat very still and attempted to work through the ramifications. "No," she said finally. "I don't buy it. Younger would never be able to hide that from the college authorities."

"He's a very smart man. I was actually looking for something and I had a tough enough time finding anything out. How would the college discover anything amiss if they didn't suspect something in the first place to even go looking for it?"

"But the students who take part—why haven't they come forward to report him?"

"He's got some sort of hold over them."

"Now that sounds a little far—"

"Please don't accuse me of being a conspiracy theorist."

Ingrid said nothing.

"I've been trying to make contact with the girl he *rescued* on Thursday afternoon, but I'm getting stonewalled. Maybe you could help me with that?"

Ingrid could only admire Tate's tenacity. "I'll see what I can do," she lied. "I still don't buy it. There would be too many people involved to keep something like that secret."

"You're having trouble believing it because I've only given you half the story." The journalist's eyes were sparkling. She wriggled in her seat and pulled out a blank sheet of paper from the file then quickly drew the spiky symbols they'd both seen painted on the wall at Loriners.

"You found out what it means?"

"Look at this." Tate proceeded to draw the lines again, but this time made them much less angular. "What do they look like now?"

Ingrid was reminded of countless physics experiments at high school, wavy lines just like these flickering on the screens of a dozen oscilloscopes. "Sine waves."

"Waves, exactly. Three waves." A satisfied smile spread across Tate's face. "The Third Wave. Heard of it?"

It rang a distant bell. "Go on—I can see you're itching to tell me all about it."

"It was a highly controversial psychological experiment carried out in the sixties. Never to be repeated. Until now, that is."

"Controversial in what way?"

"I'm just getting on to that." Tate cleared her throat. "Picture it—1967, Palo Alto, California."

Tate certainly knew how to string a story out.

"Am I boring you, agent?"

"No, not at all."

"Good. Where was I?"

"Palo Alto."

"Ah, yes. A high school history teacher was having trouble convincing his students of the inevitable rise of fascism in Germany in the 1930s. They were skeptical otherwise ordinary people could turn against their fellow citizens. That they could lose their humanity quite so comprehensively."

Ingrid nodded encouragingly.

"So… rather than teaching them from textbooks, he decided to demonstrate the phenomenon in action." She pulled out another piece of paper and read aloud: "Strength through discipline, strength through community, strength through action, strength through pride."

"Is that supposed to mean something to me?"

"It's the manifesto the teacher invented for the experiment. Naturally, none of the students knew they were participating in an experiment at all."

"How did he manage that?"

"It was the start of a new week. The class had been discussing Nazi Germany the week before. But on the Monday the teacher started his lesson not even mentioning history, but talking about the beauty of discipline." Tate paused and sipped her drink. "You know, how an athlete or an artist has to be focused and hard-working to achieve success. You're part of an organization that runs on a similar basis—doesn't FBI training involve drills and routines a bit like an army?"

"Something like that, I guess."

"I'm too much of a bloody-minded old bugger for any of that to wash with me." She slipped the hip flask from her pocket and drained its contents into her glass. "The teacher got them all sitting up straight, eyes front, no talking, and asked them how much better they felt. How it was easier to breathe, easier to concentrate. Then he got them doing drills, marching in and out of the classroom in double quick time and in silence. And the surprising thing was, the students loved being told what to do."

She paused for a moment and Ingrid took her opportunity to interject.

"The high school students were what, fifteen, sixteen? Impressionable. I can't see anything like that working with twenty-year-olds."

"Just let me tell you the rest. The teacher invented three simple rules the class had to follow to the letter." She started to count them off on her fingers. "One, they always had to carry a notebook and a pencil—now that's a rule I'd subscribe to myself—two, they had to sit to attention before the class bell rang, and three, they had to answer questions in three words or less, standing beside their desks and prefacing each response with the teacher's name."

"That doesn't sound sinister."

"But the students got into it. Suddenly they wanted to please the teacher, and each other. Quiet or badly performing students started to participate for the first time, supported by their peers. The whole class found it empowering."

"Which encouraged them to carry on."

"Exactly. And the teacher assumed the role of dictator. After he got them enthusiastic, he was really smart—he talked about the importance of community, about supporting the members of the class, taking action to preserve and protect it from outsiders. He even distributed membership cards and invented a salute." Tate brought her right hand up to her right shoulder, the palm facing outwards, the fingers curled. "The cupped hand is meant to symbolize a wave." She uncurled her fingers and picked up her glass and took a large mouthful of whisky. "As news spread of the exclusive group, more students wanted to be part of it to enjoy that sense of belonging. After just two days there were over two hundred active members, a lot of them prepared to report any of their group for rule-breaking. After four days the experiment had got completely out of hand. Students were adopting fascist-like behavior with no prompting from the teacher. It was like an organism that had taken on a life of its own."

"Are you suggesting Younger is doing the same thing at

Loriners? That he's appointed himself as some sort of benevolent dictator?"

"I'm not sure there's anything benevolent about that man."

"But you really think he's brainwashed the participants of his research program into some kind of… Hitler Youth?"

"There's no need to sound so skeptical. Not just the participants. The whole of his research group too. It was something you said the other day, about how perfect they all looked in their exclusive purple and green polo shirts. There is something deliberately homogenous about them. They're part of Younger's group, fiercely loyal to him and the research program. They'd do anything to protect it, and they shun people who aren't like them."

Ingrid now wondered if it really was possible Younger was linked to Lauren's death. He might not have done it, but maybe she was about to expose him? "And you think it's gotten out of control at Loriners?"

Tate shrugged. "In California the experiment was halted after five days. God only knows how long it's been going on at Loriners." She pulled a pack of cigarettes and an antique lighter from her purse. "Two student deaths and one near miss? Yes—I'd say it was out of control."

Ingrid took a moment to take everything in, to order the information in her mind.

"Looking at your face," Tate said, "I would say you're starting to believe me."

She was. But unless they could prove a link between the experiments and the suicides, and possibly also to Lauren's death, there was no point in going to the police. "Do you think anyone you've spoken to would be willing to testify?"

"Christ no! I've got one or two students who are prepared to break ranks, but they need very careful handling. They've effectively been brainwashed into a cult and need to be deprogrammed gradually. If I mentioned the police to them at this stage, they'd totally freak out."

Ingrid leaned back in her chair and drained the last of her vodka. She would put nothing past Younger. He was sly, he was vain, but she couldn't just accuse him of involvement with Lauren's death. Angela Tate waved a hand in front of her face.

"Earth to Skyberg, come in, agent."

"Sorry."

"So." Tate rested her elbows on the table. "Now it's your turn."

32

Ingrid stepped off the train in the East Sussex town of Lewes and was immediately struck by the sweetness and warmth of the air. It was the first time she'd left London for months, and it felt good to be out of the city. A big part of her would always be a Minnesota farm girl. Small-town life was in her blood.

In the interests of road safety—she was too badly injured to handle the Triumph on the freeway—Ingrid had opted for the train to convey her to Emily Taylor's parents' home fifty miles south of the capital. The journey had given her time to think about what Angela Tate had told her. If Stuart Younger really was running some kind of cult at Loriners, it would fit the charismatic-leader playbook if he was sleeping with his students.

Overwhelmed by the softness and fragrance of the air, she decided she should breathe as much of it as possible and set off on foot from the station as fast as her battered body could carry her. She realized her error when, after following the route suggested by the GPS app on her phone, she encountered a steep cobblestone street rising at an alarming gradient. She drew in a deep breath and started the near-vertical march, taking her time to admire the dinky little cottages lining both sides of the street. Her legs were aching as much as her ribs when she reached the top. Ten minutes later she approached her destination. A middle-aged man dressed in tweed pants and a woolen vest over a crisp white shirt was clipping a neat yew hedge that ran the length of the front yard.

"Mr Taylor?"

The man stopped clipping but didn't lower the large and menacing shears. He eyed her suspiciously, his lined forehead puckering into a network of deep furrows.

"I spoke to your wife on the phone," Ingrid continued, countering his grave expression with a much sunnier one of her own. "My name's Ingrid Skyberg—I work at the US Embassy. I explained everything—"

"Yes, yes, I know. I thought for a moment you might be a reporter. I've already seen two off this morning." He waved the shears at her by way of demonstration.

"John! What do you think you're doing?" A woman dressed in a wraparound apron appeared at the open front door, wiping her hands on a dish towel. "I'm sorry. He's just thinking of Emily."

"Of course—it's only natural." Ingrid smiled broadly and followed Mrs. Taylor through the door and into an interior lobby. The place smelled of furniture wax and lavender. As they walked further down the hall, the unmistakable aroma of roast beef filled the air. Ingrid's mouth started to water. She'd forgotten breakfast again and wished she'd had time to pick up a sandwich at the train station before leaving London.

"I'll pop the kettle on. Make us a nice pot of tea." She smiled at Ingrid. "Unless you'd prefer coffee, of course."

In Ingrid's experience, all home-brewed coffee she'd been offered in the UK was pretty much undrinkable. "Tea would be perfect."

After being shown into a light-filled living room, a room that looked out over a backyard stuffed with plants of all kinds and a cherry tree in full pink blossom, Ingrid waited for one of the Taylors to reappear. Finally John Taylor materialized at the door, hovering on the threshold of his own living room, apparently reluctant to be alone with her.

"Your house is beautiful," she said.

"That's Julia's doing. I can't take the credit for it."

"The garden too—really lovely."

He pulled back his shoulders and stood a little taller. "Oh yes. Well. There's always something to do. Especially this time of year. I can spend the whole weekend tending to it."

"Your efforts are certainly paying off."

He offered her a begrudging smile. "I should see how my wife's getting on in the kitchen." He started to turn.

"How's Emily today?"

Taylor flinched as if he'd taken a physical blow. His nose twitched and he stared at the carpet. "Well as can be expected, I suppose."

"Mind out of my way." Mrs Taylor appeared at his side, holding a tray. She squeezed past him and carefully unloaded the contents of the tray onto a side table. Bone china tea service and a large round walnut-encrusted cake safely transferred, she shoved the tray at her husband. "Make yourself useful." She turned back to Ingrid as her husband wandered toward the kitchen. "Has John been bending your ear?"

"We didn't really get a chance to—"

"I'm teasing you. He's not great with strangers. Especially not in his own house. He goes into caveman mode: protect and survive."

Ingrid thought that sounded like a pretty good strategy.

"Though I suppose he's got good reason to at the moment." She let out a sigh. "He blames himself for what happened."

"He does?"

"He thinks he's been pushing Emily too much to do well in her studies. Putting too much pressure on her."

"Do you think that's true?"

"Good grief, no. He's just a proud dad who wants the best for his daughter."

"How is Emily?"

Another sigh. "I only wish I knew. She's been holed up in her room ever since she came home."

"Do you think she might speak to me?"

"You can try. But like I said on the phone, she's not really talking to anyone. Not even us."

"How about her friends?"

Mrs. Taylor shook her head. "All her friends are at uni. I haven't even heard her speaking on the phone. I suppose she might have been texting them." She poured tea into one of the neat china cups. "Milk and sugar?"

"Just as it comes. Thank you."

"Carrot cake? It's a new recipe I'm trying out."

"I'd love some." Ingrid smiled again. "But first, do you think I might be able to speak to Emily?"

"Why would she speak to you if she won't talk to her own mother and father?" Mr. Taylor was in the doorway again.

"I'll show you where her room is." Julia Taylor led Ingrid out of the room, scowling at her husband on the way. "I really don't think she'll respond," the woman said when they were standing on the second-floor landing. She tapped lightly on a door still adorned with an 'Emily's room—DO NOT ENTER' plaque. "Emily, sweetheart. There's someone here to see you. She'd like to speak to you about Lauren Shelbourne."

Ingrid and Mrs. Taylor both held their breath and listened for sounds on the other side of the door. There was a definite creaking of floorboards. Then nothing. Ingrid exhaled.

"May I?" she said. Mrs Taylor stepped to one side. "Hello, Emily. My name's Ingrid. I'm from the American embassy in London. Did you know Lauren?" She turned to the girl's mother. "Could I have a moment alone with Emily?"

"Be my guest." She raised her voice. "I'll be in the kitchen, if you need anything, love."

Ingrid watched the woman trudge wearily down the stairs. "I know about the experiments, Emily. There's nothing to be afraid of. You're quite safe." She heard a noise from within the room. A crash of something being dropped on the floor? "Emily? Why don't you open the door and we can speak more privately?" Silence for a moment followed by the boom of dance music at top volume.

"I did tell you." Mr. Taylor was standing at the bottom of the staircase. "But you wouldn't listen."

Back in the living room, half a cup of tea and a few crumbs of carrot cake later, Mr Taylor was in full swing, berating the welfare services at Loriners College. "Students are in their care. They should be keeping a closer eye on them. One look at her and you could see she's in a terrible state. Do the tutors just leave them to their own devices? First time away from home, they're not more than schoolchildren, really. It's a dereliction of duty. I've a good mind to sue." He paused for breath and Ingrid took the opportunity to broach the subject she'd been avoiding.

"Does Emily have any history of…"

"Depression? Is that what you want to know? It's none of your bloody business!"

"Don't be like that, John. Miss Skyberg's come all this way," Julia Taylor said. "Emily's always been a happy child. She never even went through that difficult teenager phase. You couldn't have met a sweeter girl. I don't know what happened. She was fine at Christmas. Spent time with us. And her friends. Went out riding on Boxing Day."

"How was she during the spring vacation?" Ingrid asked, keen not to get sidetracked.

The Taylors looked at her blankly.

"The, ah… Easter holidays?"

"She didn't come home for Easter. She stayed up in London. She said her friends were staying at college, so she would too," Julia Taylor said. "They were taking part in some experiment or other. She said it was important she didn't miss it."

"Experiment?" Ingrid did her best not to sound too interested.

"Something in the psychology department, she said."

"Not part of her medical studies?"

"She wants to specialize in neuroscience," Mr Taylor said. "Apparently, participating in the research program helps with that." He stared blankly into space. "Though God knows how all this will affect her degree. She might have to repeat this whole year. She should be preparing for her exams right now."

"Have you met any of the teachers at Loriners? Do you know Professor Younger?"

"Younger?" Julia Taylor said and rolled her eyes. "At

Christmas she wouldn't stop talking about the man. Stuart this, Stuart that. How brilliant he is. Such an important pioneer in the field."

"And has she mentioned him or the research program since she's been home this time?"

"She hasn't spoken about any of it."

"I'd like to see Younger," her husband added. "Shake him by the hand. Buy him a bloody big drink. If it wasn't for him and what he did…" He shook his head. "I can't even think about what might have happened."

"The professor hasn't made contact with you?"

"No—and we haven't had any luck reaching him. But then if he's as brilliant as Emily says, I don't suppose he has much spare time." Julia Taylor started to clear away the tea things.

"But you'd think he might have made the effort," Mr Taylor said, "in the circumstances."

With some difficulty Ingrid got to her feet. "I should let you folks get on with your Sunday lunch. Thank you so much for seeing me." She handed Julia Taylor a business card. "If Emily changes her mind about speaking to me, please call me. Anytime."

Back on the tree-lined sidewalk, Ingrid looked up toward the second floor of the building. A drape fluttered at a small side window, a figure in shadow quickly moving away from the glass.

33

"Do you ever take a day off?" McKittrick said when Ingrid approached. Not the response she was hoping for. McKittrick set down the 1950s butter dish she was holding and moved on to the next table of secondhand objects. The flea market, or as McKittrick insisted on calling it, the 'car boot sale,' was the biggest Ingrid had ever seen, taking up most of a two-acre high school field in Kentish Town, the district of London where McKittrick lived. McKittrick had invited her to similar events before, but rummaging through other people's unwanted castoffs was not something that appealed to Ingrid, and she'd always made the excuse of a prior engagement.

"You never know what little gem you might stumble upon," McKittrick had said, in an attempt to convey what Ingrid was missing. So far they had stumbled on trash fit only for the garbage truck. "So. Why are you here, Ingrid, or do I need to report you to the ambassador for interfering with a Metropolitan Police investigation?"

Ingrid was taken aback.

"It's a joke."

"Right." Ingrid exhaled. "Phew."

McKittrick gave her a playful slap on the arm and Ingrid winced.

"Serves you right for jumping off buildings."

Ingrid didn't know how to respond.

"Think we're having a communication breakdown here. That was another attempt at humor."

"Ah."

As McKittrick browsed the stalls, Ingrid told her most of what she'd learned about Stuart Younger. The inquest into Lauren Shelbourne's death had been scheduled for first thing on Wednesday morning, and that meant they had sixty hours to present any evidence that would cast doubt on the accidental-death verdict.

"Can you at least go talk to Stuart Younger?" Ingrid asked the detective before McKittrick sifted through the next pile of random junk.

"Why? I'm not sure you've mentioned which law he's broken."

"You don't think appointing himself dictator of the research program, setting up controversial experiments that have driven at least one student to her death, is worth investigating?"

"From what you've told me, the experiments sound… unscrupulous maybe, unethical at worst. Not illegal. You should report him to the university, but it's not a matter for the police. Unless you have hard proof of Younger administering Class A drugs to the research participants, or brainwashing them to jump from tall buildings."

"Hard proof? What about the Canadian student? Are you telling me there wasn't either LSD or meth… or both in her bloodstream when she died?"

"I can't tell you that. Not because she did—I'm not saying that—but because I don't actually know. Like I explained to you before, it wasn't my case. The Homicide and Serious Crime Command didn't pick it up. There was no need. It was called as a suicide at the scene." She wandered over to the next table. "I can have a quiet word with my colleagues in CID, if you like. See if I can get hold of a blood-analysis report." She turned to Ingrid. "I'm not promising anything, mind."

"Thank you."

"But you don't have any evidence of an affair with one of his students, do you? All you've got is hearsay."

"No, but you could put Faber on the stand—"

McKittrick snorted. "No jury would believe her. She's obviously got mental health issues."

Ingrid wasn't going to be shut down so easily. "In a few weeks, I'm sure Emily Taylor will be up to being interviewed. And you could try talking to Younger's wife. She might have plenty of evidence of his affair. Wives often do."

"Alleged affair."

McKittrick had a point. She picked up an unopened rusty tin of crackers. They looked as if they'd survived the Second World War. "They'd go down a treat with some foie gras and a glass of claret."

"But if it is true," Ingrid said, determined to make her case, "the affair could be a motive for murder. What if Lauren was going to expose his experiments?"

"This isn't an episode of *Miss Marple*, Ingrid."

"You really think I'm that..." Ingrid searched for the right word. "Inept?"

McKittrick looked shocked.

"I'm an FBI agent, Natasha. I do know how you build a case, how you need evidence for a conviction, but there's a clock ticking here. Once the coroner releases Lauren's body on Wednesday, we've lost our chance to... we've lost our strongest piece of forensic evidence. Right now, I think there are enough loose ends to put the inquest on pause."

McKittrick examined a bright green teapot.

"Have you even questioned Younger?" Ingrid asked.

"Saw one of these at my first crime scene," she said, and put it down.

"Natasha! Stay with me here. If this were the States, we'd be questioning Younger."

McKittrick's expression turned icy. "Would you now?" She had found a pair of long earrings made of orange, red and yellow glass. She held them up to her ears. "What do you think?"

"They match your eyes." Ingrid managed a smile.

"Charming. Remind me never to ask for your opinion again."

Ingrid stared directly into McKittrick's face, forcing the detective to make eye contact. "What do I have to get you for you to take this seriously?"

McKittrick considered the request. "OK, from what I'm piecing together here, you're suggesting Younger buys drugs from Klaason to give to students as part of his experiments. Have I got that straight?"

Ingrid nodded.

"I'd need proper, solid evidence proving Younger has received drugs from Klaason—LSD and methamphetamine specifically—then I'd have no choice but to consider the impact on the Shelbourne case. I'd at least suggest my colleagues in the London Crime Squad invite Younger in for questioning."

"You would?"

"I'm not deliberately setting out to be obstructive, you know. You get me the evidence. I'll follow it up."

"Thank you." A firework of elation burned and fizzed inside her. She wasn't an idiot. She did know what she was doing. And if someone was killing kids, there was no way in hell she would let them get away with it.

McKittrick picked up a black-and-white photograph, the edges ragged with age. She held it up to show Ingrid. "Look at those sad eyes. I bet she had some stories to tell." She flipped over the picture. "1941. Wow, middle of the Blitz. No wonder she looks sad."

Ingrid wasn't familiar with McKittrick's sentimental side. Perhaps it was the right time to speak to her about whatever 'stuff' was going on at work. She had promised Mills she'd broach the subject. They wandered to the next table, which was selling home-baked pies and cakes. Only a few items remained so late in the afternoon. Ingrid selected a slice of cold pizza, piled high with goat cheese, sun-dried tomatoes and olives. It was gone in two bites. McKittrick raised her eyebrows.

"Want anything?" Ingrid asked her and bought the last slice of cheesecake before she'd had a chance to answer.

"I'm fine."

"Really? Are you *really* fine?" Ingrid could have kicked herself for sounding like such a klutz.

"I had a late lunch."

"No... I mean..." This wasn't going the way Ingrid had hoped. She took a bite and tried to chew the mouthful of sweet, vanilla-flavored cream cheese and dark, caramelized cookie base slowly, but the whole thing melted on her tongue. She swallowed and started the sentence again. "When I spoke to Mills yesterday, he said—"

"Mills?"

Ingrid nodded.

"Oooh."

"Not like that!"

"Ralph and Ingrid sitting in a tree..."

"Stop it!"

"K-I-S-S-I-N-G!"

Ingrid said nothing.

"You should know you're blushing."

Ingrid gathered herself. "He said he was worried about you. And, well, you were a little off-kilter at the meth bust yesterday." Ingrid shoved what was left of her cheesecake into a nearby trash can.

McKittrick was seething.

"Look, he barely said a thing. He certainly didn't betray any confidences, but if you need someone to talk to, consider me a pair of ears."

McKittrick's nostrils flared. "Bloody Mills. He's way too soft to be a copper."

She headed for the exit and Ingrid hurried after her.

"I'm sure his intentions were honorable. He's just watching your back."

"I suppose you might as well know." McKittrick finally slowed down as they reached the gate. "Professional Standards are investigating my... *conduct* at the moment. I've got to keep a low profile. Keep my head down to prevent it being shot off. I'm this far—" she held up her finger and thumb, leaving a tiny gap in between "—from being sent on gardening leave. I have to play everything by the book." She ran a hand through her hair.

"I had no idea—"

"So apart from chasing CID about that blood test, I really can't help you." She stared Ingrid hard in the face. "As far as Lauren Shelbourne is concerned… you're on your own, kid."

"Understood." Now wasn't the time to question why Natasha was being investigated, but she could guess. "There is one more favor I have to ask."

McKittrick narrowed her eyes. "Before you do, can I just remind you, this is meant to be my day off."

"It's a small thing. A favor for me, nothing to do with the Shelbourne case." Ingrid paused. "Don't agree to do this if it'll cause you any problems. I don't want you getting into trouble on my account."

"I think you know by now I have absolutely no problem saying no." McKittrick smiled at her.

"That's certainly true."

"Come on, then. Spit it out."

"My predecessor at the embassy, a guy named Dennis Mulroony… I'd really like to speak to his main contact in the Met. I'm not sure who that is. All I need from you is a name."

34

The two women said an awkward goodbye at the high school gates, neither of them quite making the 'to hug or not to hug' decision before the moment had passed. Ingrid at least felt she was getting her friendship with the detective back on track. Like McKittrick had said, she wasn't being obstructive over the Shelbourne case. Just objective. Which only highlighted how much her own objectivity had been tested. She knew she'd let her judgment be influenced by events from the past. And that was unprofessional.

Ingrid's cell buzzed as she walked toward the Tube station on Kentish Town Road. When she saw Madison Faber's number, she considered not answering. But with only two and a half days till the inquest, now wasn't the moment to shut down on Faber.

"Hi, Madison, are you OK?" She braced herself for a panicky rant.

"I have something I need you to see." Faber sounded calm.

"What is it?" She wasn't sure she could face another meeting with Faber right now. Calm or not. She felt like she needed a little distance from the student. Get some of her objectivity back.

"I have proof," Faber said, her voice even and quiet. "The proof you said you needed. To take me seriously."

Ingrid didn't remember asking her for anything. "Proof of what?"

"Come see—it's much better if I show you."

Ingrid approached the Tube station. She was pretty certain the Northern line train would take her straight up to Hampstead, so, wearily, Ingrid agreed to another trip to the house where Madison was staying near Hampstead Heath. She didn't have the energy to even begin to imagine what Faber might want her to look at. She didn't suppose it would be anything that useful. But she felt obliged to check it out.

Down on the platform at Kentish Town Tube station, Ingrid discovered she'd have to travel south to Camden Town, then switch to the Hampstead branch of the Northern line, making this particular endeavor seem like even more of a wild-goose chase. The thought of soaking in a soothing warm bubble bath that would ease her battered ribs and aching back was suddenly overwhelmingly appealing.

She emerged from the deep station in Hampstead grateful for air and daylight. Ten minutes later she arrived at Faber's impressive temporary home, and when the front door opened, an excited Madison Faber grabbed her by the arm and guided her to an annex at the rear. She was being put up in considerable style and had been gifted her own suite decorated with mid-century modern furniture. It looked like something from a magazine.

"You know I was getting some clothes from home?"

"Yes." Ingrid was being slowly engulfed by tiredness.

"That's when I noticed it." She nodded at a short red cocktail dress laid flat on a large rectangle of tissue paper spread carefully over the bed.

"This belonged to Lauren?"

"She only wore it on special occasions."

Why would Lauren leave it behind, if it were that special? Ingrid's heart sank. Maybe she should have ignored Faber's call after all. "I'm sorry, Madison, I really don't see how this is relevant."

"Special occasions—like dates. Don't you see? Dates with Stuart… with Professor Younger."

"We don't know for sure the poem was about him."

"But we will!" There was a trill of excitement in her voice. The calmness Faber had demonstrated on the phone had vanished completely. Ingrid steeled herself for whatever revelation was coming next.

"Look at that mark, down at the bottom there." She pointed to a dried white stain, a patch roughly two inches by three.

Ingrid hoped this wasn't about to go in the direction she feared it was headed. She said nothing.

"I couldn't believe it when I saw it. I'd almost finished getting Lauren's things collected together—to send them to her parents —when I discovered it."

Ingrid remained silent.

"It's the evidence we needed. All you have to do now is get it analyzed."

"Are you suggesting the stain is semen?"

"It doesn't take a genius to work it out."

"And you think it's Stuart Younger's?"

"Of course I do! Who else's would it be?"

Ingrid took a moment to work out the best way to dampen Faber's excitement as gently as possible. She needed her to calm down. "Even if I get this analyzed—"

"What do you mean, 'even'?"

"Please—just let me finish. I get this analyzed and prove it's semen. I prove it's Stuart Younger's semen. And from that I assume that Lauren was having an affair with him?"

Faber was nodding at her vigorously. "You can more than assume it! You'll know it for an indisputable, incontrovertible fact."

She laid a hand gently on Faber's arm. "But even if it is, how does that prove Younger had anything to do with her death?"

"Don't you see? It's obvious. Lauren *kept* the dress with the stain on it. This was her best dress, remember. She didn't take it to be dry cleaned. Yet she wrapped it in tissue paper. Why would she keep a dirty dress carefully wrapped up like that? It's not like this doesn't have a precedent."

Ingrid waited for Faber to draw the inevitable comparison.

"Didn't a certain White House intern do exactly the same thing?"

"Maybe Lauren just hadn't gotten around to taking it to the dry cleaner's."

"It was carefully wrapped in tissue paper, laid flat in plastic on top of her closet. She wanted to keep the dress just as it was, *with* the stain. She even left it at my apartment when she moved out. She wanted to store it someplace safe. Somewhere Younger wouldn't find it."

This wasn't adding up, but Ingrid was so fatigued she wasn't able to figure it out. "Why?"

"Why else? To blackmail him. She wanted to blackmail him into leaving his wife."

She sounded delusional. "Don't you think that all sounds a little... extreme?"

"I told you Lauren could be off beam sometimes. This was her insurance policy. If the relationship didn't go the way she wanted... if Younger proved to be reluctant in choosing Lauren over his wife, she had this stored away to persuade him." Faber had worked herself up so much her cheeks had flushed and her eyes were wet. "Only it didn't persuade him. Not in the way she'd intended. Lauren blackmailed Younger and he had to silence her." She pointed at the dress again, quite breathless. "There's all the proof you need."

35

Ingrid's exhaustion was such that she fell asleep in her clothes. The pain in her ribs woke her up at five thirty when she undressed and got under the covers, but she didn't go back to sleep. There was something creepy about Faber's glee at the stain on the dress, and it bothered Ingrid. The girl couldn't believe Ingrid wasn't taking it away for testing. Once she explained that, under UK law, only a British investigator could do that, Faber was equally exasperated Ingrid didn't call the Met.

"The thing is, Madison, that dress has your DNA on it. It was found by you in your apartment. Even the greenest, most newly qualified defender in the country could create enough doubt in a jury's mind for the dress to be worthless to a prosecution."

Faber's features had pinched and her lips pursed like she was sucking on a lemon slice. "Oh." But her deflation only lasted a second. "But you believe me, don't you?"

Wearily, Ingrid had said that she did, and as she lay awake in her hotel bed, she hated herself for lying. She had been so focused on getting justice for Lauren that she had failed to arrange some support for Faber. When the college office opened, she would report her concerns and suggest they urgently get her a counselor. She would also ask Jennifer to research therapeutic options for the girl in case the embassy could help. Given every-thing Faber had been through since finding Lauren's body, her odd and erratic behavior was understandable, but Ingrid was fearful the girl was on the cusp of some kind of psychiatric episode.

She arrived at Loriners just after eight. The place was quiet: it was far too early for most students to be up on a Monday morning, but the cafeteria was open, so she got herself a coffee then sat in the early morning sun in the piazza. When three tall, blond, unusually handsome men entered the science building together, Ingrid's curiosity meant she followed them. She reached Professor Younger's office to discover the door half-open. Through the gap she saw the men removing files from cabinets, shifting piles of CDs from shelves into waiting cardboard cartons, and feeding sheets of paper into an industrial-sized shredder. Such was their industry that they didn't notice her until she tapped lightly on the door.

"I'm looking for Professor Younger. Is he in yet?"

The young man hunched over the shredder looked up and eyed her suspiciously. For a long and agonizing moment, she wondered if he recognized her. Although he wasn't wearing the trademark green and purple uniform, it was possible he'd been one of the men pursuing her across warehouse rooftops on a Deptford industrial estate. She didn't recognize him.

"Who're you?" he said finally.

Ingrid let go of the breath she'd been holding. "Sarah Charles. Prospective PhD student." She smiled warmly at him, eager to make the lie more believable.

"Stuart didn't mention anything to me about a meeting."

"And you are?"

He didn't answer.

The other two men had stopped what they were doing and studied her as closely as the first. Again, she hoped neither of them had been at the meth factory on Saturday.

"Stuart's in the lab all morning."

"Really? I'm sure our meeting was today."

"He's busy."

"That's a shame. I've heard so many exciting things about his research. I was looking forward to meeting him."

"I can pass on a message." The man threw an armful of files into a box at his feet.

"Never mind. I can rearrange for another time."

Ingrid turned on her heels and headed toward the exit, keen to get to the lab while Younger was still there. Assuming, of course, the shredding man was telling her the truth.

The cleanup operation was puzzling. Angela Tate's story about Stuart Younger's research methods wasn't due to hit the streets for a while yet. Had Younger found out about her plans for publication? She picked up her pace, grateful her sore bones were complaining just a little less than they had the day before.

She found the research laboratories and followed the signs to the psychology section, peering into rooms as she went. Each one she passed was empty, the lights off. Younger and his merry gang of industrious students were the only people on campus. She came to the end of a corridor and stepped into a larger space lined on both sides with small booths. She opened the door of one of them. The booths were no more than ten feet square. A single chair was tucked beneath a waist-high workbench. On the bench sat a pair of headphones connected to a socket in the wall. She supposed this was where some of the experiments took place, a willing volunteer isolated in each booth. She closed the door and continued toward a bank of file cabinets that divided the space in two. Professor Younger appeared suddenly from behind one of the cabinets, his head turned away from her.

Ingrid crept a little closer and watched as he opened a drawer, retrieved a handful of files and dumped them with a *thwump* on the floor.

Was this all part of the cleanup operation she'd witnessed in his office?

"Professor!" she called.

Younger spun round, saw it was her, then looked past her, over her shoulder. He seemed relieved to discover she was alone. He'd aged ten years since she'd last seen him, his face grayer, the skin around his eyes more lined, the eyes themselves bloodshot. With some obvious effort he managed to smile at her. "Agent Skyberg, to what do I owe this unexpected pleasure?" He looked at his watch. "I'm afraid I don't have much time for you. I'm very busy at the moment."

Ingrid looked at the pile of files by his feet. "A spring clean?"

"Something like that. I do like to get my house in order as we move further into the summer term. Clear the decks."

"Seems like quite a clearing out. At least you got some help."

He gave her a puzzled look.

"I was just over at your office."

"You were?" He touched his shirt pocket, running his fingers along the outline of his cell phone, no doubt wondering why no one had warned him to expect a visitor. "Look—I really am up to my eyeballs with all this. What do you want?" He slammed shut a cabinet drawer.

"I was wondering if you'd seen anything of our Dutch friend lately—Timo Klaason?"

"He doesn't study here anymore. We discussed that the last time you were here."

"You told me you didn't know him. Yet it turns out he was actually part of your research group."

"You're mistaken."

"I have it on good authority."

"Whose?"

"One of your other students. Madison Faber."

He flinched at the mention of her name. "She is, as usual, mistaken. Don't you think I'd remember him if he was part of the group?"

"The police are pursuing Klaason in connection with a drugs offense." She watched Younger's reaction.

He paused before answering. Calculating. Judging the best way to respond, maybe. "Drugs? One of my students?" He tilted his head to one side. "I suppose that sort of thing goes on within every student body."

Ingrid folded her arms schoolmarmishly.

"Are you telling me you never experimented while you were at college? A little weed?"

"Never appealed."

He gave her a wry smile.

"They want to question him about a *serious* drugs offense. We're not talking about smoking the odd joint here and there."

"Just as well he left the college. We don't want that kind of thing at Loriners." He wetted his dry lips with his tongue. "How serious?"

"You don't know?"

"How on earth would I? I don't even remember him." He glanced at his watch. "Look, if we're done here, I really must ask you to leave." He opened a drawer in the next file cabinet. "I take it you can see yourself out." He didn't bother to look at her.

Either he wasn't even curious about Klaason's offense, or he knew about it already?

"I'm not sure that we are... done, that is," Ingrid said.

He blew out an irritated sigh.

"When we spoke before, you told me Lauren Shelbourne was an exceptional student."

Younger tensed slightly but recovered quickly. "She was. She'll be greatly missed." His shoulders slumped, his hands dropping inside the drawer. "By everyone."

"By you in particular?"

"What do you mean by that?"

"I got the impression Lauren was a favorite of yours."

"She was intelligent, hardworking, energetic. Students like Lauren don't come along that often. It was a pleasure to work with her." He straightened up, pulling back his shoulders, and fixed Ingrid with a cold stare. "Where are you going with this?"

"So much of a pleasure you... made it personal?" She stepped up close. She could smell coffee and a metallic tang on his breath.

"What?" He leaned toward her.

"Were you having a sexual relationship with Lauren Shelbourne?"

His mouth dropped open and his eyes widened. "You've really got the gall to ask me that? Incredible. Is that what the US government is paying you for? To harass British citizens?"

"I'm just pursuing a line a of inquiry—"

"How dare you!" He fumbled in the rear pocket of his pants and retrieved a wallet, then pulled out a small square color photograph of a dark-haired woman in her late thirties. She had perfectly proportioned features. Full lips, straight nose, chiseled cheekbones. Younger prodded the picture with a finger. "That, if you're in any way interested, is my beautiful wife. The mother of my children. We've been together fifteen years. Claire is my best friend, closest ally and confidante. Do you think I would jeopardize a relationship like that for the sake of… what? A sordid little affair with a research student?"

She had certainly hit a nerve. He glared at her, his chest rising and falling rapidly. "Get out!"

Ingrid stood her ground.

"You have no jurisdiction here. I've only been speaking to you out of courtesy. Leave now before I get security to escort you from the premises." He squared up to her. "Get. Out."

"I'd think about your answer very carefully when you're asked that question again."

"No one in their right mind would even ask it." He grabbed the phone from his pocket and waved it at her. "What's it to be? You leave now, or I have you forcibly removed?"

Ingrid backed away. She scanned the rows of file cabinets. "This cleanup of yours…"

"What about it?"

"You're wasting your time. It'll be impossible to destroy all the evidence."

"What are you talking about?"

"I think you know."

"You're out of your mind." He swiped the screen of his phone and tapped in a number.

"It's OK—I'm leaving."

As she passed the long row of narrow booths, Ingrid heard Younger raise his voice.

"For Christ's sake," she heard him say into his phone, "please tell me you're about to leave the country."

36

She reached the main piazza and dialed Angela Tate's number. The journalist answered after a half dozen rings.

"What?"

She had obviously woken her up.

"This is Ingrid Skyberg. Have you coaxed your sources to go on the record yet?"

"What?"

"Is your story about Younger's program about to hit the streets?"

There was a silence on the line. "Why are you asking?"

"I've just seen Younger. He's covering his tracks. What isn't being moved is being destroyed. Files, CDs, paperwork, you name it. I could practically smell smoke coming out of the shredding machine."

"Shit."

"Maybe one of your sources told him. Perhaps his hold over them is stronger than you thought."

Ingrid kept a close eye on the main entrance of the research block, expecting to see more of Younger's acolytes arrive to help with the cleanup operation. What she didn't expect to see was Younger himself racing through the doors, his cell phone clamped to one ear, a dark gray baseball cap pulled low over his head. She snuck into a doorway.

"You've got to stop him destroying the evidence," Tate said.

"I'm not in a position to do that."

"Inform the college authorities."

"I'm kinda busy right now." Ingrid hung up, and when Younger had crossed the square, she emerged from her hiding place. The professor exited through the main gates, and Ingrid followed, staying a good fifty yards behind him. Where did he have to be so urgently he could abandon the task of sanitizing his office and laboratory?

Ingrid trailed Younger all the way along the street, watching and waiting as he stopped at three different ATMs, withdrawing cash from each one. He stuffed the money in his pocket and continued until he reached the next cross lights, where he turned right. When she reached the corner, she scanned the sea of faces for Younger, but couldn't pick him out. This street was busier, lined with stores on either side, and full of rush-hour commuters. She'd lost him.

Dammit.

She stared at the bobbing heads, but the professor had vanished. Her heart thudded. He could be in any one of the stores. She headed up the street, hoping she was still going in the right direction, praying he hadn't hopped on a bus. Mostly she hoped he hadn't already spotted her. She kept her eyes peeled and her legs moving. Then she spotted his baseball cap. He had picked up his pace. Wherever he was headed, he needed to get there fast. Younger took the next left, and Ingrid hurried to the corner.

It was a residential street and much quieter. There was only a handful of people on the sidewalk, and Ingrid had no choice but to let the gap widen between them, even if it meant the risk of losing him again.

She followed him for a half mile through a network of quiet roads until his pace slowed. Younger was checking the numbers of the large duplex, two-story houses as he passed them. Each house had a garage out front and a narrow alley running along-side it. Most front yards were neat and clean. Smart cars on the driveways. After another fifty yards Younger stopped abruptly, and Ingrid ducked behind an SUV. She peered through its windows and saw him glance left and right before walking up the front path of a house that had a bright red motorcycle parked on the driveway. Younger banged a fist against the door, which was opened almost immediately. Younger slipped inside, the door closing quickly behind him. Less than a minute later he was back out on the street, adjusting his cap and retracing his steps.

Ingrid waited behind the SUV until Younger reached the end of the street. Then she watched the house and the corner for another five minutes until she was happy the professor wasn't returning.

She hurried across the road and made straight for the alleyway that ran along the side of the house. She pushed open a wooden gate to discover a ramshackle backyard. A square lawn overgrown with weeds took up most of the space, discarded plastic toys strewn over it. She stopped for a moment. Was this a family home? Would there be children inside? She continued into the yard, where she found the back door, a cigarette smoldering in a saucer on the ground beside it. She crept up to the door and tried the handle. It wasn't locked. She pushed it open a fraction then waited for a response from someone inside. There wasn't one. She held her breath and stepped over the threshold, feeling exposed without a weapon. All she could do was work quietly and slowly, listening and watching as she went. She entered a long, narrow galley-style kitchen. Pots and pans were stacked high in the sink and on the drainer. Empty cans of beer littered the counter. The room smelled of tobacco and Chinese takeout.

She stopped. Listened. No sign of activity.

She continued through the kitchen until she reached a gloomy hallway. A staircase to her right, with a low, narrow door set into some wooden paneling. On her left was a closed door—the living room presumably—and straight ahead was the front door leading out onto the street. She crept forward and listened at the door on the left. All she heard was her own heartbeat banging in her ears.

Someone had to be in the house. Judging by the silence of the room on her left, that someone was upstairs. She inhaled.

Listened again. Somebody coughed. The sound came from somewhere above and behind her, perhaps on the second-floor landing.

"Now's as good a time as any." A woman's voice.

"No, it'll wait until tonight." A man's voice.

"What's there to hang around for?" The woman again.

Both voices English. Not foreign. Not Dutch. Not Timo Klaason.

Dammit.

She'd been so sure. She continued to listen, but the conversation had ended. She moved toward the front door. No point in staying now. She tried the door. It was locked. No sign of a key. She turned back to the kitchen, but before she could take a step, the door beneath the stairs opened. She froze for a microsecond before instinct kicked in. She levered down the handle of the door into the living room and ducked inside. In the gap between the door and frame, a tall figure emerged from the cellar door under the stairs.

Timo Klaason. No question.

He had a small duffel bag slung over one shoulder, a motorcycle helmet in his other hand. He leaned over the banister and shouted up the stairs, "Hey, you guys! I'm leaving now. Thanks for everything, yeah?"

Scraping and thumping overhead was swiftly followed by heavy footsteps clattering down the stairs. The leaving committee. Ingrid pushed the door further toward the jamb. She heard the sound of a key in the lock, then the front door opening.

"Send us a postcard, yeah?" the woman said.

"Sure—I'll upload my holiday photos to Flickr for you."

"All right, whatever. Take care of yourself, though, I mean it."

"I always do," Klaason called from outside.

The motorbike in the front yard started to roar. Ingrid reached for her cell phone and dialed 999. Without hanging up, she shoved the phone in her pocket and threw open the door.

"What the fu—"

The woman and man wheeled around toward her, their jaws dropping wide. Ingrid pushed a path between them and threw herself through the front door. The bike revved again. Ingrid leaped toward it, clawing at Klaason's back. He half turned, his right arm swinging at her, making contact with her ribs. She flinched but tightened her hold. She felt a pair of hands grip her shoulders, trying to yank her off the bike. She gripped him even harder.

"Help! Police!" she shouted. "I'm being attacked!" She screamed the address of the house at the top of her voice, hoping she was still connected to emergency services. The hands on her shoulders let go.

The engine revved again and Klaason accelerated out of the front yard and into the street. Ingrid held on tight. Klaason couldn't control the bike, but she clung on.

They went twenty yards down the street, thirty, forty. He started swinging the bike, trying to throw her off. This wasn't going to end well. She pressed her thighs against the bike, freeing her hands. She reached forward and grabbed his right arm. He accelerated harder. She didn't even want to look at the speedometer. He took his left hand off the clutch and whacked her right hand, but she tightened her grip. They were coming up to a junction. They were going too fast to take the corner safely. He braked hard and the bike slid sideways beneath them. Ingrid let go and slammed, shoulder first, into a parked car. Her body thumped down onto the road. She heard sirens in the distance.

And then everything went dark.

37

The embassy staff doctor typed up his medical report, alternately sucking his teeth and sighing as he pecked at his keyboard.

"Bed rest," he said after he'd tapped the final key with a flourish. "It's all I can suggest. Painkillers every four hours, every two if you switch between ibuprofen and acetaminophen." He looked at her over the top of the glasses balancing on his thick nose. "I'll sign you off duty for the rest of the week."

Ingrid shook her head. "Not possible. I'm in the middle of an investigation."

"Tough."

Two hours earlier, much to the dismay of the medical staff at King's College Hospital, Ingrid had discharged herself shortly after arriving there by ambulance. The doctors had wanted to keep her in overnight for observation, a precaution for all concussion sufferers, they'd explained. They told her how lucky she had been to have escaped such a serious accident with no broken bones or ruptured organs. She'd listened politely to them until they were done, then demanded they give her back her clothes so she could get out of there.

As she sat staring into the embassy MD's rheumy eyes, she felt anything but lucky. Every part of her was either bruised or grazed, and every time she moved, she set off a new tsunami of pain through her entire body. Lucky or not, she sure as hell wasn't going to be confined to quarters.

"Really, Doc, I look a lot worse than I am. It's my coloring—I bruise easily. I'm fine to carry out desk duties, wouldn't you say?"

The doctor pushed his glasses onto his head and noisily drew in air through his teeth. He sat back in his chair and folded his arms. "Very well. But make sure you perform light duties only. Here in the embassy, where I can keep an eye on you."

When she walked into the criminal division office, Jennifer's mouth fell open, making her look even younger than her twenty-three years. She looked like she should still be selling Girl Scout cookies.

"Don't ask."

Jen got up. "I, like, have to ask. Did you come off your motorcycle?"

"Not exactly."

Ingrid gave her the basic outline of what had happened. Jen perched on her desk, peering at the grazes on Ingrid's face, her luscious strawberry-blond hair framing increasingly concerned features.

"I don't understand," Jen said. "This guy is Dutch, right?"

"Correct."

"And he's a drug dealer, like, in the UK? Selling drugs to British students?"

Ingrid fired up her computer. "He doesn't care about their nationality."

"But, like, this might sound really stupid, but what's it got to do with us? First you find his... his *factory*, then you track him down. Are the British police paying you or something?"

Jen was not being stupid. Her summary was totally correct. It didn't really matter that Ingrid was after answers in the Shelbourne case, the Klaason thing had been an unnecessary detour. The whole reason she'd checked out of the hospital was to stop Sol and Louden finding out just how far off track she'd gotten.

Among her emails was one from the forensics lab in DC with the subject line Sample request ready. The paint analysis. She clicked on it. Ingrid scanned through the explanatory notes, registered something about the delay due to the sample not matching US databases, and found what she was looking for. The paint used to write *lauren shelbourne = whore* on the walls of Loriners the day after her death was made by Dulux, and the shade was Sun Dust 2.

Her desk phone rang. Normally calls to the department went to Jen's phone.

"You want me to get that?"

Ingrid waved her away. "Criminal Division, Agent Skyberg speaking."

"Hi, sweetie."

"Marshall! Did someone call you?"

"I don't understand."

"It's nothing." Ingrid had thought maybe someone had let him know about her hospitalization. No need to tell him she was OK. "How are you?"

"Sweetie, listen." He was talking very quietly. "You need to leave the building. Go for a walk. And take your cell."

"Marsh?"

"I can't say any more."

"Marsh, I—"

"Just pick up your coat, and go. You've got five minutes, OK?"

What the hell was going on with him? It was not like Marshall, which was why she was going to do as he said. "Jen, I'm just heading out to pick up some painkillers, OK?"

"You want me to go?"

"Thanks, but I think a gentle walk would do me good."

"I've got Tylenol," she said as Ingrid reached the threshold.

There was no way Ingrid was up to taking the stairs, so she punched the button and called the elevator. Two minutes later, she passed the security barriers in the lobby and walked out into Grosvenor Square. It was almost dusk, and the spring warmth had gone from the air. She buttoned up her coat, checked for traffic and stepped into the garden square, where crocuses and primroses welcomed her. The cinder path led her past several empty benches, but it was a little too cold to sit down. She breathed as deeply as her battered ribs would allow, and held tightly to her cell.

An out-of-area message flashed on her screen. She hit the connect button.

"Agent Skyberg."

There was a slight delay on the line. "Hi. Is that Ingrid?"

"Speaking."

"I have some information for you."

She kept walking. "Who is this, please?"

"You made an inquiry about an agent called Mulroony."

"Is that you?" Ingrid's mouth was dry. She pushed a finger in her ear, determined not to miss anything.

"We have only one record of a Dennis Mulroony." The voice was male, East Coast, and educated. He sounded middle-aged, but with the quality of the line, it wasn't possible to be sure.

Ingrid's pace had picked up. She still couldn't quite believe Marshall had come through for her. "And what is that record?"

"London, Legal Attaché Program, April till December 2012."

"That's it?" Mulroony had only worked at the embassy for eight months? She was sure, when Sol had recruited her, he'd said her predecessor had been there for years.

"There are no other records." He paused. "No college records, no public records, no birth or death certificate."

"You're kidding." Ingrid strode out of the square and walked north toward Oxford Street. "He's disappeared?"

"Right off the map. You have any other questions, agent?"

"Any idea what his security clearance was when he worked in London?"

"Negative, agent."

Ingrid's thoughts were spinning, trying to work out which questions to put forward, but leery of asking any when she did not know whom she was speaking to. "Thank you. Were you also asked to research Greg Brewster—" she stopped herself, considered the ramifications of revealing she knew his occupation, then proceeded "—the arms dealer?"

"Affirmative. Gregory James Brewster is an alias for Sidney

Joseph Baxter. He is booked on a flight from Oman to London, arriving Heathrow twelve twenty-five tomorrow." The line went dead.

Ingrid checked the last-number feature on her phone. It only said 'international,' but she dialed it anyway. She wasn't surprised to get a message saying the company was unable to connect her call, with the helpful suggestion she should check the number and try again. Her stride had slowed to a shuffle as she absorbed not only what she'd just been told, but also that Marshall had put himself out for her. She should call him. She was scrolling for his number when an incoming call vibrated her phone. It was Ralph Mills.

"Hey, Ralph."

"How are you? I heard about what happened."

"I'm fine." She shifted the phone from left hand to right, the soreness in her left arm suddenly too painful to ignore.

"I have some news. Thought you might like to know Lauren Shelbourne's mobile phone has become active."

38

"I had no idea your injuries were so bad." Ralph Mills rushed toward her. "Should I take you to the hospital?"

It was her face, Ingrid realized. Her hip, right thigh and ribs were in much worse shape, but a woman with a grazed cheek and bruised eye was guaranteed to attract the wrong sort of attention.

"Really—it's nothing." Ingrid was tempted to say 'stop acting like my mother' except Svetlana Skyberg had never shown as much sympathy and concern in all the years she'd raised her. Mills offered her his hand, and reluctantly she took it. The visitors chairs in Lewisham police station were particularly low, and she was actually grateful of the gesture. He led them out of reception and swiped them through into a network of corridors that was starting to be familiar.

"Tell me about Lauren's phone."

"Like I explained earlier, it was switched off again before we had a chance to triangulate."

"Do you have a rough idea where it was used?"

"Greater London."

"Oh. How long was it on for?"

"Less than five minutes. And it didn't make any calls or send any texts."

"But Natash... DI McKittrick has called off the inquest?"

Mills pushed open a door. "I haven't had confirmation, but I imagine that's a formality. If Lauren's phone was stolen, that puts a whole other spin on the crime scene. We'll go over everything again."

Part of Ingrid was elated—she'd always thought there was enough about Lauren's death to suspect foul play—but she also knew the pain that knowledge would inflict on the girl's parents.

"And any sign of Younger? Do we know where he went after visiting Klaason?"

Mills shrugged apologetically. "We've got officers watching his house and the college."

"What about airports and train stations?"

"We don't have that kind of manpower available. But his wife has surrendered his passport, so we don't think he'll try to leave the country." He pulled an apologetic face. "Right now the London Crime Squad, whom I am about to introduce you to, are trying to match up the serial numbers of the twenty-pound notes Klaason had on him with the cash withdrawn using Younger's bank card. As soon as they've proved that link, they'll issue a 'perverting the course of justice' arrest warrant." He held open another door for her and they entered a corridor lined with doors and plastic seating. "Delivering cash to a known felon to aid his escape is serious enough for us to lock him up for a while."

That was something.

"Millsy!"

Ahead of them a short, female detective with a huge smile bowled over to them and slapped a hand on Mills's, shaking it hard.

"You might have to be gentler with Ingrid," Mills said. "Agent Skyberg, this is Detective Constable Cath Murray. We used to work together."

"Ooh, yes, you do look a bit ropey." Cath had a northern accent and scruffy short hairstyle that made her look like she was up to no good. Ingrid took an instant liking to her. "Call me Cath. It's a real pleasure to meet you. I've heard so much about you."

"Really?" Ingrid was incredulous.

"Ralph's been singing your praises nonstop."

Mills's cheeks reddened. "I'll, um, be next door. If you need anything at all, Cath'll sort you out."

"I'm sure I'll be fine—thank you."

Mills shut the door behind him, and Murray led Ingrid into an observation room. She pulled a chair out from under a wide desk, with two huge TV monitors set on top. "You look like you need all the rest you can get. Take a seat."

Ingrid eased herself onto the chair, careful to avoid any sudden jarring movements. "Ralph mentioned you were part of the initial interviewing team when you brought Klaason in."

"I work in the London Crime Squad. Just started, as a matter of fact." She beamed at Ingrid. "I sat in while the SIO questioned Klaason about his industrious little setup in Deptford."

Ingrid focused her attention on the left-hand TV monitor.

"But now Homicide and Serious Crime Command—"

"McKittrick's team?"

"Exactly. They want to talk to him about the girl they found in New Cross."

The monitor showed Klaason sitting very calmly at a three-foot-by-four-foot table. He had a shaven head, sallow skin and broad, dark features. His ethnicity was hard to determine, but Ingrid would guess he had ancestors from central Asia. There were no obvious signs of injury from falling off the bike. But then Klaason had been wearing a motorcycle helmet and a thick leather jacket when they'd hit the ground. His face was completely blank. The right-hand monitor displayed a wide shot of the interview room. Sitting next to Klaason was a neat woman in a smart suit. Her face was set in a scowl. Neither of them spoke.

"What did Klaason tell you during the first interview?" Ingrid asked.

"Bugger all. It was as much as we could do to get him to confirm his name and date of birth. He didn't even give us an address."

"And you're here in case he says anything relevant to your investigation?"

"Correct." Murray shuffled in her seat. "Great detective work, by the way, finding him like that. Not to mention brave. Really impressive."

Ingrid smiled. "Thanks."

The monitor showed McKittrick and Mills enter the interview room. They made their preliminary introductions, stated clearly that the interview was being recorded—Klaason glanced up at the camera and blinked—and McKittrick kicked off the interview.

"When did you start supplying narcotics to Lauren Shelbourne?"

For an opening gambit, it was nothing if not direct. Klaason stiffened. But remained silent. It was a bold move by McKittrick.

"OK," McKittrick said, "let's start with something easy. How long have you known Professor Younger?"

"I'm sorry, my English is not so good. Can you repeat the question?" She did and Klaason responded with: "No comment."

The microphones in the interview room were very sensitive— Ingrid heard McKittrick failing to suppress a sigh.

"He did the exact same thing with us," Murray said, her voice low, as if the four people in the room at the other end of the corridor might hear her. "His English is perfect—he refused an interpreter."

McKittrick cleared her throat, then said, "We've checked with the college's admission records. You started at Loriners last October. Studying psychology. Under Professor Younger."

"If you already have the information, why are you asking me?"

"Where were you on Monday the fourteenth of April between the hours of midnight and eight a.m.?"

"How would I know that?"

"The date may have stuck in your memory, given it's the day Lauren Shelbourne died."

Again there was a definite tensing across Klaason's shoulders. Ingrid leaned forward, closer to the monitor, wishing she were conducting the interview herself.

"I don't see why." Klaason stretched his neck left, then right, then rolled his shoulders.

"You knew Lauren Shelbourne?"

"No."

"You were a member of the same research group."

"It's a big project. Lots of people take part."

"Are you denying you met Miss Shelbourne?"

Klaason folded his arms and stretched out his legs under the table, kicking Mills's feet in the process. He didn't apologize. "I'm not *denying* anything. My English, sorry… I mean I didn't know Lauren well."

"Did you ever visit her in her flat?"

Klaason started to answer, but his lawyer grabbed his arm. "No comment," he said.

"Here we go again," Murray chimed in. "We had nothing but 'no comments.' Even when we told him we had masses of forensic evidence placing him at the meth factory. But at least that wiped the smile off his face."

Ingrid pulled back from the monitor and turned to Murray. "Do you know how many DNA samples were collected from Lauren's apartment?"

"No, I'm not on that team."

"So we don't know if Klaason's DNA was found in her apartment?"

"Don't quote me on it, but I doubt it. When the pathologist said it was accidental death, the lab wouldn't have prioritized samples from that investigation."

"But now the case has reopened, there might be samples to test?"

"Not my area, I'm afraid." Murray nodded at the screen. "You'd need to ask those two."

Ingrid switched her attention back to the monitor, aware the conversation had restarted in the interview room. She caught the final few words of a sentence. "… my client has already been answering questions for several hours."

"Not answering them, more like," Murray said.

McKittrick forced a smile. "He had a lengthy break between interviews."

"My client hasn't eaten."

"Answer a few more questions and we'll get him a sandwich, how about that?"

"Make sure it's no more than two."

McKittrick rolled her eyes. "I'll decide how many questions I ask. Mr. Klaason, I realize your solicitor has advised you to assert your right to silence, but you have to remember that if you fail to tell us something that may help your—"

Klaason held up a hand. "It's too complicated. My English... I told you..."

"Is good enough to study a degree course at one of the UK's top universities." McKittrick forced another smile. "If we discover you have visited Miss Shelbourne in her home, it won't be—"

"I never did!"

"So you didn't provide a delivery service when Miss Shelbourne requested more drugs?"

"You're crazy. I never supplied her with drugs."

"Is that so?"

The lawyer grabbed Klaason's arm again; he batted her hand away.

"Ask Younger—he knew her better than anyone."

"What do you mean?"

Klaason slumped forward, resting his elbows on the table. "He was screwing her."

"How do you know that?"

"He told me."

"So you and Professor Younger are quite close?"

"I wouldn't say that."

"But he told you about his sex life. Isn't that quite an admission, given he's a married man?"

"I'm sorry, my English..."

"Change the bloody record!" Murray shouted unhelpfully at the monitor.

"You say you never supplied Lauren Shelbourne with drugs?"

"That's right."

"So how do you explain the high levels of methamphetamine in her bloodstream at the time of her death?"

"What?"

"You're the man manufacturing the stuff, not two miles away from her home. You studied with her. You can understand why we might think there's a connection."

"I never gave her anything. If she was taking meth, it has nothing to do with me."

"Nothing?"

"No comment."

"I think we've moved beyond that now, Timo." McKittrick sniffed loudly, then spread her fingers flat against her notes. "Let me ask you a different question. Did you supply Stuart Younger with LSD and methamphetamine?"

Klaason didn't reply.

"Mr Klaason, a young woman has died. A brilliant young woman, by all accounts, a woman whose life revolved around Loriners College. Her only friends in London study at the college. Her Oyster card shows she hasn't moved more than a mile from the college in the past month. Her mobile phone records show she had not made or received calls to any person we have not been able to speak to—"

A flicker of alarm on Mills's face confirmed that McKittrick was lying about that.

"—so as far as we have been able to establish, it is extremely probable that she obtained the drugs that killed her from the campus. A campus where you appear to be the main dealer—"

The lawyer interrupted. "My client is highly unlikely to be the only dealer at the college."

McKittrick ignored her. "—and it seems worthy of my time to see if you can help me find out why this bright and brilliant woman, with no previous history of substance misuse, had such large quantities of drugs in her system."

Klaason was silent.

McKittrick circled something in her notes. "Mr Klaason, you are looking at a minimum of eight years in prison for the production of methamphetamine, but I am willing to put in a good word with the London Crime Squad if you tell me what you know about Lauren Shelbourne and how she came to have drugs—very likely *your* drugs—in her system."

His lawyer cleared her throat and whispered something to Klaason, who nodded.

"I have nothing to do with Lauren dying, OK?"

McKittrick and Mills said nothing.

"But I did give stuff to the professor." The lawyer held onto his arm. He pushed her away. "Ask Younger how come she was taking meth. Ask him why she ended up dead."

There was a knock on the interview room door and a uniformed PC stuck her head through the door. McKittrick got up and spoke to her. They exchanged a handful of words before the inspector returned to the table and officially suspended the interview. Mills followed her eagerly out of the room.

The observation room door opened a moment later and the two of them walked in.

"What a result!" Murray said. "Great work."

She high-fived a beaming Mills. "It gets better than that," he said.

Ingrid's eyes widened. "What's happened?"

He looked to McKittrick. "Can I?"

She was smiling too. "Go for it."

"Uniforms say Lauren Shelbourne's phone is active again."

"And this time they've got a location." McKittrick paused for dramatic effect. "It's within a fifty-meter radius of Stuart Younger's house."

39

Jen got such a shock seeing Ingrid at her desk, she almost dropped her coffee.

"Sorry, didn't mean to scare you."

"Please tell me you didn't sleep here last night." Jen took off her coat, opened her umbrella to dry, and switched on her computer. It had been raining hard since Ingrid had got up at six.

"Do I look that bad?"

"Jeez, no. Totally no. Except for, you know…" She gestured to the bruising on Ingrid's cheek, which was now deepening from mauve to eggplant. "How come you're in so early?"

Ingrid explained she was in no state to go for a run, and even lying flat was painful. There was also the small matter of Greg Brewster's return to the UK at lunchtime, and she had much to plan. "Also, the Deputy wants to see me."

Jen turned round, her mouth agape, her eyes wide. "What have you done?"

Ingrid scrunched up her face. "I find out at eight thirty." She looked at the clock: she still had fifteen minutes to put her pieces in play. She called the St Pancras hotel and asked to be put through to the concierge.

"Good morning, I'm hoping you can assist me today."

"Of course, madam."

"My boss, Mr. Greg Brewster, is checking in with you this afternoon, and I would like to make some reservations for him."

"Of course."

Ingrid was calculating that whoever had stolen Brewster's laptop had not got what they wanted. Its encryption had almost certainly held up to attempts to access the information they had stolen it for. What they needed was the passwords that would unlock the laptop's secrets. The other calculation she made was that Brewster always stayed at the St. Pancras hotel because he felt well taken care of by the staff there. It was her guess that the reason they took such good care of him was because someone at the hotel was tipping off the people who were targeting him. If she was right, the appointments she was lining up for him after he checked in would make him the victim of a second crime, and this time she would be there to intercept the criminal. Getting him to play along might prove impossible, but she would cross that bridge when she met his plane at lunchtime.

At exactly eight thirty, Ingrid knocked on Amy Louden's door. She straightened the collar of her shirt while she waited to be told to come in. When she entered, Louden couldn't keep the surprise from her face.

"My God. The medical report was comprehensive, but I couldn't have guessed you'd look so... beaten."

"Just a few superficial injuries. I heal quickly," Ingrid said. "A couple of days before I'm back to full strength. Max. I promise I won't scare any members of the public between now and then."

"The MD authorized desk duties."

"Yes, ma'am."

"So where were you yesterday afternoon?" She indicated Ingrid should take a seat opposite her desk.

A flash of fear engulfed Ingrid. Did Louden know about her anonymous call?

"I came looking for you about five o'clock."

"Oh. Right. I was at Lewisham police station. The investigation into Lauren Shelbourne's death has been reopened."

"Ah. Have you told her parents?"

"Not yet, no." Ingrid chewed her lip. "Why did you want to see me?"

"I received a call from the senior investigating officer in the London Crime Squad yesterday afternoon."

"You did?"

"He called to thank me for your intervention. Explained how useful you've been to his investigation."

Ingrid blinked. She'd assumed she was going to be rebuked.

"But I thought I should point out that jumping off a roof isn't very smart. You're needed here, Ingrid, and you can't go putting yourself in danger or taking unnecessary risks."

Louden had called her 'Ingrid' and not 'agent.' That was a first. "I didn't have much choice. If I hadn't jumped, I could well have been pushed."

"And jumping on the back of a drug dealer's motorcycle? Was your life in danger then?"

Ingrid fidgeted awkwardly. "I guess that Quantico training just kinda kicked in."

At least that dragged a smile onto Louden's lips. "Listen, it's clear you are a very committed investigator, but this is just a friendly reminder to take better care of yourself. I'm all for awarding bravery medals to my agents, but I'd prefer not to hand them out posthumously, you understand?"

"Got it."

Louden walked over to her window and looked at the torrential rain. "Now, what about Mr. Brewster's laptop? Are you getting anywhere?"

Ingrid outlined her plan to set a trap for the thief—or more likely whoever had hired the thief—when they came back to complete the job. Louden listened without interrupting.

"If we had the manpower," Ingrid said, "we could also set up meetings for Sidney Baxter, an alias used by Brewster—"

Louden turned sharply away from the window. "Where did you find that out?"

Ingrid felt heat rising up her neck. "It was something that came to light during the course of my investigation."

Louden returned to her desk, positioned herself within inches of Ingrid and leaned against it. "Yes, but someone must have told you that information?"

Sweat formed between Ingrid's shoulder blades. "I interrogated Met archives. It wasn't the first time Brewster has been the victim of a crime in London. Ma'am?"

"Yes?"

"What's really going on? Why are you so personally interested in Greg Brewster?"

Louden pressed her lips together.

"I have been trying to investigate this robbery with one hand tied behind my back. I have a great deal of respect for you, and for your rank, and I know that you know how hard it is in these circumstances to find evidence and unmask the perpetrator." Ingrid paused to assess from Louden's expression if she had gone too far. "Yet you keep pushing me for more information. I just want to understand why."

Louden nodded slowly. She walked round to the other side of her desk, sat down, then steepled her fingers under her chin. "You're right. We haven't made this easy for you. Let me reassure you that you are doing excellent work."

Ingrid waited for her to say more, but that was it. "Thank you. If there's nothing else, I should go and speak to the Shelbournes, update them on the case."

Louden nodded.

"Thank you for your time." Ingrid winced as she got to her feet. By the time she had reached the door, Louden had picked up the phone. She waited until Ingrid had left the room before she dialed.

Ingrid closed the door behind her and leaned against the wall in the corridor outside, trying to work out her next move. The painkillers were wearing off and she felt a little nauseous. She needed air. She would walk to the Shelbournes' hotel.

It wasn't until she reached reception she remembered it was raining. She was about to go back upstairs to borrow Jen's umbrella when she saw a familiar face standing on the sidewalk in the pouring rain. She grabbed a magazine from a rack and headed out to join her.

40

Alex Shelbourne was drenched. By the looks of her, she'd been standing in the rain for hours. Ingrid held the magazine over her head and raced toward the girl.

"What did you do to your face?" the teenager asked as she approached.

"Had a fight with a parked car."

"You've got blood on your cheek."

"It's just a graze."

"No, I mean fresh blood. It's running down your face."

Ingrid lifted a hand to her cheek and it came away pink, where the blood had mingled with rainwater.

"Here." Alex Shelbourne handed Ingrid her scarf.

"It's OK—it'll stop soon enough."

"Take it." She thrust the scarf at her and Ingrid blotted her cheek.

"Why didn't you get security to call me? How long have you been here?"

"I didn't want anyone else to know I was here. So I waited."

"You'll catch cold. Let's get you inside." Ingrid started back toward the embassy, but Alex tugged on her arm.

"Not there."

They headed down North Audley Street and stopped at the first café they came to. Ingrid threw the sodden magazine into the trash and handed Alex back her scarf, scooping up a handful of paper napkins from a nearby table. She pressed the wad of tissue against her face.

A hot chocolate and double espresso ordered, they took the table furthest from the window.

"How long have you been waiting?" Ingrid asked.

"A couple of hours."

"You must be soaked."

"I'm OK."

She didn't look it.

"Do your parents know you're here?"

Alex stared into her hot chocolate. She scooped the froth backward and forward across its surface with a teaspoon. "I told them I wanted to visit the Apple Store." There was no attitude now. The goth makeup had gone, to be replaced with a palpable sadness. Alex Shelbourne seemed a completely different girl.

"They were relieved to get me out of the way so they could fight some more without an audience. They've never been like this with one another before. Mom blames Dad. And Dad…"

"Blames himself?"

"I don't know. Maybe. But mostly he just pretends it's not really happening."

"I'm so sorry."

"Me too." Alex Shelbourne shivered as she gazed blankly at her hot chocolate. Ingrid wanted to tell her the case into her sister's death had been reopened, but she needed to tell the parents first. Alex put down the spoon and looked up suddenly at Ingrid. "Why did you ignore the note I gave you?"

"I didn't. I would have gotten in touch. But events kind of overtook me."

The teenager pointed to Ingrid's face. "You mean your fight with a car?"

"Among other things. Plus I had no way of contacting you without going through your parents first. I'm guessing that's the last thing you wanted me to do."

The girl nodded slowly. "I hoped I'd get a chance to speak to you after the meeting on Saturday."

"I was kept behind by my boss."

"You make it sound like she's your teacher or something."

"More like the principal." Ingrid gave her a smile. "What was it you wanted to tell me about your sister?"

Alex took a deep breath, her shoulders rising almost to her ears then slumping down again. "I wasn't one hundred percent sure I should even tell you, but when she came to the hotel, pretending to be so upset, I knew I couldn't keep it to myself. I wanted to scream at her."

"Who?"

"Madison. She's a two-faced bitch."

"Madison Faber? You saw her when she visited your parents?" Why had Alex Shelbourne taken such a strong dislike to a woman she didn't even know?

"I saw her—but she didn't see me. I stayed in the room next door. No way was I going to speak to her. She hated Lauren. And Lauren hated her right back. How could she cry like that in front of Mom and Dad? She's so fake."

"Are you sure? Weren't Madison and Lauren good friends?"

"If they were, why did Lauren move out of the apartment? She should have made that bitch leave instead."

"I'm sorry, I don't follow." Ingrid's head was foggier than she'd realized.

"The apartment, it was Lauren's. She should never have let Madison move in."

"Lauren's? Are you sure about that?"

"Yeah—why wouldn't I be?"

"So you're saying Madison moved into *Lauren's* apartment?"

"Yes!" The girl sniffed. "I'm sorry—I didn't mean to shout."

"That's OK." Ingrid took a sip of coffee. "Is that what you wanted to tell me about Lauren?"

"No—I thought you should know why she and Madison had such a big fight."

Ingrid blinked. Where the hell was this going? "I want you to take this slowly. Make allowances for me, I've taken a lot of painkillers. I want to be clear exactly what you're saying."

"Lauren and Madison had a big fight. Lauren asked her to

leave, but Madison refused. She's such a spoiled bitch. She wouldn't move out."

"So Lauren was forced to leave instead?"

"She didn't want to stay a moment longer with that weirdo."

"Weirdo?" Ingrid wasn't going to correct the kid's language—she was only sixteen—but it was a reminder to arrange proper support for Faber.

A sob erupted from Alex's throat. Her eyes started to water.

"It's OK—take your time."

"She told me they had a fight over some guy she was seeing."

"A man your sister was seeing?"

Alex nodded. A tear dropped into her cup.

"Did she tell you who that was?"

"Lauren never said who she was dating. Not even when she lived at home. She always kept her boyfriends secret." She sobbed again. "I mean, I thought for about a year she was gay she was so damn secretive."

Ingrid laid a hand over the girl's. "Drink some hot chocolate —you're chilled right to the bone. I'm going to sit here and watch you drink it."

"I don't really want any."

"Just a little, come on."

With shaking hands, the girl lifted the wide cup to her lips, took a sip and put the cup straight back down. She dabbed her mouth with a paper napkin. "It was weird Madison knew who the guy was because I don't think Lauren would have told her. I guess she must have found out some other way."

Faber had always said she didn't know who Lauren was dating, but Alex Shelbourne seemed sure of her facts.

"And that's why they fought?"

Alex nodded. "Madison was jealous as hell. She wanted to go out with the same guy. She accused my sister of stealing him from her. Lauren told me he couldn't even bear to look at Madison. When I saw her crying at the hotel with Mom and Dad, I just wanted to punch her. I wish I had."

Ingrid wished there was a pause button she could press. She

needed time to think. "Drink some more hot chocolate, Alex. Just a little."

Faber had told the police she and Lauren never fought. Not once, she'd said. The inconsistencies were mounting up. Why would Alex make any of this up? What could she gain from fabricating something like this? The girl looked up and saw Ingrid staring at her.

"What is it?"

"You are sure about what you've told me? You couldn't have misinterpreted what your sister said?"

"She was clear enough. I think she needed someone to talk to about it all. She didn't really have many friends here." Her bottom lip quivered.

Ingrid's phone buzzed in her pocket. She took it out and glanced at the screen. It was Ralph Mills.

"I'm OK—you should take it," Alex told her.

"I won't be long." Ingrid turned away to answer the call. "Ralph." She got to her feet and headed toward the exit. "What have you got?"

"We've picked up Professor Younger."

41

Ingrid waited in the embassy limousine. She decided it was better if the driver was the one holding up the sign that said 'Greg Brewster.' She saw them approach, Brewster on the phone, and realized her palms were moist. First, the driver opened the trunk and placed Brewster's bag in the back, and then he opened one of the rear doors. Brewster ducked his head inside.

"You?"

"Good flight?" Ingrid gave him a smile, certain the ten-mile journey into central London was going to feel more like a hundred.

Brewster's podgy face reddened with fury. "I will have to call you back." He sat down beside her, carefully placed a laptop case between his feet, and the driver pulled away. "Is this a trap?"

Had he already been in contact with the concierge?

"Well, sort of."

He looked puzzled. "I don't understand."

Ingrid explained her theory that someone would attempt to complete the job by trying to get hold of his passwords on his return trip to London. She then told him of the appointments she had arranged with the concierge.

"But I have appointments of my own," he blustered.

"I appreciate that, sir, but when I put this plan into action, you were already in the air and uncontactable." She breathed in deeply, sending pain spiraling round her torso. "I was hoping we could use this journey to work out which of the appointments you would be able to keep. I will then, posing as your assistant, shake the tree a little and see who falls out."

"Shake the tree?"

"Let it be known where you'll be at what time, and then I'm going to watch you like a goddamn hawk and see who turns up."

The driver navigated the limousine through the parking lot barriers and, once in the open, the rain hammered down on the roof.

"My bet is at some point on this trip you're going to be asked to set up a password to use the Wi-Fi, or asked to authorize a card payment, or to access the gym in the hotel—" she glanced at his corpulent belly as he stared out the window: Greg Brewster was not a user of hotel gyms "—and one of the people doing the asking is going to use the information you give them to de-encrypt your laptop."

Brewster said nothing. Instead he breathed so heavily it sounded like light snoring. "Are you saying that you are actually trying to investigate the theft?"

Ingrid pursed her lips. "Of course I'm investigating it. Why wouldn't I investigate?"

He turned to her. "Because no other fucker in the past few years has bothered."

On the remainder of their journey into the center of London, they went through Brewster's appointments for the rest of the day. A visit to the Iranian embassy. A private meeting at the Reform Club with a representative of the Malawian army. An opening night at an art gallery, where he hoped to meet a member of the Kazakh government. It was a snapshot of how central the UK capital was to the international arms trade. Ingrid got on the phone and, posing as Brewster's secretary, started to give the tree a shake. When she had finished, Brewster turned to her.

"There is, of course, one major problem with your plan."

Just the one?

"With those bruises on your face, you're a little, well…" He struggled to find the right words. "The thing is, no one is going to believe you're my secretary. There is no way anyone in my industry would let you come to work like that—" He leaned forward and tapped the glass screen separating them from the driver. "This isn't the right way. I'm staying at the St Pancras."

The driver nodded.

"Then you can't leave at this junction. It's straight ahead."

The driver turned south.

"You need to turn back." Brewster was agitated. He looked at Ingrid for an explanation. "Where are we going?"

Ingrid met the driver's gaze in the rearview mirror. His eyes were smiling. "Heavy traffic on Marylebone Road," the driver said. "Taking a detour."

Ingrid knew the area well—they weren't far from her own hotel—and she could see the driver was taking them on a very long detour. He accelerated, moving them quickly south down Edgware Road.

"What's going on?" Brewster demanded.

The driver said nothing.

"Answer me!"

The car came to a halt at a set of traffic lights. "Sorry." The driver turned round. "There's been some kind of incident. I need to take you the long way round."

"What sort of incident?" Ingrid asked.

The driver shrugged. "Think a truck has tipped over. Whole road's blocked. Probably take another ten minutes."

The road ahead hadn't looked blocked. The traffic hadn't been grinding to a halt.

The lights changed and the driver carried on south, quickly reaching the Marble Arch oneway system. Ingrid was familiar with the route: it was one of her regular runs into the embassy. When the driver didn't turn left onto Oxford Street, she got suspicious. She hadn't checked him out. She'd just assumed the embassy had approved him. She swallowed hard. Her skin shivered. They had just spent the entire journey laying out their plan. Shit. She hadn't even considered the driver might be the one to try to get the password. She got out her phone surreptitiously, ready to call the police and report a kidnapping, when the limousine turned sharply off Park Lane and into the back streets of Mayfair. They passed the Shelbournes' hotel at speed then swung right into the street running along the rear entrance of the embassy. The barriers lifted and the car descended urgently into the embassy's underground parking lot.

Brewster turned to Ingrid. "What the hell?"

She didn't know what to tell him.

The car screeched to a stop and the rear doors of the limousine were yanked open. Sol Franklin bent down and introduced himself.

"Sidney Joseph Baxter, you are in the US Embassy. That means you are officially on American soil, and as a federal officer I am arresting you on suspicion of selling privileged information given to you by the Department of Defense. Will you please step out of the car?"

Brewster didn't know what to do. Behind Sol was a Marine. An armed Marine.

"Sir," Sol said, "please step out of the car."

Dumbfounded, Ingrid turned to see that Amy Louden was holding open the door on her side. "Do you want to come with me, Ingrid? I think we need to have a little chat."

42

Deputy Louden took Ingrid straight to her office, asking her assistant to make sure they weren't disturbed. Louden gestured to a couch facing a coffee table and indicated Ingrid take a seat.

"So much for 'desk duties,' eh?" Louden said.

Ingrid eased herself onto the couch. She still had no idea what was going on. "Am I in trouble?"

Louden sat on the couch opposite. "Good grief, no! Gosh, you've not been thinking that the whole way up here, have you?"

"You said we needed to talk privately."

"Well, I'm sorry you got that impression." Louden smoothed down her skirt. "I thought you deserved a proper explanation."

Ingrid was disoriented at the turn of events and chose careful silence instead of the nervous small talk she often ended up spewing in situations like these.

"Yesterday, when we were sitting in this office, you said you'd found out Greg Brewster was an alias for Sidney Baxter. You also said you had been informed this wasn't the first time Brewster's property had been stolen." Louden paused. "I'm sorry, I didn't offer you a drink, did I? Would you like a coffee?"

"No, thank you."

"I need to ask you how you found out that Brewster and Baxter were the same person."

Ingrid held her gaze and snapped her brain out of the disbelief she was experiencing to come up with an answer. When she remembered, she felt a stone fall from her throat to her stomach. "I cannot tell you that."

Louden stiffened. "Why not?"

Ingrid thought about the anonymous call in Grosvenor Square, five minutes after Marshall had instructed her to leave the office. "I received that information from an anonymous informer."

Louden's chest heaved as she inhaled sharply. "I see. Do you mean anonymous to you? Or is that you are not prepared to reveal their identity?"

Ingrid scratched her forearms, a nervous tic. "Anonymous to me. Why are you asking me this?"

Louden stretched her fingers, then curled them into fists. "That is rather delicate, I'm afraid. If your source was anonymous, what reasons did you have for thinking he or she was a credible source of information?"

Ingrid looked down at her hands, trying to avoid Louden's scrutiny. She had to keep Marshall's name out of the conversation. She couldn't recall any other time he had put himself out for her, and their relationship was on shaky ground at the moment. Revealing his role had the potential to... well, she wasn't prepared to consider the consequences. Ingrid ran through what she was about to say in her head and, reckoning it stacked up, gave her response. "I'd put out a few feelers, asked around for background—"

"From who?"

"Oh, um." Ingrid's train of thought had been interrupted. "Contacts in the Met, here in the building, associates elsewhere in the Bureau." Damn. She'd said too much.

Louden looked at her intensely. "And then what happened?"

"My phone rang. Out of the blue. It was a short conversation." Ingrid's discomfort was mounting. She couldn't just sit there and take the inquisition. "You told me I haven't done anything wrong, which I appreciate, but I would like to know what is going on."

Louden paced over to the window. "You will have gathered,

from what Sol said when he arrested Baxter, he is believed to have sold defense secrets."

Ingrid had indeed worked out that much.

"It is suspected"—Louden adjusted the wooden slats of the window shade—"one of the intermediaries he used was…"

Yes? Ingrid willed her to tell her.

"And this is completely confidential."

"Yes."

"Never to be repeated outside this room."

"Of course."

"Dennis Mulroony." Louden turned to check Ingrid's reaction.

Ingrid felt a little dizzy. "My predecessor?"

"Which makes sense of why I was getting pressure from above to keep asking you about the Brewster case."

Ingrid's thoughts spiraled. It also explained the hostility Ingrid had gotten from other agents and CIA officers since her move to London. "And you thought, what, that I was… what? Going to take Mulroony's place?"

"There was a possibility Baxter would have tried to recruit you—"

"He wouldn't have stood a chance."

Louden almost laughed. "I think we know that now, Ingrid. You've been here for four months, maybe five, and we're all getting to understand your tenacity and dedication. You're gaining a lot of fans here, Ingrid, both among the London police and your colleagues at the embassy."

Ingrid wasn't used to flattery. "Thank you."

"I suppose it was a test of your loyalty." Louden perched herself on the arm of the couch Ingrid was sitting on. "Am I right in thinking your mother is a Russian national?"

Ingrid blinked: she had not been expecting that. "My mother is a US citizen. She defected from the Soviet Union in 1976."

Louden nodded. "I've read your personnel file, Ingrid. After she competed at the Montreal Olympics, am I right?"

"Yes." What the hell was going on?

"And I can see nothing in your career that would explain the

scrutiny you've been under since you arrived in London."
Louden grimaced slightly. "Mulroony's behavior got everyone
nervous about double agents."

Ingrid felt a fire burn in her chest. "And because my mom
grew up in Russia—"

"I think it's more likely to do with the fact that you speak
Russian, fluently, I believe."

Ingrid had joined the FBI as a languages expert. French,
Italian and Russian. She was too mad to speak any of them right
at that moment.

"I mention it as something to keep in mind. You probably
haven't had this sort of… oversight… before. But now that you're
working overseas… Well, I wanted to give you a heads-up."

"What? That I've been earmarked as a potential traitor?"
Ingrid needed to rein in her fury.

Louden got to her feet. "I didn't mean to upset you."

Ingrid wasn't upset, she was angry.

"I may be completely wrong, but I sense that someone, somewhere, was setting a trap for you with this Brewster thing."
Louden walked over to the door. "And I wanted to alert you to
that fact."

Louden opened the door. The meeting was suddenly over.
Ingrid wriggled forward and pushed herself painfully to standing. "Thank you, ma'am."

"For the record," Louden said as Ingrid approached, "I think
you're a real asset to the team here. I'm sorry the actions of your
predecessor have impacted on you in this way."

"Thank you."

"And your behavior with Brewster… Baxter this afternoon
has been exemplary. I'll be letting that be known."

"Thank you again."

"But"—Louden stopped Ingrid as she was leaving—"I will
have to report something about ignoring doctors' orders. Desk
duties, remember?"

"Yes, ma'am."

"Please," Louden said, holding out her hand, "call me Amy."

When Ingrid got back to her office, she was relieved Jennifer wasn't around. She needed to process what she'd just heard. Her predecessor, of whom almost all records had been destroyed, was some kind of double agent? And her bosses way up the food chain, higher than Louden, had potentially set a deliberate trap for her? She felt blindsided, hollowed out, stunned. Her head slumped into her hands.

"Hey there!" Jen was as bright and breezy as ever. "Looked what I picked up for you."

Wearily, Ingrid lifted her head to see Jen deposit a copy of the lunchtime edition of the *Evening News* on her desk.

"Thought you'd like to see it."

Ingrid stared at the headline. It was something to do with a delay to a new underground line being built. "I don't get it," she said to Jen. "What am I missing?"

Jen put down her take-out coffee and donut and pointed to a strap line printed above the newspaper's masthead. 'College scandal: prize-winning professor arrested. Turn to Page 5'. "That's your investigation, isn't it?"

Ingrid turned to page five, eager to see what Angela Tate had written. She scanned it quickly. It didn't even mention Stuart Younger by name. It said nothing about Lauren Shelbourne. It was all about his close relationship with a drug dealer who was referred to as 'a Dutch national now in custody.' Ingrid checked again. There was no mention of his experiments either. And certainly no mention of Lauren's phone being used within a fifty-meter radius of his house? What was Tate playing at?

"Damn."

"You need help?" Jen asked, now beavering away at her desk.

"No. Thank you."

If Younger's arrest was in the papers, she really had to speak to the Shelbournes. They shouldn't be getting their updates from the *Evening News*.

"Well, actually, maybe," Ingrid said. "Could you get me the number for the hotel the Shelbournes are staying at?"

"I have it right here."

Jen was efficient, but that was ridiculous. "How come?"

"Sol asked me for it a couple of hours ago. Said he wanted to update them on the investigation."

"Oh." Ingrid knew it should have been her to make the call, but she was grateful—and a little embarrassed—that Sol had stepped up.

"Still need it?"

"I guess not."

However, there was still someone else who needed an update: Madison Faber. Ingrid guessed the girl would know by now Timo Klaason was in custody and not likely to walk free for several years. But now that Younger was being questioned, Ingrid thought Faber might feel free to say more about the egotistical professor. Ingrid dialed her number. Voicemail.

"Hello, Madison, Ingrid Skyberg here from the embassy. Just checking up on you. Am assuming you've heard the news that Stuart Younger has been arrested, but as far as I know, he is only being questioned in relation to the distribution of methamphetamine, not Lauren. If I hear any more, I'll let you know. In the meantime, you have my number if you have any questions." Ingrid ended the call and instantly relaxed. She exhaled loud enough for Jen to check over her shoulder and make sure she was OK. Why had leaving a message for Faber got her so tense? Her body was sending her a message and she needed to pay attention.

Ingrid picked up a pen and flicked it between her fingers. Something had been bothering her about Faber for some time. The girl's focus changed every time they met. First she was worried about Lauren's parents, then about Klaason, then about Stuart Younger. Particularly about Younger. She only had Faber's word that Lauren had been sleeping with the professor, and she only had sixteen-year-old Alex Shelbourne's word that Lauren and Faber were dating the same man. Ingrid had cut Faber a lot of slack—she was a young woman living through a horrific trauma without a support system—but it was definitely time she did a bit of digging on the mercurial Madison Faber. If Ingrid was limited to desk duties, she was going to use her time wisely.

Her initial search for a criminal record for Madison Faber

drew no results: Faber was completely clean. Ingrid then searched the alumni records for the major colleges in the US. Luckily, there was only one Madison Faber of the right age listed. The search returned results for two colleges. The first in upstate New York and the second just outside Boston. Faber had excelled academically, finishing top of her year in both institutions. A disappointingly blemish-free record. Ingrid trawled further back to Faber's school career.

And things got a lot more interesting.

According to the records, from the age of sixteen, Faber was homeschooled. Given both her parents, lawyers with major firms in New York, had hectic work schedules, Ingrid supposed she must have been tutored by someone other than her mother or father. Homeschooling was an unusual choice. Not something she expected. She trawled back a few more years and found out why.

Madison Faber had been forced to leave her private school just a few days after her sixteenth birthday. Three weeks before that she had made a complaint about a member of the faculty that led to the teacher's dismissal. She made a note to find out exactly what became of him after she'd finished looking into Faber's past. According to a teenage Madison Faber, her chemistry teacher, a young man fresh out of college himself, had kept her late after school one day, trapping her in the lab technician's room—the only room with a lock on its door—and sexually assaulted her. As soon as she reported the assault, he was suspended from duties awaiting criminal investigation. He was never reinstated even though just a week after Faber made her initial complaint, she withdrew it. Along with the statement she'd given to the NYPD.

Ingrid sat very still, trying hard to shut out the sound of Jen's eighty-word-a-minute typing frenzy.

Ingrid went over the reports again, trying to work out what motivations Faber would have for withdrawing her claim. She had been fifteen when she made the complaint against the teacher, and it was entirely possible the school put pressure on her, eager not to have their otherwise excellent reputation tarnished. But would Faber's parents have allowed that to happen? Another trawl revealed that the chairman of the board of trustees of the exclusive school was none other than Faber's father.

Now Ingrid didn't know what to think. Was Faber an innocent student forced to back down because of school board politics? Or the instigator of a nasty lie that had caught up with her?

43

The next morning, Ingrid lasted till midday before she felt compelled to abandon her desk duties and headed to Loriners. She wanted to test how many of Faber's outrageous claims stacked up to a little investigation. Still not strong enough to handle the bike, she made her way to southeast London on public transport. Her phone rang when she was on a surprisingly packed lunchtime train. It was DC Ralph Mills. Just seeing his name on her phone made her smile.

"Was wondering if I could buy you a drink? Got something you might like to hear."

When she told him she would shortly be in what he called 'his manor,' Mills sounded childishly excited and said he would meet her at the train when it arrived at New Cross. He was holding two paper cups of coffee, a bag of sandwiches from a local shop and a Clark Swanson smile.

"I guessed you took it black?"

She took the cup from him. "You guessed correctly." Eye contact was a little more difficult than it ought to be.

"So what brings you to the hood?" he asked, leading her out of New Cross station and into the sunshine.

"Still have a few loose ends to tie up."

"Relating to?"

There was a chance her plan would do more than ruffle

feathers at Lewisham police station. "Just getting some answers for Lauren Shelbourne's parents." It was bland and opaque, but it was true. She changed the subject. "You made it seem pretty intriguing on the phone," she said. "I didn't realize you were letting me in on state secrets." They came to a pedestrian crossing —for some unfathomable reason the Brits called them 'pelican crossings'—and she pressed the button that started a countdown to the traffic lights changing color.

Mills took a sip of coffee and licked his lips. "The boss has given me the OK, but you have to understand she's sticking her neck out for you."

"Tell Natasha I appreciate it."

"She reckoned she owed you a favor, not letting go of the whole Shelbourne thing."

The lights changed and they crossed the road.

"Where are you headed?" he asked.

"Loriners."

"I know a shortcut."

He led her down a side street where once grand houses looked ashamed of the mattresses and broken appliances littering their front yards. Even in broad daylight it was menacing.

"So. What was it you wanted to tell me?"

"I'm an idiot," he said. "I haven't asked you how you are."

"I'm healing. Ralph, what is it you need to say?"

He raised his eyebrows. "Right. Yes. Remember the Canadian student who died at Loriners week before last?"

"Of course."

"It's taken a while, because suicides aren't high priority, but we got her blood tests back."

Ingrid stopped herself from taking a sip of coffee. "And?"

"High levels of methamphetamine and LSD."

"Really?" Somehow it wasn't much of a surprise. "What does that mean for Younger?"

He guided her through a back alley running behind several neglected backyards. It was the kind of shortcut only a cop or a drug dealer would know about.

"He's still in custody. We get seventy-two hours before we have to charge or release him."

"And what are you going to charge him with?"

Ralph chucked his empty coffee cup onto an aluminum trash can overflowing with food waste. "Assisting an offender."

"I don't get it."

"For assisting Timo Klaason's attempt to leave the country."

"Come on! You've got to be able to pin more on him than that?"

"We can, and we will. I'm sure. The DI's going gently with him. We still have another forty-eight hours for him to panic and incriminate himself."

They came to the end of the alley and Ingrid recognized where they were. A high brick wall ahead of them marked the perimeter of the college grounds.

"And what has he said about Lauren Shelbourne?" An image of the wound taking a chunk out of the girl's skull flashed through Ingrid's thoughts. "Are you questioning him about her?"

"Ah, yes, there's quite a lot I need to bring you up to speed on. We actually recovered Lauren Shelbourne's phone from Younger's house."

"When the hell were you going to tell me that?" She slapped him on the arm.

"Sorry. It's all been moving pretty quickly." He nodded at a narrow gate in the wall. "See, told you it was quicker." They entered the campus grounds and followed a signed path that led to the main piazza.

"Tell me about the goddamn phone, Ralph."

"Ah, yes, right." He really needed to get out of the habit of stringing out a story like a comedian building up to a punch line. "The phone was discovered by none other than Mrs Younger herself. She found it in Professor Younger's underwear drawer."

Ingrid held fire on her questions to prevent Mills from taking hours to get through his story. She took a sip and let him continue.

"So here she is, dutiful and faithful wife, putting away the laundry, and voilà, she discovers a strange mobile phone nestling amongst his underpants and woolly socks. Odd, she thinks, what's this? She then proceeds to turn the phone on and read all the text messages stored in the memory." They came to a bench that was neither covered in bird mess nor chewing gum. "Shall we?"

"Sure."

They sat down and Ralph handed her a sandwich out of the paper bag. A steady stream of students poured through a gap in the buildings and disappeared into their accommodation blocks. No doubt the poor kids who couldn't afford lunch in the canteen.

"So," he continued, "she's shocked to discover over ninety percent of the texts are *from* her husband. She's even more shocked by the nature of their contents. Once she's got through all of those, she takes a look at the 'sent' folder. In here we have such X-rated missives that they make her husband's texts look positively tame. Understandably, she's getting a tad angry over all of this. Angrier with each new description of what the phone's owner—whose identity, remember, is still unknown to her—has planned for the good professor next time she gets her hands on him. By now Mrs Younger wants to get her hands on him herself, but we're talking X-rated horror movie, not soft porn."

He paused for breath, but Ingrid thought it wise not to interrupt and ate her sandwich. BLT. Good choice.

"Then things get even worse. Mrs Y reads texts that mention her in a less than flattering light. How fantastic her husband's and his mystery lover's lives will be when he dumps his nagging wife and runs away into the sunset—I'm paraphrasing—with said lover." He stopped again and picked a slice of tomato out of his sandwich and threw it onto the patch lawn. Pigeons descended on it within seconds. "That's the final straw. Next thing, she's marching out to the two uniformed officers sitting in the squad car parked outside—I wish I'd been there—telling them she's ready to answer any questions they might have concerning her husband, and offering to provide an exhaustive list of the places the professor might be. And this was all playing out just about the same time we'd pinned down the location of the phone."

He paused again and Ingrid took her chance to interject. "Yet it still took a couple of hours for you to pick Younger up."

He lifted his eyebrows.

"I'm yanking your chain."

"Right." His face gradually broke into a smile.

"So there's no doubt Younger was having an affair with Shelbourne. You've got so much proof now, he can't deny it." Madison Faber's lurid allegations had been proved right. Just because she was excitable, it didn't mean the girl was wrong. She really didn't know what to make of Faber's reliability as a witness.

Ralph nodded.

"So are you talking to him about Lauren's death? Do those texts give him motive to get her... out of the way? What's he got to say for himself?"

Ralph rapidly swallowed a mouthful. "Nothing at all. Not a murmur."

"Even his connection to Timo Klaason?"

"His prints are all over the money we found in Klaason's possession. Klaason has confirmed Younger gave him the cash. But still Younger won't say anything. His lawyer's a hot shot from a firm in the city, and he's advising the professor to keep quiet."

"And you haven't charged Younger with anything yet?"

"Like I say, we've still got plenty of hours on the clock before we have to do that."

"And what might you be able to charge him with?"

"Assisting an offender. Definitely perversion of the course of justice. It'd be hard for him to get off that one."

"But nothing to do with Lauren's death? Or the drugs used in his experiments?"

"We've got him on the line and we're reeling him in. Be patient with us. We're using his phone data and diary to piece together his movements the night Lauren died. DNA samples from her flat will almost certainly confirm his presence there, but that won't be a surprise—he must have visited her there loads of times—so wouldn't necessarily be helpful with implicating him in killing her."

"But you think he might have?"

"He's an arrogant twat, so I'd put nothing past him, but…"

"Yes?" Ingrid was electrified at the prospect of nailing the bastard.

"There's nothing in the texts he exchanged with Lauren that suggested their relationship was on the rocks."

That was true. The phone could just as easily exonerate him. Ingrid thought about things for a second. "He explained how come he had Lauren's phone?"

"Nope."

Ingrid wanted desperately to be in on the interrogation. "Is DI McKittrick doing the interviews herself?"

"Yep—I'm her number two." He looked at his watch. "I should get back over there. Our next crack at him starts in fifteen minutes." He drummed his fingers on his knees.

"Well, thanks for the update. And lunch."

He stood up. "I almost forgot. Your predecessor's main liaison in the Met?"

Ingrid looked up at him. Now wasn't the time to tell him it didn't really matter anymore. "You have a name for me?"

"Not exactly." He screwed up his face. "McKittrick told me to tell you your predecessor's primary contact was a high-ranking officer in SO15—Counter Terrorism Command. She couldn't get his name. For reasons of national security, apparently. You want a hand up?"

She didn't, but accepted his offer, wincing as she got to her feet. "Thanks so much. Hope it didn't get you into any trouble."

He gave her a Clark Swanson special. "I hope so too."

"Say thank you to Natasha for me," she called after him.

"Will do."

She turned toward a gap between buildings that she hoped would lead her to the administration block. Out of the sunshine, the spring air was cool. The atmosphere on campus was febrile, with students and staff hurrying between buildings as they gossiped. Ingrid found the administration block and was given a map marking out where she would find the buildings used by the medical faculty. A few minutes after that, she was outside the lecture theater she was looking for. She was about to let herself in when her phone buzzed in her pocket. It was Ralph again.

"Hi." She spoke quietly, keen not to disturb the students on the other side of the door.

"Hi." He was a little out of breath. "You'll never guess who was in reception when I got back to the station."

She could.

"Madison."

No surprise there.

"She wants to give us a statement. She's claiming Stuart Younger confessed to killing Lauren Shelbourne."

44

"When?" Ingrid asked, her voice rising several decibels.

"She says he came to her two days ago."

"Why the hell did she wait two days?"

"Listen, I don't know. I have to go. I thought you'd want the heads-up."

Mills hung up, leaving Ingrid stunned. She leaned against the wall; the lecturer's drone permeated through the door. She was more than willing to believe the sly Professor Younger was involved in Lauren's death, but somehow Faber's allegation undermined that belief. The revelation that she had withdrawn the accusation of assault against her teacher made Ingrid doubt every word that came out of Faber's mouth. She could no longer put her erratic behavior down to recent trauma.

The doors to the lecture theater swung open and students filed out, chatting excitedly, talking over one another, as if they'd just been released from a silent order of monks. Or more accurately, nuns. Almost all of the people emerging from the hall were women. A few moments later she saw the person she'd been waiting for and hurried toward him before he was lost in the stream of bodies.

"Mohammed!"

The medical student pulled up sharply and quickly turned his head left then right.

"Mo," she said again when she was just a few feet away.

"Hello. Man!" He reared away from her. "What did you do to your face?"

"It's OK—it's not as bad as it looks."

"I never expected to see you again. I thought you wouldn't want to get anywhere near this place after what's happened. You'd be better off getting your PhD somewhere else."

"Ah… yes. About that." She explained who she was and apologized for the earlier deception.

"You're kidding me. FBI? No way, man."

She pulled out her badge. He snatched it from her and inspected it closely, front and reverse, only reluctantly handing it back to her when she wrapped her fingers around it.

"Are you here because of Younger? Did you suspect him all that time?"

"I can't discuss the details of the police investigation."

"I won't say a word. Honest."

Ingrid told Mohammed the bare minimum to get the result she needed. Ten minutes later she was climbing the stairs of a small accommodation block just around the corner from campus.

"Jamil probably won't want to talk—you'll have to use your best interrogation techniques to get him to open up. He hardly even told me what happened to him. And we've been mates since, like… infants. We go way back." He stopped at a door halfway along a corridor on the third floor and thumped his fist against it. "Jamil! It's me, man. I know you're in there."

They listened for noises inside the room. There weren't any.

"Jay! Come on! I got a hot lady out here desperate to speak to you." He glanced sideways at Ingrid and smiled at her with one corner of his mouth. "No offense—any means necessary—you get me?"

"Piss off," a muffled voice called from the other side of the door. "I'm busy."

"Seriously, man. She ain't gonna take no for an answer."

"Jamil?" Ingrid raised her voice. "I'm Special Agent Ingrid Skyberg. I work out of the US Embassy here in London."

The noisy metal rattle of a lock unfastening was followed by the creak of the door. A sliver of face appeared and a single eyeball inspected first Ingrid, then Mohammed. "Ouch! Who mashed your face?" Jamil said, opening the door wide.

Ingrid followed him into a dark study-cum-bedroom, a podlike bathroom right next to the door, a narrow single bed along one long wall, a desk against the other, drapes drawn shut at the window. The room stank of toasted cheese and adolescent sweat. Two laptops sat on the desk, glowing in the dark.

"Jamil here is a regular Mark Zuckerberg. He makes apps in his spare time. He's an entrepreneur, innit." Mohammed pulled out the chair so that it stood in the narrow space between the bed and the desk. "How about some light in this dungeon, yeah?" He opened the drapes and bright sunshine came streaming in. Jamil held up a hand to shield his eyes.

"And maybe some fresh air too?" Ingrid suggested.

Mohammed pushed open the window a crack while Jamil threw a cover over his unmade bed. He and Mohammed sat down. Ingrid smiled at them both. "Mo tells me you took part in the psychology department research program last semester."

Jamil glared at his friend.

"It's all right, bro. Nothing can happen to you now, can it?"

Ingrid showed him her badge. "Anything you tell me will be treated in the strictest confidence."

Jamil stared at the badge with wide eyes. "Why are the FBI interested in what I've got to say?"

"It's in connection with an ongoing investigation. I can't share the details, I'm afraid."

"But I signed a nondisclosure agreement—I don't want to get sued."

"Jamil's loaded," Mohammed said. "He's been stashing away millions, innit. He thinks I don't know."

"A nondisclosure agreement signed under duress wouldn't stand up in court." Ingrid kept her voice as gentle as she could. "Trust me."

"Yanks know everything about all that legal stuff, suing and that—they practically invented it," Mohammed offered. Ingrid wished he'd shut up.

"I'm curious—why did you sign up for the experiment in the first place?"

Mohammed started to answer for his friend, but quickly stopped when Ingrid held up an admonishing finger.

"The researcher was really nice to me. Girls normally just ignore me. Or take the piss. She was different." He sighed. "And gorgeous. She said she'd selected me specially. Because I wasn't like the other students. She told me I would be part of something really important. It was an exclusive group, she said." His head dropped into his hands. "I can't believe I fell for it."

"Who was this?" Ingrid pictured one of Younger's acolytes dressed in her green and purple shirt, ingratiating herself. Preying on a vulnerable student.

"Her name's Madison Faber. She's American."

Faber? Ingrid took a deep breath, her mouth suddenly dry. She moistened her lips with her tongue.

"You know her, don't you?" Jamil said, reading Ingrid's face. He was trembling, a faint tremor making his upper body vibrate.

"You're sure it was Madison Faber who enrolled you in the program?" Ingrid asked.

Jamil nodded. "She told me she was running a side project of her own. She made me…" He stopped himself.

"It's OK—take as long as you need."

"There was this one experiment where I had to… *hurt* somebody." He blinked rapidly, as if he were reliving the event in his head. "There was this machine. It electrocuted people. I actually heard them scream in the next room. But Madison said it was OK —the pain only lasted a fraction of a second. She said it was important for me to carry on. To put the person in the other room out of my mind." His breath caught in his throat.

"I'm not in a hurry, Jamil."

The experiment he was describing wasn't new to Ingrid. Anyone studying psychology 101 would have heard of the Milgram Experiment. And most of them would know it was no longer carried out due to ethical concerns. Faber would have known it too.

"How could I put them out of my mind when I actually had to speak to them? I had to ask them questions. If they got the answer wrong… that's when I flipped a switch on this big machine. They were wired up to it. They got a shock if they didn't know the answer." He shuddered. "I had to stop. I told Madison I couldn't go on. She got really angry. She told me I was putting her project in jeopardy. Then she said if I was so concerned about the person in the next room, maybe I'd like to take their place. I'd be connected to the machine, and she'd ask the questions." He swallowed another wet gulp.

"You're certain it was Madison who was running the experiment? Not Professor Younger?"

"She told me Younger was in overall charge. She carried out other experiments for Younger. I'm not sure exactly what they were. I didn't ask. I didn't want to know."

"Can you tell me what happened next?"

He started gnawing at one of his fingernails.

"You're doing really well. What you're telling me is really helping my investigation."

Jamil looked at his friend, who urged him on, nodding encouragingly. "I said I'd report her to the college authorities. Tell them about her twisted experiment."

Ingrid nodded. "And how did Madison react to that?"

"She went mental. Told me I didn't understand anything. Called me a moron. She said no one would listen to a loser like me." He shook his head. "Maybe I was a moron—to actually believe she liked me in the first place."

"Did she say anything else?"

"She threatened me." He shivered more violently. Mohammed jumped up and closed the window. "She said she'd get the guardians to come and speak to me, see if I might change my mind about ratting on her then."

"The guardians?"

"It's a private group in the psychology department."

"Private army more like," Mohammed added. "You spoke to

me about them in the cafeteria when I first met you. I said I didn't know what you were talking about. You remember? The blokes in the polo shirts? You don't see the shirts anymore, but the guardians are still around. I steer well clear of them."

"Me too," Jamil said. "And Madison. Every time I see her, I get the shits. I ran right into her after my tutorial last week. She threatened me again."

"Man, I'm sorry," Mohammed said, "you should have told me. I didn't realize it was that bad. Is that why you've been locked up in here since Thursday?"

Jamil nodded. "After I saw her, I came straight back. Been living on pot noodle ever since."

No wonder the room smelled. Ingrid had heard enough and she didn't want to make Jamil relive any more of his pain. "Jamil, you've been incredibly helpful. I really appreciate it." She handed him a card. "You should know, the experiment you took part in? I've seen it before, and you don't need to worry about what you did to the other students."

"You didn't hear them scream."

"Really—it's OK. You weren't torturing anyone. You were the *subject* of the experiment. Madison Faber was testing just how far she could push you. And from what you've told me, that wasn't very far at all. You've done nothing wrong."

"You're sure?"

"Absolutely." She offered him her hand. "Thank you, Jamil. You too, Mo."

Ingrid got to her feet. Mohammed did the same. "I'll walk you down to the street."

"It's OK, I can find my way." Ingrid opened the door and stopped just outside the room. She turned back. Something Jamil had told her wasn't right. "You said you've been holed up in here since last week?"

The student nodded at her. "Since Thursday."

"Last Thursday, that's when you ran into Madison? You're certain?"

"Why wouldn't I be?"

Ingrid smiled at him. "No reason. Don't worry about it.

Thanks again." She closed the door quickly and hurried in the direction of the exit.

What was Madison Faber doing at Loriners on Thursday when she'd told Ingrid on Wednesday morning that she was too terrified to set foot back on campus?

45

Ingrid stood on the street for over ten minutes waiting for a black London cab with its light on to drive past. She told the driver to take her to Lewisham police station. With any luck, she could get there while Madison Faber was still giving her statement.

Her phone rang. It wasn't a number she recognized.

"Ingrid Skyberg."

"Miss Skyberg, is that you?" A polite, male voice.

"Speaking."

"This is John Taylor." He paused. "Emily's father."

Ingrid's brain trawled through its databases, trying to place him.

"You came to our house in Lewes the other day."

Ah! "Yes, yes of course. How is Emily?"

"She's much better, thank you for asking. My wife and I are just bringing her back to Loriners College, so I think that's a good sign."

"That's excellent news. I'm so pleased to hear that." Ingrid still had no idea why he was calling.

"She said she would like to talk to you." There was some chatter in the background. "Now, if you're free."

Ingrid asked the driver to turn around and take her back toward Loriners. Emily had rented a room in an apartment in a street identical to the one Ralph had walked her down earlier in the day. The buildings were large, five-story houses with bay fronts and would once have been respectable family homes. But in recent decades, they had been bought up and divided by landlords seeking to exploit the transient student market. Ingrid wasn't able to stop herself from thinking that, if Emily had been living somewhere a bit nicer, she might not have found herself standing on a window ledge contemplating suicide.

John Taylor opened the door before Ingrid got a chance to knock. "That didn't take long."

"I was in the neighborhood."

He showed her into a tattered kitchen at the rear of the house. Cabinet doors were hanging off their hinges; dirty dishes were stacked in the sink. Ingrid remembered the nice, well-maintained house she had visited in Lewes with its clipped yew hedge. Coming back to such a student dive would be hard on Emily's fragile psychology.

The girl smiled when Ingrid walked into the room. "Hi," she said. "I'm Emily."

Ingrid noticed a tattoo of an infinity symbol on the girl's wrist as they shook hands. "Ingrid, nice to meet you."

"Would you like a cuppa?" she asked.

Ingrid looked at the counter, imagined the dirt in the cups and the Legionnaires' in the pipes and declined. Emily's father hovered in the doorway, just as he had done in Lewes.

"We're OK, Dad," Emily said.

"Right, yes. I'll bring some more things in from the car."

Ingrid joined Emily at a small square dining table that wobbled. "Sorry about the state of things. Mum's gone to the supermarket to buy a year's supply of cleaning products."

Ingrid smiled nervously.

"I know, we still have to use them."

"Perhaps your mom will draw up a cleaning roster for everyone too?" Ingrid reached out a hand toward Emily, stopping short of touching her. "How are you doing?"

Emily's eye twitched. "Good, I think. The worst bit was the drugs. I feel like they're out of my system now, so almost back to normal, really."

"And," Ingrid lowered her voice, "have you spoken to a therapist or a counselor?"

"Nah. I would never have tried anything like that if it hadn't been for the drugs. That's why I wanted to talk to you, and also kind of why I came back."

Ingrid waited for her to explain.

"I read that Younger's in prison—"

"Not yet. He's been arrested, but they haven't charged him yet."

"So he's in police custody, is that what they call it?"

"Yes, that's right."

"So he hasn't actually been found guilty of anything yet?"

"No, that would require a judge and a court case." Ingrid was amazed at how naïve the girl was about criminal proceedings. It was one of the hallmarks of a middle-class upbringing where no one she knew had ever been in trouble with the police. "But it seems very likely that he will be charged, and he will serve time. Do you think you know something pertinent to his case?"

The girl nodded and gave her a brief, weak smile. "I'm not sure where to start."

"How about I ask some questions, and we'll see where we get to? Why don't you start by telling me how you got involved in Professor Younger's research program?"

Emily shook her head.

"You don't need to worry. He can't hurt you anymore."

Emily Taylor frowned. "Why would he want to hurt me?"

Ingrid was confused. "I assumed you felt able to speak to me now because he's not around."

"No! It's the opposite of that. You have to tell the police they've made a mistake. I don't suppose they'll listen to me; that's why I thought you could help. They've probably labeled me as unstable or unreliable. Or just mad. I want you to tell the police that Stuart's not a bad man. He shouldn't go to prison. You have to believe that."

Ingrid pressed her palms against her thighs. "He systematically gave drugs to students, Emily. It was part of how he controlled everyone."

"No." She tapped the table firmly for emphasis. "I went into it with my eyes open. I knew exactly what was involved. So did everyone else. Look, I'm interested in the brain, right? It's what I want to specialize in. Psychology is all part of the same whole. Being involved that closely with live experiments was a fantastic opportunity for me. It's why I chose Loriners in the first place. There are better colleges in London to study medicine. But none of them has a psychology department that even gets close to Stuart's."

Emily was yet another student with a crush on the handsome professor. Which made her testimony dubious at best, useless at worst. "So tell me about the experiments."

Emily craned her head close to Ingrid's. "It's the drugs you're really interested in, isn't it? That's the important thing as far as the investigation is concerned, isn't it?"

"It's almost certainly what he'll be charged with."

"Then you need to understand the drugs were why I was taking part. They produce transformative results. Ground-breaking."

"You took drugs voluntarily?"

"Of course I did. Did you think they were forced down my throat?"

Ingrid rubbed her chin. "How were they administered?"

"I swallowed them with a glass of water. How else? No one forced me to do anything. I knew what I was doing." Emily's eyes were bright and alert. "I can't be sure whether I was given real drugs or a placebo—these were proper robust trials—but I certainly felt the effects. The whole experiment was carefully designed and properly monitored. I didn't leave the lab for four hours after I took the pills. I was under observation the whole time."

"So what happened this last time? How did you end up—"

"You want to know how come I was on the top floor of the admin block, dangling out of the window?"

Ingrid nodded.

"I'm not sure. I don't understand what happened, and I've been trying to analyze it myself. Maybe the purity of the drugs was different. Maybe it was a new batch. Or I was given the wrong dose."

"Is that possible? That something could go that wrong?"

The girl shrugged. "With Lauren not around to double-check everything? Sure. I nearly didn't continue in the program after she died. I thought it would be disrespectful to her somehow. But then if I hadn't, it would have messed up all the results."

"Who was supposed to be watching you?"

"They were short-staffed. Stuart popped in at regular intervals to make sure I was OK."

"Did he give you the drugs himself?"

"No, it was another of the researchers."

"And was there a staff shortage the week before? When the other student jumped from the same window? Could she have been administered the wrong dose?"

"I spoke to Lauren about that right after it happened. Jessica—the Canadian student—was taking a placebo. It couldn't have been the drugs that made her jump."

"She had high levels of LSD in her system."

"What?"

"According to the blood tests the police carried out."

"She couldn't have. She was definitely taking a sugar pill."

"Not before she died she wasn't."

"That doesn't make any sense. That means someone switched her from the control group to the active group without letting Lauren know. Who would do something like that?"

Ingrid took a moment to figure things out. "Is it possible someone was deliberately trying to meddle with the experiment?"

"It's possible, I guess."

"Is it possible you were previously on the placebo, but your dose was also switched last week?"

Emily covered her mouth with her hand. "I guess."

Ingrid felt she was getting somewhere. "Do you remember which researchers gave you the drugs the last time?"

She nodded. "Yeah. I don't know her name, but I'd seen her

around the lab now and then. I got the impression she was more senior than the other researchers. She certainly acted that way."

"Can you describe her?"

"Oh, you'd be able to track her down if you need to speak to her, I'm sure. She was the only other American in the program."

46

Ingrid left Emily Taylor and called Natasha McKittrick. When she got her voicemail, she called Ralph Mills and left a message for him too. She thought about calling Madison Faber on the pretense she was concerned for her welfare, but the girl was smart, she was manipulative, and Ingrid wasn't convinced she could keep her ulterior motive out of the tone of her voice.

If Madison was at Lewisham police station, Ingrid was willing to risk that at some point while she was in the neighborhood, she would pay a visit to her apartment, so that was where she headed. Ingrid wanted to see her face when she confronted her.

The street Madison Faber's apartment was on felt like genteel suburbia compared to the house share Emily Taylor had rented. The cars parked in the street were newer and larger, and the front gardens were tended and abundant. Either Faber was taking on a lot of debt to get her master's, or her parents were footing a size-able bill.

Ingrid looked up at Madison's apartment from the sidewalk. The shades were open, but that didn't mean Faber was at home. She rang the bell, one of four buttons on the intercom panel. No answer. She tried all the other buttons.

"Hello?" A woman's voice.

"Hi." Ingrid leaned into the intercom. "I'm from the American embassy. I need to get hold of the girl who lives on the top floor."

"Sorry, haven't seen her."

The woman disconnected. Ingrid buzzed again.

"Hello."

"I'm so sorry to disturb you, but I think she might be in trouble."

The crackle on the intercom ceased, and Ingrid was ready to turn.

"Who did you say you were?"

"Ingrid Skyberg. US Embassy."

The locked clicked and Ingrid pushed the door open. Ahead of her was a neatly decorated hallway, a table on the right-hand side with mail in piles, a staircase straight ahead. A door on her left opened and a middle-aged white woman in pajamas and a heavy cardigan stood in the doorway.

"I'm sorry, did I wake you?"

The woman smiled. "I work from home."

Ingrid smiled at her. "Thanks for letting me in. So you haven't seen Madison?"

"No, I don't really know her. Only know her name from the post." She didn't open the door further.

"When was the last time you saw her?"

She shrugged. "I'd have to think. Day before yesterday maybe. When you work from home, the days sort of merge. Why are the embassy interested in her?"

"We think she might be in some difficulty."

"Is it to do with what's going on at the university?"

Ingrid dodged answering directly. "It may be adding to her stress. Have you ever seen her come home with anyone?"

"What kind of trouble?" the woman asked. "Should we be taking precautions?"

"I think she's in danger more than she's in trouble, which is why I want to trace her." Ingrid reached into her pocket and pulled out a business card. "If you do see her, would you please give me a call? No matter what time of day."

The woman looked at the card. "You work for the FBI? Really?"

Ingrid smiled apologetically. "Yup, there's a bunch of us in most embassies around the world."

"So she's committed a crime?"

Ingrid didn't reply.

"Is she dangerous? I've got a kid."

"Mostly I'd say she was a danger to herself. The moment you see her, please call me."

The neighbor looked at the card again. "OK. You need me to do anything else?"

"You don't have the number for a local taxi company, do you?"

The woman nodded to the table where the mail was. "You'll probably find a flyer amongst that lot."

Ingrid leaned against the wall separating the front yard from the sidewalk and called herself a taxi. It would be a ten-minute wait. She tried calling Ralph Mills again. This time his phone didn't go straight to voicemail, but rang and rang until she got the automated message. Neither he nor McKittrick had returned her calls. She left another message for Natasha, saying she had spoken to credible witnesses and that she had concerns Faber had deliberately sabotaged Younger's experiment.

When her phone rang, she was disappointed to see it was an embassy number.

"Ingrid Skyberg."

"It's Sol."

Ingrid ran her fingers through her short hair. "Hi, Sol."

"I notice you're not at your desk." His voice rasped with forty years of cigarette addiction.

"Ah. About that."

"Where are you?"

"Outside Madison Faber's apartment."

"Who's she?"

Ingrid was taken aback. She had been so consumed by Faber and her erratic behavior over the past few days it seemed impossible that Sol wouldn't know who she was. "The girl who found Lauren Shelbourne's body."

"And why are you there?"

That wasn't an easy thing to explain. "I'm helping the Met."

He said nothing.

"But I'm taking it easy. No motorcycle. In fact, I'm waiting for a taxi. Is there a reason you're checking up on me?"

"It's called pastoral care, Ingrid. Just checking you hadn't jumped off another building or a moving vehicle."

"All limbs still in working order."

"Also."

Ingrid knew that hadn't been why he was calling.

"The Met have been in touch. Concerned there may have been a security breach. Counter Terrorism Command. Starting to ring any bells?"

Ingrid's blood turned to ice. "Is this to do with Mulroony?"

"You tell me."

Ingrid closed her eyes, silently hoping she hadn't got McKittrick or Mills into trouble. "I was only hoping to speak to his Met handler. I never even got a name."

Sol inhaled audibly. "Do yourself a favor, agent, when it comes to your predecessor, ditch your tenacity, lose your curiosity and discover a blind eye that will stand you in good stead. You hear me?"

"Do I get to ask why?"

"It's better if you don't."

Neither of them said anything for several moments.

"My taxi's here." It was a lie, but she hung up anyway, too annoyed to talk anymore to her boss. She scrolled for Mills number, but stopped herself from calling him. Leaving three messages might just send the wrong signal, even if all three were genuinely about work. She was, she reminded herself, engaged, and that came with certain obligations she intended to honor.

The taxi came and took her toward Hampstead. She wanted to speak to the family friend Faber was staying with. Perhaps she could shed more light on the young woman's mental stability. Her phone illuminated in her lap with a text. It was from Mills.

Sorry. Not ignoring you. Been flat out. Big news. Stuart Younger has been charged with Lauren Shelbourne's murder. He was remanded in custody about an hour ago.

Ingrid dropped the phone onto the seat and gazed out the window. She didn't know how to feel. A tiny bit proud that she had been the one who hadn't let it lie? Pleased the smug smile would have been wiped off Younger's face? Desperately sad a young woman's life had been ended not by misadventure, but by force? Her head fell against the window and she watched the traffic.

If Younger had been charged, that meant Natasha and the Crown Prosecution Service felt there was sufficient evidence. They wouldn't just be taking Faber's word for it. Maybe he had even confessed.

Damn.

There was somewhere else she needed to be.

"Excuse me," she said to the driver. "Can you take me to the Ixion Hotel in Mayfair?"

He looked at her in the rearview mirror. "It'll be extra."

"Whatever."

Somebody had to tell the Shelbournes their daughter had been murdered.

47

Ingrid walked slowly back to the embassy. Lisa Shelbourne had screamed when she'd told her. Alex had remained perfectly still apart from the tears rolling down her cheeks. Anthony Shelbourne had paced like a caged animal. Ingrid absorbed as much of their pain as she could, but she had to put up a barrier. Their grief, their anger, added to her own about the friend she had lost. She didn't know what had happened to Megan after her abduction, but every crime scene, every murder report she read, Ingrid could never quite stop herself from imagining her friend was the victim. She made her apologies and her excuses and left them to their anguish and heartbreak.

By the time she got back to her desk, most of the civilian staff had gone home. A few other agents were still working, but the place had a weekend feel. She closed her office door and signed in to the computer network, pulled up a browser and logged in to her personal Skype account. An icon told her Marshall was online. But that wasn't whom she had arranged to call. She tapped in the details, and her call was answered almost immediately, and the Skype window was filled with the surprisingly healthy features of an ex-schoolteacher from Washington Heights.

"Hello, Mr. Timms," she said.

A beat later the tanned face beamed back at her. "Agent Skyberg, please, call me Kevin."

The years had been kinder to Kevin Timms than she had been expecting. After being forced out of his chosen profession by the false claims of a fifteen-year-old Madison Faber, his reputation ruined, Ingrid had supposed the man would have turned to drink or drugs. According to the records, Timms had moved to Mexico shortly after leaving the school and hadn't returned to the US. She'd only managed to trace him by searching social media sites.

"OK," he said, "you have to put me out of my misery. My mind has been racing since you first contacted me. What does the FBI want with a simple man eking out an honest existence south of the border? I'm assuming you don't want to haul my ass back to the US, else you wouldn't have gotten in touch first." He smiled at her again and leaned back in his seat. Behind him, through the glass of patio doors, Ingrid spotted a generously proportioned swimming pool, two very tanned children playing noiselessly. It seemed Kevin Timms had done very well for himself in the last seven years.

"Don't worry, sir—you're quite safe."

"Good, because I've no intention of *ever* coming back." He picked up a tall glass of yellow liquid, an umbrella sticking out the top, and lifted it toward the webcam of his laptop. "Giving up teaching was the best thing that could have happened to me." He took a sip of his juice. At least she assumed it was juice. It was just after lunch in Lake Chapala.

"That's why I'm calling. I'd like to talk to you about Madison Faber."

He put down his glass with a clunk. "Why, what has she done now, murdered somebody?"

Ingrid's heart missed a beat, but she ignored the remark. "I wondered whether you could go over the details of—"

He cut her off. "Do you know, I thank that twisted bitch every single day of my life. If it weren't for her, I'd probably still be teaching."

"I've read the report of what happened, but I was hoping you'd be able to fill in the blanks for me."

"I'd really rather not relive that time in my life," he said. And then spent the next ten minutes doing exactly that.

When he reached the part of his story Ingrid hadn't heard before, she stopped him. "Wait a minute, are you saying Madison Faber was stalking you?"

"She was always waiting for me after school. At my house on the weekend. Dressed like a whore, might I add. Then, when I'd made it clear I wasn't interested, she turned on me. Twisting reality so that suddenly it was me stalking her day and night. Harassing her any chance I got. Until finally I supposedly attacked her one afternoon in the chemistry lab."

"She withdrew all her claims."

"Too late for my career. Still, as I say, I've never looked back. I make more now in a month than I did in a year." He waved a paperback book at the webcam. "Romantic fiction. Quite ironic, don't you think? I can churn out one of these every two months. More than covers my extravagant lifestyle."

"Do you know why she withdrew her story?"

"Not for certain. Though if you put a gun to my head, I'd guess the school leaned on her. And her family."

Though the image of his face on her screen had started to break up a little, Ingrid couldn't mistake the change in his expression. Gone were the toothy grin and raised eyebrows, replaced by a thin-lipped scowl and furrowed brow. A few moments later he snapped himself out of whatever reverie had come over him, and he clapped his hands together. "So, what do you need from me, Agent? A character reference for Miss Faber? A report on the standard of her high school chemistry?"

"I think you've given me enough information for now, thank you."

"You're kidding me. I've only just gotten started." He lifted his glass. "You still haven't told me what she's done to come to the attention of the FBI. Must be some serious shit. *Did* she murder somebody?"

Ingrid glanced away from the screen, aware someone was

standing at the threshold of the office. "Mr Timms, I'm sorry, but I have to go." She thanked him again and turned to the woman in her doorway. "Hi."

"Hi. I'm Christine. I work with the counterespionage group."

"Hi, yes, come in."

Christine, a robust-looking woman in her thirties with a formidable power suit, strode toward her with a piece of paper in her hand. "I've taken a couple of calls for you today."

"That's weird."

"I know, I think there's a divert on the system, so I couldn't put this through to you." She placed the paper on Ingrid's desk. "This man was quite insistent you call him back."

Ingrid looked down at the name. Julian Granger. "Who is he?"

"An arrogant asshole is all I can tell you."

"Well, thanks for bringing it to me."

Christine called out a 'you're welcome' on her way out.

Ingrid picked up her phone and dialed.

"Julian Granger." The man was upper class. He sounded like he was in a BBC adaptation of a Le Carré thriller.

"Ingrid Skyberg. I understand you wanted me to call."

"Ah, yes, Miss Skyberg, where have you been?"

Christine's description of him was so far wholly accurate.

"I only just got your message."

"Hmmm."

"Mr Granger? Why are we speaking?"

"I am Stuart Younger's solicitor. He is asking to see you."

"What?"

"In fact, he is insisting."

48

Early the following morning, Ingrid got off the Triumph, pleased her body had healed well enough to handle being on two wheels again, and walked up the steps of Lewisham police station. With any luck she could have a quick word with McKittrick before visiting Stuart Younger in the cells. She unzipped her motorcycle jacket and realized she had got a smudge of engine oil on the pants leg of her shabby suit. She really did have to buy some new clothes.

"Miss Skyberg?"

"Yes?"

"Julian Granger." She had already guessed as much. He looked as upper class as he sounded with a double-breasted pinstripe suit and a perfect triangle of a silk pocket square poking out of his suit jacket. It was almost impossible to tell his age, as his outfit was so old-fashioned, but she'd hazard he was early thirties. His gold watch rattled as they shook hands. "I hope you don't mind, but I've taken the liberty of signing you in. If you would come this way."

A uniformed officer led them into a stairwell and took them down two flights. So much for getting the latest from McKittrick.

"He's being transferred to Thameside later," Granger said.

"What's Thameside?" Ingrid asked.

"A category B prison. I'm very grateful you came. The professor is convinced you can help."

Ingrid gripped the chin guard of her helmet as they trotted quickly downwards. "What has he been charged with?"

"You don't know?"

"I want to hear it from you."

The constable opened a door that led into a waiting area. "Desk sergeant will sort you out," he said before leaving.

An aroma of stale body odor mingled with the more subtle scent of disinfectant and overcooked food. They were now underground in the bowels of the Victorian building, and there were no windows and no phone signal. The tile floor beneath their feet gleamed only in patches: decades of shuffling footsteps had scuffed and scraped the surface so badly that no amount of polishing could fix it.

"Mr Granger," the sergeant said from behind a counter, "I see you have company this morning."

Granger made the introductions and Ingrid signed a succession of forms the sergeant put in front of her. Once the paperwork was out of the way, the sergeant gestured for Ingrid to follow him.

"What about you?" she said to Granger.

"He wants to speak to you alone."

At the end of a long corridor lined with cells, Ingrid was shown into a visitor room, where she was patted down by a female constable. "I need to take that." She nodded to the helmet. "You could knock him out with that."

Ingrid handed it over and opened her shoulder bag for inspection. Satisfied she was free of offensive weapons, the constable told Ingrid to take a seat. "We'll bring him out in a minute."

Ingrid sat on an orange plastic chair on one side of a wooden table that was covered in graffiti and scratched messages. Protestations of innocence, profanities and women's names predominated. She heard footsteps.

Stuart Younger appeared in the doorway, accompanied by an officer.

"I'll be right outside," he said. "Knock when you want to leave."

Younger was dressed in his own clothes, presumably the ones he'd been arrested in, and the pants were grimy, his shirt crumpled and creased. His hair was damp against his scalp. His eyes were puffed and red-rimmed; a slick of sweat covered his forehead. "Thank you so much for agreeing to see me," he said, his hand outstretched as she approached.

Ingrid ignored the hand. She didn't want him to think she was doing him any favors. Younger took his seat and she waited for him to speak.

"She's out to destroy me. You know that, don't you?" Younger leaned in close. "My work, my career, my marriage." The last word snagged in his throat. For a second Ingrid thought he might cry. "It's a tissue of lies. Everything she told the police."

"Take a moment," Ingrid told him. "Breathe slowly. Then back right up and start at the beginning. Do you need a glass of water?"

"No, I'm fine. I just need you to listen to me. The police won't take me seriously."

She wasn't sure she would either.

"I started to tell them about her, how evil she is, but they weren't interested. They insisted on repeating the same questions over and over. Like a stuck record. My solicitor advised me to stay silent. I've provided a written statement about her. But the way things stand, I can't be sure anyone in authority has even read it." He rubbed a hand over his head. "Why are they listening to her?"

Ingrid studied him carefully.

"Why would they believe her and not me?" He clasped his hands together and stared with wild, wide eyes into Ingrid's face.

"If you need me to listen to you, then you have to do what I say." Ingrid spoke very clearly and slowly, as she might to an overexcited child. "Do you understand?"

He nodded, his face pinched.

"Good. Now—tell me who you're talking about."

"It's bloody obvious, isn't it?"

"I need to hear you say the name."

"Madison fucking Faber. Is that clear enough for you?" He squeezed his hands into tight fists and thumped the table.

"Take it easy," Ingrid said.

"For Christ's sake, they've charged me with murder."

"I can get up and leave, anytime. Walk straight out that door and not look back. Give me a reason to keep listening—start from the beginning."

He sat back in his chair and shoved his fists under his arms. "I've got to get out of here."

"Then start talking."

He closed his eyes for a moment then gazed down at the tabletop. "Madison Faber started at Loriners in October last year. She was enrolled on the MSc course. It became clear very quickly she was a gifted student—a sharp, forensic mind, hardworking, energetic. Before the end of the first term, she was working with me and a handful of other postgraduate students in my research program. A program I began five years ago. A program all my previous work has been leading towards." He let out a sarcastic snort. "My life's work." He glanced up at Ingrid.

"Who else was working with you?"

"Shouldn't you be taking notes? Or recording our conversation?" She stared at him until he realized he hadn't earned the right to ask questions. He bit his lip. "It's vital you get the details straight."

"No, it's vital you do. Right now you're shoveling a load of horseshit."

He swallowed hard and looked at his hands. "Everything seemed to be going along swimmingly right up until the middle of the autumn term. Then Faber's attitude changed. She wanted to be given more responsibility in the program. Said she'd like to take a leading role in the planning of experiments, be more hands-on with the subjects."

"What triggered the change?"

"I think she may have been bored. As I said, she's a very bright young woman." He sighed. "Unfortunately for me."

"And you agreed?"

"I got the impression she wanted to compete with Lauren, prove herself smarter, more industrious and so on—a healthy rivalry can lead to greater discoveries. It's happened many times in the history of experimental science. I'm sure I don't need to tell you that. So, yes—I agreed to her request, hoping the other students would up their game."

"And did that happen?"

"After a short while one or two of the others came to me, complaining about the way Madison was behaving. The way she was treating them. Using them as if they were *her* research assistants."

"And was Lauren one of them?"

"I'm forgetting—you never met Lauren. She was the sweetest... She wasn't the complaining type."

"So what did you do about the complaints?"

"I had a quiet word."

"And did Madison modify her behavior?"

"Initially. But she's a clever manipulator. On the surface things seemed to have changed; meanwhile Madison was busy devising other plans. Obviously I had no idea at the time."

Ingrid would have labeled Younger paranoid if she hadn't had so many misgivings about Faber herself.

"Things came to a head in January. Madison wanted to work more and more closely with me. Normally I would have been thrilled to be sharing the work with such a talented student, but... well, I didn't really *like* her. She was brilliant... and enthusiastic, but difficult. Too intense. Too demanding. Of my time. Of my attention."

"Why January?"

He buried his face in his hands and shook his head. "I was so bloody stupid." He pounded a fist on the table. "Stupid, stupid, stupid."

"Did something happen over Christmas?"

He hesitated.

"You have one chance to tell me everything. I'd seize the opportunity if I were you."

"I... Oh God. I... slept with Madison."

49

Ingrid had suspected a liaison ever since Alex Shelbourne's revelation her sister and Faber had fallen out over a man.

"I don't need you to judge me. It was a mistake. One I bitterly regret." He sniffed. "My God, that's an understatement."

"How did it happen?"

He was bewildered by the question. "How do these things usually happen? We got together at the end-of-term Christmas party—you know the sort of thing—too much booze, a letting off of steam... a slow dance." He opened his eyes wide. "Jesus, if I'd known then..."

"How often did you see each other... romantically?"

"We didn't! It was a one-night stand. Instantly regrettable. Quickly forgotten. For me at least. But Madison had other ideas. All over the holidays... she wouldn't leave me alone. Texts, phone calls. Visits to my house."

"Your house? How did you explain that to your wife?"

"Madison's clever. She made sure to come round when she knew my wife would be out. Which means she must have been watching the house. I mean... watching the house, for God's sake."

"What did she do?"

"She'd bang on the door, scream at me through the letterbox

until I let her in. She said she just wanted to talk. She was interested in my mind, she said. But the number of phone calls increased. She started calling me in the middle of the night. I told Claire the phone calls were from marketing companies. Claire threatened to answer my phone herself, give the marketers a mouthful. It was a constant struggle to get to it in time. I couldn't risk my wife speaking to her." He ran a hand over his face. "In the end I agreed to meet with Madison—to spend some time with her on New Year's Eve—it was the only way I could think to get her to stop… harassing me."

Ingrid despised him. An arrogant man in a position of power over young women thousands of miles from family and friends. A bit of her admired Madison for standing up to him. "What did you say to her?"

"I explained I couldn't see her again. I mean, sleep with her. I told her I wouldn't betray my wife. She seemed to accept it. She was very mature about it, in fact. She even apologized for the calls and visits. I was so relieved." He rubbed his eyes. "Unfortunately the relief was short-lived. When the new term started, she kept her promise to leave me alone. But went too far the other way—she was positively hostile towards me." Younger sounded rehearsed. "Her treatment of the other students in the program deteriorated, generating more complaints than before. The only way to deal with it was to let her work alone. She devised her own experiments and executed them quite separately from the rest of the group."

"But in a way the situation was resolved? She'd stopped harassing you."

"It was resolved temporarily. As I said before, things came to a head in January. It all… it all got out of control."

"What did?"

"I take full responsibility. I should never have let it happen. I'm weak. I know I am. There's absolutely no excuse." He looked down at his hands resting on the table. "In the middle of January —the twelfth, to be precise—I started seeing Lauren."

"Seeing her?"

"Do you need me to spell it out?"

"It was a sexual relationship?"

"Of course it bloody well was!"

He was a pitiful sight. A once mighty alpha male slayed by his own libido.

"No one knew," Younger said. "We were very discreet, Lauren and I. Such a sweet, sweet girl. I fell for her. I hated myself, yet could do nothing to stop it. I still love my wife."

Ingrid made no comment.

"I know what you're thinking. I know how pathetic I must sound… I'm not going to blame a midlife crisis. There was something very special about Lauren." He sighed. "Oh God, if I'd known… Somehow Madison found out about us. I don't know how, Lauren swore she never told her. Madison probably spied on Lauren, going through her mail, her text messages. Who knows what else? I wouldn't put anything past her."

"What did Madison do?"

"That's the incredible thing. I would have expected her to go straight to the college registrar—report me for gross misconduct. Or worse—tell Claire about it. But she did nothing. Absolutely nothing. Nothing to me. She let rip with Lauren though. They had a huge row. Madison started throwing things, breaking Lauren's stuff. Lauren had to move out of the apartment in a hurry. It was obvious Madison wasn't going to leave. I'm not even sure Lauren managed to pack all her things before she left."

Something was nagging at Ingrid, some fact that didn't fit. "So that was it?" Ingrid pushed back her chair, indicating she would leave if he didn't come up with something that resembled actual facts and believable evidence.

"Far from it. She was just biding her time. She visited my house—actually had tea with my wife. Chatted with her as if she were an old friend. Claire said she practically had to throw her out. But Madison never breathed a word about my relationship with Lauren. She was planning something though. It's amazing how clear hindsight is. I realize now that annoying little things that were happening then must have been her doing."

"Such as?"

"Items of clothing going missing. Expensive things: a silk tie, a cashmere sweater, some kid leather gloves. I still don't know what she's done with them. Maybe she has something else planned." He blinked rapidly as if he were imagining what that something might be.

"When did those things go missing?"

"I don't know for certain."

Ingrid was getting fed up. "When was the last time you saw Faber?"

"She…" He gulped and stared into space for a moment. "I still find it almost impossible to believe."

The constable opened the door and looked at them both. "You need anything?"

Ingrid eyeballed him. "No. Thanks."

Alone again, Younger continued. "Madison Faber is evil. She's trying to frame me. You have to trust me. I have nowhere else to turn."

"The last time you saw her?" Ingrid prompted.

"She arrived at the lab long after all the other students had gone and… Madison tried to *seduce* me. Right there in the lab. What was going through her mind? I told her in no uncertain terms that I wasn't interested in her, not then, not ever." He stood up. "God—especially not then. Maybe she thought she'd strike while I was vulnerable. While I was still grieving."

"Wait." Ingrid got to her feet. "Grieving? When was this?"

"Just a day after Lauren's death."

Ingrid had seen her that day. The girl was still numb from discovering the body. They had walked across the campus—it had been the morning the whore graffiti had appeared—they had drunk coffee. The girl had seemed detached, but not deranged.

"She said that now that Lauren was dead, there was no reason we couldn't be together."

Ingrid planted her elbows on the table and interlocked her fingers. She stared hard at Younger.

"What she actually said was 'Now that Lauren is out of the way.'" His eyes bored into hers. "You have to believe me, I've got no proof, but I've gone back over that night again and again, and there was something in the way she said 'out of the way'…" His words trailed off.

Ingrid rested her chin on her hands, bringing her head closer to Younger's. "Are you saying Faber killed Lauren?"

A tear fell from his left eye. "I'm convinced of it."

50

Ingrid asked the desk sergeant to phone Detective Inspector McKittrick for her. When the call was connected, he handed over the receiver.

"Natasha, hi, it's me."

"This is Detective Inspector McKittrick's office." It was a young woman's voice.

Oh. "Can I speak to Natasha? This is Special Agent Ingrid Skyberg from the US Embassy."

"The inspector is in a meeting right now."

Damn. "Is Ralph Mills around?"

"One moment."

Ingrid rested her head on the counter while she waited.

"He's in the same meeting. Can I take a message?"

"Please ask DI McKittrick to call me urgently. It's to do with the Shelbourne case. I may have more evidence."

Ingrid grabbed her helmet and ran up the stairs to ground level to get a phone signal. She reached reception and dialed McKittrick's cell and left a message. While she was speaking, her phone bleeped with an incoming call. She didn't even check the number before answering.

"Hi."

"Is that Ingrid Skyberg?" The woman's voice was tentative.

"Speaking."

"This is Gail Mooney, Madison Faber's neighbor."

"Yes, hi."

"You wanted to know if she showed up. Well, she's here. Just bolted up the stairs."

Ingrid ran her fingers through her hair. She wasn't expecting that. "Great. Right. Thank you for calling."

"You want me to give her a message?"

Ingrid thought for a second. "No, probably best not to."

Ingrid looked at the doorway she knew led toward McKittrick's incident room. She considered making a run for it. Slipping past the reception staff and tracking her down, yanking her out of her meeting and... and what? She had no evidence Faber killed Lauren. McKittrick had interviewed the girl herself. As she said, Faber was found covered in Lauren's blood but had been eliminated from the investigation. The neighbor had confirmed her arrival at the apartment at eight in the morning, hours after the time of death. Ingrid couldn't tell an inspector in the Metropolitan Police, even if she was a friend, that she had let the killer go without giving her some proof.

Ingrid pushed on the door and stepped into the bright spring sunshine. She texted Mills as she walked. *Are you with Natasha? I really need to speak to her about Lauren Shelbourne.* Ingrid unlocked her bike, pulled on her helmet and kicked the Triumph into life.

Ingrid didn't know if Faber had killed Lauren, but she thought it was entirely plausible she had used Lauren's death to put Younger in the frame for murder. She didn't know if Faber was capable of smashing Lauren's head against a coffee table, but she was convinced she was more than able to persuade her former roommate to take a cocktail of drugs that contributed to her death.

She accelerated through the streets of south London, fairly sure she could find her way to Faber's apartment without checking the route. Her phone rang and she tapped the Bluetooth headset attached to her helmet to take the call.

"What's so bloody urgent?" McKittrick's voice.

Ingrid needed to concentrate on the traffic. "Hi. I've just spoken to Younger. He asked to see me."

"Uh-huh."

"Do you think he did it?"

McKittrick sighed. "That's why we charged him. You know how it works." She sounded fed up.

"Listen, I've been doing some background checks into Faber. You know she has a history of making allegations against her teachers?"

McKittrick said something to someone, her hand over her phone. "I've got about two minutes before I need to go back into this meeting. It's a major case review for a multiple homicide."

"Do you think there's any chance Faber was involved in Lauren's death?"

McKittrick came back quickly and emphatically. "No."

Ingrid filtered down a line of cars and came to a junction she didn't recognize.

"We eliminated her from our inquiries. The postmortem report exonerated her. Her story was confirmed by the neighbor. She didn't get to Shelbourne's apartment until eight hours after the estimated time of death."

"But that doesn't mean she didn't visit the night before, does it? Just because no one saw her the first time doesn't mean she wasn't there. Have you even found a witness confirming Younger was at Lauren's apartment that night?"

"We're still checking the CCTV recordings."

"So you don't have confirmation Younger was there at the time of death either?"

"No. Listen, mate."

Ingrid didn't like the way she said 'mate.'

"I know you like to be all superhero about this stuff, but we do know what we're doing. If you think we've charged Younger on the basis of hearsay, you can fuck off."

"Shit." Ingrid braked hard to avoid a pedestrian stepping out between parked cars.

"What?"

"I know you've got more than that, Natasha, and I appreciate you're very busy, but there's something about Faber that isn't stacking up."

"Ingrid, I like you. I consider you a friend, but you are pushing our friendship to the absolute fucking limit right now." She was in fearsome form. "Yesterday, we carried out a second search of Younger's property. With dogs this time."

"A second search, why?"

"Something that came up in Faber's statement prompted us to check again."

"But you can't trust anything she says. Whatever she's told you—"

"Enough!"

Ingrid was gripping the throttle too hard. She was going way too fast.

"There's some shit you don't know," McKittrick said, fury soaking her words. "At the back of Younger's garden, in the vegetable patch, sniffer dogs found a half-burned cashmere sweater."

Ingrid was listening.

"The burned remains of Younger's sweater was drenched with blood. The case is closed, Ingrid, a slimy predator of vulnerable young women is behind bars, and I really don't need your shit right now."

McKittrick hung up, leaving Ingrid in no doubt how close she'd come to burning their friendship. It took a few blocks for her to calm down, but she eventually got her bearings and found Faber's street. There was no answer from Faber's intercom. She tried the ground-floor apartment.

"You just missed her," Gail Mooney said.

Ingrid slammed her hand against the wall of the house before the locked clicked and Ingrid pushed open the door. Gail Mooney was standing in the open doorway to her apartment. "You might want to come and take a look at this."

She beckoned Ingrid inside and led her into her kitchen at the rear of her flat.

"See that?" She pointed out the window to a large garden. A row of fruit trees lined the edge of an overgrown lawn.

"What am I looking at?"

"The smoke."

Beyond the trees, a narrow plume of smoke curled up into the sky.

"She was out there for about twenty minutes, and then a cab came and took her away."

Gail Mooney unlocked her back door and Ingrid ran down some stone steps, across the lawn and dashed between the fruit trees. In the middle of a neglected vegetable garden was a trash can, flames licking up the sides. Ingrid rushed over to it and peered in. The heat pushed her back. She looked round for a stick.

"I was right to call you, then?" Gail Mooney appeared between the trees in her slippers.

Ingrid pulled out a bamboo cane that might once have supported beans and prodded the fire. The flames leapt higher. Shielding her face, Ingrid looked again. A hunk of smashed metal smoldered, its surface blackened. It took her a moment to realize she was looking at a hard drive.

Ingrid turned to Gail. "Is there a hose here, a pail?"

"I don't know. The garden's not really my thing."

Ingrid pushed past her and ran toward a dilapidated shed. She almost ripped the door off its hinges. She searched for a watering can or a bucket of some kind. She scanned a selection of rusted tools and half-used tins of paint. On the floor she looked for anything she could put the fire out with, any way she could preserve evidence. For some reason her eyes were drawn back to the paint tins. Why am I staring at the goddamn paint?

Sun Dust 2. By Dulux.

Ingrid wheeled round. *Damn you, Faber.* She ran down the side of the house. There had to be a faucet. Or a hose.

She found a brass spigot and used all her strength to turn it.

"I've got this. If it helps."

Gail proffered a washing-up bowl. Ingrid swiped it from her and shoved it under the flow of water. Why wasn't it filling more quickly? Come on! Half full she grabbed it and dashed back to the trash can, trying not to lose too much water. She sloshed it into the can, releasing a geyser of sizzle and steam.

"Can you fill this again?"

Gail ran back to the outdoor tap. Ingrid picked up the bamboo and prodded. Definitely a motherboard. There was no way she could lift anything out without burning the skin off her fingers. She thought she could see bits of broken keyboard. She grabbed her phone and snapped away, hoping a forensics team could confirm it was the make and model of Lauren's laptop. Maybe they'd be able to read the serial number. Gail came back and tipped more water onto the dying flames.

"What's going on?" she asked.

Ingrid scratched her scalp. "You said a taxi took her away. Any idea where she was going? Did you speak to her?"

Gail pulled her cardigan tight around her. "No, but it wasn't the local cab company, if that helps. Had a sticker on the passenger door. Heathrow Transfers."

Ingrid felt the air escape her lungs. She bent over, resting her hands on her knees. "She was heading to the airport?"

51

Ingrid told Gail Mooney to put the fire out and make sure no one touched the trash can. Ingrid ran back through Gail's apartment and out onto the street. She clasped her phone, wondering who to call first.

"Jen, it's me."

"Hi, Ingrid. Where are you?"

There was no time to answer. "I need your help. Madison Faber is booked on a flight out of Heathrow. I need you to find out which airline, which terminal and text me, OK?"

"I'm on it."

"You're a star."

Ingrid switched her phone to Bluetooth settings, pulled on her helmet and sat astride her bike. She dialed McKittrick and got her voicemail yet again. She didn't want to sound like an idiot, and she didn't want to piss off her friend.

"Natasha, it's your favorite FBI agent. I'm sorry about earlier, but I have new information. Madison Faber is leaving the country. Right now." Ingrid worked out what to say next. "I'm at her apartment. She's been burning things, evidence, I believe. You need to speak to her downstairs neighbor. Ground floor. I can't be sure, but I think she's destroyed Lauren Shelbourne's missing laptop." Ingrid turned the key in the ignition. "Also, you know that tissue with the paint on it? Well, I had it analyzed. There's a tin of the exact same paint in Faber's garden shed." She knocked back the stand and kicked the bike into life. "I'm going to Heathrow. I'm going to try to stop her getting on a plane, but, Natasha, that's all I can do. I've got no powers of arrest here. If you want to stop her leaving the country, you're going to have to send someone to the airport."

Ingrid tapped Heathrow into her satnav app, pulled down her visor and roared out into the road.

Faber's taxi had no more than a twenty-minute head start on her, probably more like fifteen minutes. The sort of lead an 800 cc motorcycle could eat up. She was in central London within ten minutes, back on familiar roads. So long as she avoided road-works and accidents, and she didn't get stopped for speeding, Ingrid was confident of beating the taxi.

Ingrid ran through all the ways to detain Faber without the authority to arrest her. Without a request from the Met, she couldn't get the Border Agency to detain her. As an FBI agent, she could make sure she was stopped at immigration in the US, but without an extradition request from the UK, they would have no reason to prevent her from entering her own country. Of course, Ingrid reminded herself, Faber might not be going home. She could be flying anywhere.

Ingrid kept an eye out for any taxi with a Heathrow Transfers logo. It was likely the driver was taking the same route, and it was just possible she would intercept Faber on the road. She didn't know what she would do if that happened.

She desperately wanted to check her phone, she wanted to call Natasha or Ralph and find out what the hell they were going to do, but it was tucked in her pocket, and she needed to keep both hands on the handlebars. She hadn't heard a bleep to tell her Jen had messaged her back either.

The traffic in Earl's Court was glacial. A bus had blocked a box junction, and cars were having to wait for the lights to change several times to get through the intersection. Even on the bike Ingrid had to pick her way through, weaving between stationary cars and irate van drivers, who all thought they had right of way. With any luck, Faber's car was somewhere in the snarl-up.

Ingrid cleared the traffic jam and swerved up onto the Hammersmith Flyover, a raised freeway that carved an elevated path over roundabouts and junctions, easing her way west toward the airport.

It wouldn't be enough to find Faber, she had to somehow stop her from boarding her plane. Persuading the police at the airport was a possibility, but a faint one. By the time she had explained who she was and what she suspected Faber of doing, the girl would be through security. Ingrid had a credit card on her: she had the means to buy a ticket if necessary and follow her through the gates, but her passport was in her hotel safe: there was only so far she could go. What she really needed was for McKittrick to pick up the phone and authorize the airport cops to arrest Faber. But for that to happen, Natasha had to leave her meeting, listen to her messages and take Ingrid seriously. The last of those things, given her tone earlier, seemed the least likely.

There were other options, but almost all of them involved breaking the law whether that was calling in a bomb scare or flying a remote control drone. There was no way Ingrid was going to shut down the entire airport and inconvenience thousands of passengers. If she'd had more warning, there were plenty of things she could have tried. She could have slipped something into Faber's bag, drugs or a weapon; she could have submitted her passport number and requested an intercept. The way she saw things, the only advantage she had was that Faber didn't know she was coming. The girl thought she was free and clear. Younger had been charged, and while the Met congratulated themselves for getting him held on remand, Faber was making her escape. The girl was as smart as Younger claimed.

Ingrid reached the outskirts of the city where the freeway began. From there it was just fifteen minutes to the airport. Her phone rang and she tapped her Bluetooth headset to answer.

"Hi." She accelerated into the fast lane.

"It's me."

"Hi, Jen."

"Sorry it's taken me so long, but there was no record of a Madison Faber booked on a Heathrow departure."

Maybe she planned to buy a ticket at the airport? Ingrid overtook a succession of cars, her speed well over the limit.

"So I thought she might use another name."

"And?" Ingrid was in danger of losing concentration.

"And then I checked the other airports. Ingrid, she's flying from Gatwick."

"Fuck."

"She's booked on a Virgin flight at fourteen forty to Las Vegas."

Booking a Heathrow taxi to take you to Gatwick? That was smart. That was *devious*. It also told Ingrid Faber was deliberately leaving a false trail. She wouldn't put anything beyond Faber, including murdering her roommate. Ingrid peeled off the freeway and took the exit for the M25, an orbital superhighway that encircled London, famous for its traffic jams and backups. But on two wheels it was also a very quick route to Gatwick, London's second airport, about thirty miles south of the city. Ingrid estimated the journey would take her twenty-five minutes, and when she got there, she was taking Madison Faber down.

52

Ingrid ran into the terminal building clutching her helmet. She checked the display boards and headed for the check-in area for Virgin.

She hung back, not wanting Faber to see her. The line of passengers waiting to dump their luggage was at least a hundred people long. Several flights were using the same check-in desks. She scanned the faces. Faber was not there.

Ingrid checked her phone. No messages. It was twelve twenty. An hour since she'd left Gail Mooney's apartment. The chances she had beaten Faber's taxi were extremely low, and in all likelihood the student had already gone through security. Ingrid turned and ran, darting between jet-lagged passengers and precariously stacked luggage carts. A public-address over the loudspeakers informed everyone that, due to unforeseen circumstances, several gates had been closed, and they needed to check the departure boards for accurate information. Ingrid kept running till she saw what she was looking for.

A sales desk. There were three people ahead of her. She didn't need to panic. Faber's flight wouldn't board for another hour. All she had to do was buy a ticket to somewhere in the UK that didn't require a passport, go through security and wait for Faber to arrive at the gate. Easy. She checked the electronic display boards and saw there was a flight to Edinburgh in two hours.

That was good enough. She called Ralph while she waited. She couldn't remember how much she'd already told him.

Damn. Voicemail. *Again.* It was like they saw it was her calling and refused to answer.

"Ralph, hi, it's Ingrid. I'm at Gatwick airport. Madison Faber is getting on a plane to Las Vegas in two hours, and I am going to stop her. I know you all think Stuart Younger killed Lauren Shelbourne, but I'm damn sure Faber is framing him. I think he can prove it, which is why she's leaving the country before you realize what she's done."

The people in front of her turned their heads, making it obvious they were listening in.

"Ralph, I have no powers of arrest. I don't have time to work the diplomatic channels. I need McKittrick to authorize her for detainment. I need you to call the Gatwick police."

She hung up, then texted him. *PLEASE LISTEN TO YOUR MESSAGES.*

Maybe she should have sent a different kind of text. One offering to meet for a drink. He'd probably reply to that.

"Can I help you?"

Ingrid put her helmet on the counter and asked for a seat on the Edinburgh flight. Out of the corner of her eye, she saw two armed police officers carrying MP5 semiautomatic carbines. Airports and government buildings were the only places in the UK where the police were routinely armed.

"Let me see if there's any availability for you." The man behind the desk had long, pointed sideburns, dyed black hair and a spray tan. His bored demeanor betrayed how much he hated his job. His words were polite, but his tone was acidic. "That will be two hundred and thirty-five pounds, please."

Ingrid pulled a bank card out of her jacket pocket and placed it next to the helmet. A few minutes later, the ticket agent placed her card, a receipt and a boarding pass in front of her. She grabbed them and ran straight to the security gates. While other passengers emptied bottles of water or sorted their liquids into plastic bags, she dashed past them. She presented the boarding pass at the electronic barrier and was allowed into the security hall, where a uniformed guard ushered her toward one of ten conveyor belts.

The hall was rammed with vacationers and travelers. Ingrid checked her bag to make sure she didn't have anything that would get picked up by the scanners. The helmet was bound to attract attention, as would the fact she was wearing a leather jacket over her tired business suit. She looked a mess. If they stopped her, she needed an explanation. A friend in need, she would say. A mercy dash. Her embassy ID should cover all eventualities.

The line moved slowly as inept travelers took off their belts and shoes and forgot to take laptops and iPads out of their bags. *Hurry up!* Ingrid had to remind herself it didn't matter: all she had to do was get to the departure gate before Faber. *Don't panic. You've got time.*

One of the other lines appeared to be moving much more quickly, adding to her frustration. She looked at them enviously, and that was when she saw her. Faber. Ingrid turned away, keen that the girl didn't recognize her. Ingrid stooped, hiding her five-foot-ten frame behind a family of Dutch tourists. She didn't want to draw attention to herself, but judiciously peered over their heads. Faber placed her bag in a shallow plastic tray, then took off her jacket and folded it before placing it another tray along with her watch. She then lined up to go through the metal detector.

Ingrid's line shuffled forward and she lost sight of Faber, but when she spotted her again, she saw the student was putting her coat back on and slipping her passport into the right-hand pocket. *That's what I have to do,* Ingrid told herself, *I need to steal her passport.* Without it, she wasn't flying anywhere.

Ten minutes later, Ingrid left the security hall and snaked her way through the endless duty-free area, searching for Faber. She wasn't browsing the perfumes or the whisky; she wasn't looking at discounted electronics. A public-address announcement issued a reminder about the late change to departure gate numbers. Once through into the lounge, Ingrid scoured the seating area. If she was really, really lucky, she would find a seat behind Faber and somehow distract her enough to get access to her jacket pocket. But Faber wasn't in the seats. Ingrid did a three-sixty. There were so many shops, countless food outlets, prayer rooms, restrooms: Faber could be anywhere.

People stared at Ingrid's helmet. It was an unusual thing to see in a departure lounge. She thought about dumping it, about making herself less conspicuous. And then she wondered if she could use it to her advantage. Could she leave it somewhere that would create an incident? Hope someone reported a suspicious item? It still wouldn't be enough to get Faber's flight delayed. She carried on through the departures lounge, hoping to spot her.

Ingrid checked the aisles in WHSmith. She scrutinized passengers at the checkouts in Boots. She studied the diners in Café Rouge, but she couldn't see Faber. *OK*, she told herself. *Back to plan A*. Intercept her at the gate. She scanned the departure board to see if the Las Vegas flight was boarding. It still said 'wait in lounge.' Ingrid searched for a place to wait, somewhere out of the way where she wouldn't be noticed. Her ears tuned in to yet another announcement over the PA system.

"Would passenger Skyberg, that's passenger Ingrid Skyberg, please proceed to gate thirty-nine, where your friend is waiting for you. That's passenger Skyberg…"

Ingrid stopped listening. She hadn't spotted Faber, but evidently the girl had seen her.

53

Ingrid followed the signs to Gate 39 down corridors, travelators, escalators and stairs. It was warm under her leather jacket and she unzipped it as she ran. The crowds thinned. The tannoy announcements faded away. Faber was leading her to the closed departure gates. A 'caution: men at work' A-frame sign kept guard, but there was no sign of maintenance workers.

Ingrid slowed down. She came to a lounge with a central rectangle of seating surrounded by four departure gates. The place was deserted. The LED signs behind the desks were blank. There was no lighting. The Coca-Cola vending machine wasn't humming. A power failure must have caused the airport to close the annex. It suddenly felt like an ambush. Sweat trickled between her shoulder blades, sending a shiver across her skin as it snaked down into her waistband. Ingrid reached into her pants pocket for her phone.

Something moved behind her and she spun round.

There was no one there.

If the power was out, that meant the CCTV cameras weren't recording. There was no surveillance. Ingrid checked the lounge again. It was almost a perfect square with a gate on each side. In front of each set of doors leading to the jet bridges were desks where airline staff would normally check passports. The only exits were the alarmed gate doors out to the empty plane stands, or the corridor she had just run down. Apart from the vending machine and trash cans, the only furniture was several rows of rigid plastic seats forming a neat square. Faber had to be hiding behind one of the desks.

Ingrid gripped the chin guard of her helmet, ready to swing it at Faber's head. "I spoke to Kevin Timms yesterday," she said, her voice surprisingly clear. "You remember Mr Timms, don't you, Madison? Your old chemistry teacher?"

There was no reply.

"He remembers you. Wanted me to thank you on his behalf. Losing his job was the best thing that ever happened to him. That's what he said. He's very successful now. Rich, happy." Ingrid's voice echoed through the empty chamber. If Faber was watching her, she might see her leg was trembling.

"It's remarkable how similar what happened seven years ago is to what's gone on with Stuart Younger. The stalking, the obsession. It's like history repeating itself. I'm sure your friends in the Met will be very interested to hear all about it."

There was a loud whacking sound behind her as a door was yanked open. Ingrid turned in time to see it close. Ingrid ran over, pulled it back open and found herself in a stairwell that led down to the airport apron. The staircase formed a series of descending U-shapes around a central void. The cinder block walls were painted white. The steps were concrete edged with steel protectors. The drop in temperature suggested the door at ground level was open.

It took Ingrid a moment to notice she couldn't hear Faber's footsteps. She turned just as Faber was revealed by the closing door. She smiled before lunging at Ingrid, pushing her against the metal railing. Ingrid yelped as her bruised ribs erupted with pain. She brought up her hand, aiming the helmet at Faber's head, but she wasn't quick enough and Faber ducked.

Madison pushed Ingrid again, sending spikes of agony through her body. Faber, sensing Ingrid's weakness, grabbed the helmet from Ingrid's grasp, lifted her arm and took a swing at Ingrid's head. Ingrid curled out of the way, and the helmet flew out of Faber's hand and clattered down the stairs. Ingrid reared up, leading with her elbow, and pushed Faber back against the wall.

"Is that your plan, Madison? You think if you silence me, you'll get away with it?" Their faces were inches away from each other. Ingrid kept her forearm against Faber's neck, pinning her against the cold wall. "You think you've been so clever, don't you?"

Faber maintained eye contact as she stamped down hard on Ingrid's toes, making her recoil before leaning in harder and pressing Faber against the wall. Faber spat in her face, but Ingrid barely blinked.

"You're not going to beat me, Madison." Ingrid stared into the girl's livid eyes. "This is going to end one of two ways." Faber relaxed and attempted to slide down, out of Ingrid's grasp, but she wasn't fast enough. "The thing you don't realize is the Metropolitan Police have found Lauren Shelbourne's laptop."

Faber's eyes widened.

"You shouldn't have left that fire unattended, Madison."

Faber's lip snarled.

"And really, if you were as smart as everyone thinks you are, you'd have added that can of yellow paint to the bonfire."

Was there a slight tensing of Faber's upper body? Was Ingrid starting to get to her?

"I'll take it one stage at a time." Ingrid paused, quickly checking Faber's impassive expression. "After all, I wouldn't want to misrepresent what happened."

"You don't know what you're talking about."

"So you are talking to me, then?"

Faber bared her teeth, and Ingrid jabbed her forearm a little harder against the girl's throat.

"Because I wouldn't want you to think I'm not impressed, Madison. Before you spend the rest of your life in prison, it's important I acknowledge how special you are."

Faber scowled.

"I mean, really, you've been so clever it's a shame you haven't gotten away with it. First, when you call the cops and tell them you've found your roommate in a pool of blood, you make damn sure you get into a fight with one of them so you get arrested. And that means the police scrutinize your story even harder than they might otherwise. But that's just what you wanted, wasn't it? That way, when they release you, you're completely exonerated. They'll never suspect you again. Why would they? Lauren was your friend. They could see for themselves how devastated you were by her death."

Faber wriggled under the force of Ingrid's restraint. "You saw it too, agent." Faber managed a smile that released a rush of anger in Ingrid's chest. Heat radiated up into her throat and face. She kept her forearm pressed against Faber's neck. Her other hand, still gripping the phone, pushed into her stomach.

"The police released you, accepting you arrived at Lauren's apartment for the first time at eight twenty a.m., the morning *after* she died. So now you're free. And clear. So you pay Professor Younger a visit. You offer him a shoulder to cry on in his time of need. You suggest that with Lauren dead, the two of you can be together."

Another flicker of reaction. Faint, but unmistakable. Distant engine noises roared up the stairwell.

"But Younger rejects you again. Again, Madison. You've removed the main obstacle between you, but he tells you where to go. And that is unforgivable. So you move to phase two of the plan. And for this you need someone on your side. Someone, perhaps, whose job it is to support US citizens in the UK. And how lucky for you this person also lost someone. What great leverage that gave you. And what an easy mark I was. Your years of studying psychology really paid off, didn't they?"

Faber raised her eyebrows, a smile faintly playing across her lips.

"Oh, you should feel smug. I went all out for Younger. Like he was public enemy number one. Choose between an American citizen in fear for her life and an arrogant, egotistical English college professor with dubious morals? It was no contest. I almost admire your cunning and inventiveness."

"My inventiveness? You're the one making the whole thing up."

"I'm congratulating you, Faber. Can't you at least congratulate me on finally working it all out?"

Faber looked right and left, but no one was coming to her rescue. "An imagination like yours is wasted at the FBI. Aren't you trained to deal in cold, hard facts?" She balled her right hand and slammed a fist into Ingrid's ribs, inflicting enough pain for Ingrid to loosen her stance. Faber wriggled free and headed for the stairs. Ingrid took a second to suck down as deep a breath as she could manage and gave chase, taking the steps three at a time. Faber reached a half-landing and pulled a fire extinguisher off the wall. It was heavier than she was expecting, and instead of aiming it at Ingrid's head, she swung it at her shins, sending her toppling downward. Ingrid's tight grip on her phone meant she couldn't break her fall properly, and she let out a yelp of pain before clambering onto all fours. She looked up at Faber. She held the fire extinguisher in both hands and brought it down hard. Ingrid rolled out of the way, making Faber lose her balance. Men's voices drifted in from outside. Maintenance workers most likely. Ground crew.

"Is that what you did to Lauren?" Ingrid was breathing hard; her entire torso was circled with pain. She forced herself to stand upright. "Did she put up a struggle too?" Ingrid lunged at Faber, holding her against the banister with her body weight, arching Faber's back over the handrail. A fall from this height was either life-changing or life-ending. "You know what always bothered me about your testimony?" Ingrid said. Her chest rose and fell with each painful breath. "It took me a while to work it out. Can you guess what it was?"

A flicker of something flitted across Faber's face. Fear or curiosity?

"You told the police you had a key to Lauren's new apartment. But why would she give you a key? She loathed you by then." Ingrid shifted her weight, pushing Faber further over the handrail. "So either you got it from Stuart Younger when you were planting her phone in his house and stealing his sweater or, much more likely, is you took it the night before. Lauren was high because you'd made sure she hadn't received the placebo. I can imagine you saying to people at college, 'Don't worry, I'll make sure she gets home OK.' And then when you're alone, something happens. Either she trips and falls, or she says something about Younger, something that makes you flip, and you shove her so hard she falls. She hits her head. She loses consciousness."

The fight went out of Faber's body. She slackened. Softened. But Ingrid held firm.

"Instead of calling the EMTs, you start planning. You wait until you're sure she's dead. You take her key. You take her phone. Her laptop. Maybe you thought you'd make it look like a robbery. Am I close, Madison?"

Faber arched her back, then brought her head forward sharply, slamming her skull into Ingrid's cheek, sending her backwards. She slipped free of Ingrid's grasp and turned on her, pushing her against the banister and bending her over the rail. Ingrid winced as it dug into her rib cage. Faber pressed her advantage. Ingrid knew Faber's only hope was to silence her and get on her flight. No one would find Ingrid's body until the annex was reopened, and by then Faber would be in the air. Ingrid stared at the concrete floor two flights down: it was plenty high enough for a fatal fall.

Faber brought up her knee. The force of the blow pressed Ingrid harder into the metal and finally ejected the phone from her hand. Ingrid watched it fall through the air and clatter to the ground below. She released the breath that had stalled in her throat, emitting a deep, guttural cry. Madison relaxed her grip and Ingrid turned painfully. Faber picked up the fire extinguisher and swung it up toward Ingrid's head. Ingrid leaned out of its path, but her momentum took her over the top, and she tumbled into the void. She reached out and managed to grab the banister with one hand, then the other, as her legs dangled below. Faber raised the fire extinguisher and brought it down hard with both hands, aiming for Ingrid's fingers.

Ingrid tucked her knees and dropped down. She aimed her feet onto the handrail below, turned and jumped again, this time reaching out for the handrail opposite. With every ounce of strength she had left, she repeated the move: tuck, drop, grab until she hit the concrete floor, rolling on impact to disperse the force. *Five years of parkour.*

Faber's footsteps echoed as she ran upward, toward the exit, toward escape. The door opened and slammed shut.

Ingrid picked up her phone. "Please tell me," she said between breaths, "you heard all that?"

Was that cheering on the other end of the line?

"The airport team have instructions to arrest," McKittrick said. "Nice work."

Ingrid stared up at the steps and took a deep, weary breath. She swiped her dented helmet from the floor and began climbing, one agonizing step at a time. Ingrid reached the top and yanked open the door into the departure lounge. Three uniformed airport police officers, two holding MK5s, had surrounded Faber. The other placed her in hand restraints.

"You do not have to say anything," he said, "but it may harm your defense if you do not mention when questioned something you later rely on in court. Anything you do say may be given in evidence."

Ingrid caught Faber's eye and the girl smiled at her. "This isn't over."

Ingrid slumped against the wall. She wanted to answer back. She wanted to tell Faber it was indeed over, that the game was up and to see the smile permanently wiped off her face. But she wasn't worth it. She could let the kid have the last word: after all, nothing Faber said now would make any difference.

The cops led Faber away. She yelled something about her father. About how they didn't know who they were dealing with. She shouted that Inspector McKittrick would explain everything. Ingrid stopped listening. She collapsed onto a plastic seat and let her head fall into her hands. As the tension left her body, she felt sobs rise up from her chest.

Her tears weren't for Lauren or the Shelbournes. They never were. She was crying for Megan and for her fourteen-year-old self, who had never given up the search for answers. Every time she figured out a new case, it was a painful reminder she was no closer to solving the one crime that really mattered. But she would, she told herself.

"One day," she said out loud. "I promise."

In KILL PLAN, the next book in the series, Ingrid is on the trail of a serial killer. Trouble is, he's also hunting her.

Available in paperback and ebook.

KILL PLAN

AN INGRID SKYBERG THRILLER BOOK 2

A banker is found dead at his desk in the City of London. Then a heavily tattooed body washes up in the Thames. Now someone is after Ingrid.

At first these crimes seem unrelated, but they are all the work of an audacious serial killer working on both sides of the Atlantic.

Special Agent Ingrid Skyberg, the FBI's criminal investigator in London, is one of the toughest agents ever to come out of Quantico. She's resilient, resourceful and a bit of a renegade, but she's never been tested like this before. With no help from her colleagues at the US embassy, Ingrid is running out of time to unmask the killer before he strikes again. But to do that, she's got to stay alive.

Available in paperback and ebook.

GET AN EXCLUSIVE SKYBERG NOVELLA

Want to read more about Ingrid Skyberg? For FREE? Join Eva's mailing list at evahudson.com and receive RUN GIRL, a novella featuring Ingrid Skyberg's first assignment in London for free. You'll also get be kept up-to-date when new books in the series are released.

Visit evahudson.com

THE INGRID SKYBERG THRILLERS

Run Girl - Prequel (A novella)

Secretary of State Jayne Whitticker is in the middle of delicate negotiations when her favorite grandchild disappears from Paris.

Special Agent Ingrid Skyberg is hauled out of her FBI training session at Scotland Yard to head the hunt for the eighteen-year-old girl, who the FBI believe is now in London. Will she succeed in her unexpected mission? Or will her failure lead to the collapse of the crucial peace talks?

FREE to download when you join Eva's mailing list.

Fresh Doubt - Book One

A story of lies, secrets and deadly mind games.

Two hours ago, brilliant American psychology student Madison Faber found her roommate lying in a pool of blood. Now she is in police custody and suspected of murder. Madison persuades Special Agent Ingrid Skyberg to find the real killer, but the investigation soon puts Ingrid in danger. Can she unmask the murderer before she becomes a victim herself?

Kill Plan - Book Two

An American trader is poisoned in his office in the City of London. Two days later, a Latvian immigrant is discovered floating face down in the River Thames. These seemingly unrelated crimes are the work of an audacious serial killer working on both sides of the Atlantic.

When Special Agent Ingrid Skyberg starts putting the pieces together, she also puts herself in the firing line.

Deep Hurt - Book Three

In a seedy hotel in central London, the baby daughter of a US Air Force pilot lies lifeless in his wife's arms. Accused of killing the fourteen-month-old in an uncontrolled rage, Kyle Foster flees, taking his eight-year-old son with him.

Will Ingrid find Foster before he hurts anyone else? Or will she succumb to the old demons she's been trying to escape for the last eighteen years?

Shoot First - Book Four

A teenage girl disappears after witnessing a gangland murder in Chicago. Nine months later, and heavily pregnant, she arrives in London only to disappear again.

Special Agent Ingrid Skyberg has just two days to find the girl and get her to testify or else a brutal killer walks free. But Ingrid isn't the only person looking for the girl, and a war that started on the streets of Chicago is about to explode in the peaceful English countryside.

Below Zero - Book Five

Stockholm is under siege. A bomb has gone off, a series of high profile people have been kidnapped, and the city is in lockdown. Unfortunately for Special Agent Ingrid Skyberg, everything is kicking off on the same day she is in town to complete a dangerous assignment that is so secret, and so illegal, that neither the FBI or the US government can ever know about it. Her instructions are simple: no ID, no credit cards, no trace. If she ends up in jail, or floating face down in the harbor, there can be no way of identifying her.

No badge, no gun, no back-up: this time Ingrid is on her own.

Final Offer - Book Six

A shadowy UK-based group has been trying to hack the US elections. When Special Agent Ingrid Skyberg is assigned to find out who's funding the hackers, she finds herself up against an invisible enemy who is extremely powerful and utterly ruthless.

To bring them to justice, Ingrid must go undercover and infiltrate the world of super-rich Russian oligarchs. But money buys all kinds of protection and Ingrid soon realizes that by taking on this battle she's putting everything on the line – her career, her future, her life.

In a nail-biting race against time, Ingrid sets out to solve the mystery and unmask the conspirators before they can silence her. Forever.

Flight Risk - Book Seven

Ingrid is ready to walk away from her life. She wants out of London. She even wants out of the FBI. But when she attempts to board a flight at Heathrow and sneak away without telling anyone, she's arrested on suspicion of causing the death of a man she's never heard of.

Now Ingrid must stay in the country, and the Bureau, to prove her innocence. There's just one problem: she can't remember if she killed him or not

———

EVA'S OTHER BOOKS

The Loyal Servant

Winner of the Lucy Cavendish Prize for Fiction, *The Loyal Servant* is a whistleblower thriller that topped the Amazon political fiction chart. Investigative reporter Angela Tate investigates scandal and corruption in the corridors of Westminster.

The Senior Moment

Sixty-five-year-old Jean Henderson arrives in New York to find her son and his pregnant wife missing from their apartment. When she reaches out to the cops for help, Jean discovers how invisible older people really are and concocts a plan to get noticed: by robbing a series of banks.

The Deadly Silence (formerly The Third Estate)

Thirty-three years ago two little girls disappeared. Today, the man convicted of murder three decades ago is back on the streets as another girl vanishes. Angela Tate covered the first disappearances and is dragged into discovering the terrible truth behind the latest.

ABOUT THE AUTHOR

Eva was born and raised in London. She worked as a local government worker, web editor, dot com entrepreneur, portrait artist and singer. In 2011, Eva won the inaugural Lucy Cavendish Prize for Fiction for her first novel, *The Loyal Servant*. The book was also shortlisted for ITV's People's Novelist Award.

In 2013, Eva published the first Ingrid Skyberg Thriller and never looked back.

To find out more about Eva or Ingrid, please visit evahudson.-com. You can get the latest on all things Skyberg at twitter.-com/eva_hudson and facebook.com/evahudsoncrimewriter.

ACKNOWLEDGMENTS

Big thanks to my editor, FC, my copy editor/proofer Lucy, and my early readers Hilary and Jose.

Made in the USA
Las Vegas, NV
04 January 2022

40371258R00194